MOURNING MEADOW

Larion Wills

MYSTERY ROMANCE

Secret Cravings Publishing
www.secretcravingspublishing.com

A Secret Cravings Publishing Book
Mystery Romance

MOURNING MEADOW

Print ISBN: 978-1-61885-217-5

First E-book Publication: January 2012
First Print Publication: March 2012

Cover design by Dawné Dominique
Edited by Ariana Gaynor
Proof read by Ariana Gaynor

PUBLISHER
Secret Cravings Publishing
www.secretcravingspublishing.com

MOURNING MEADOW

Larion Wills

Prologue

To the casual observer Robert's hand on Steven's broad shoulder looked to be no more than camaraderie. In truth, Steven struggled not to wince and pull away from the fingers hooked into his flesh. At six foot four inches tall, two inches taller than Steven, and a retired football player with an appropriate build, Robert had quite a grip.

"Would you relax?" Steven implored. "You're going to blow everything before I even get us an introduction."

"This could be worth millions," Robert hissed. "Millions."

“If you don't relax, there won't be any chance of a deal."

Robert's voice dropped. "You shouldn't have brought me. These rich, white folks ain't gonna talk to no black man.”

"You're black?”

Robert chuckled. He was about as black as a man could be with equally dark hair and eyes. "Never have been to you, that's for certain." He took a deep breath, let it out slowly, and uncurled his fingers. "Okay, boss, let's go scalp these riches of their millions."

They started through the crowd of the ultra rich with the appearance—they hoped—of having no particular objective in mind. They received many double-take looks, Steven for his natural blue-eyed, blond good looks, athletic build at a comfortable thirty-five years of age, and devastating smile. Robert because a black man, at any age and build, was so rare among them.

Steven made a sudden stop and turned to a small group they were passing. "Did you say Morning Meadow? Fulton DeBain's Morning Meadow?"

The tall slender woman, late twenties, dark auburn hair, and sapphire blue eyes looked him over appreciatively. When she smiled, it was only her mouth while her eyes held a look of cool calculation, but her voice purred. "You've heard of my home?"

The man beside her drawled out slowly with a slight English accent. "Not everyone has, love." His manner was one of lazy insouciance with a well tailored look of a modern slim, fair-haired David Niven right down to the narrow mustache. "Perhaps he has a special interest."

"Only professional," Steven said stiffly. He didn't miss the innuendo or sweep of eyes the man gave him. "Sorry, I interrupted you."

"Oh, don't rush off, handsome." She hooked her arm through Steven's to hold him. "Just what profession would that be?"

"Architect, but it was rude of me to interrupt a private conversation." He removed his arm. "As your friend so subtly pointed out."

"Oh, dear." The man yawned behind a raised hand. "How boring to be called subtle."

"And how boring to be a boor," she countered. "I'm Caroleigh Fitzhugh. And you are?"

"Steven Chase." He turned to Robert. "This is Robert Brown."

She barely nodded to acknowledge the introduction. "This boring fellow is Edward Van Philips." She indicated a slender blond who looked barely twenty years old standing beside Edward. "This is Evelyn Goodman, new to Denver."

While Evelyn gave Steven a haughty look and ignored Robert, Edward said, "Charmed, I'm sure." He managed to sound as if he was anything but. His next words were a snide accusation. "And as an architect you would simply love to see the Meadow?"

"What a delightful idea," Caroleigh exclaimed, drawing an exasperated roll of the eyes from Edward. "Evelyn and I are driving up tomorrow. Won't you join us?"

"Caroleigh?" Edward conveyed an unvoiced question with the single word; what in the world are you doing?

Evelyn voiced hers. "Is it wise to invite a total stranger that way?"

"We haven't met before, but I've heard of the handsome Mr. Chase, architect and developer. Who better to get advice from?"

With one eyebrow raised, Edward asked, "Advice on what?"

"Whether I should sell the Meadow or develop it."

Edward's mouth opened only to snap shut. Whatever he started to say stayed behind pressed lips and a speculative expression.

Caroleigh laughed softly. "You may come as well to protect us, but I'm sure Steven will be more interested in the Meadow as a possible project than murdering us in our beds."

"Kari would be much more a candidate for that," Edward answered dryly.

"Kari? Who is that?" Evelyn asked in alarm.

"My little sister," Caroleigh answered.

"Who," Edward supplied, with a twist of his lips and another flip of his eyebrow, "just happens to live there."

Caroleigh laughed again. "And who is—I will admit—a little strange, but never violent. She just has difficulty dealing with anything too complicated and needs some special care."

Edward's brow rose yet again. "And so generous and kind of you to care for her the way you do."

She responded with a side-ways glance at him and opened her small clutch purse to hand a card to Steven. "Now that's all settled, meet us at noon, and we will be there in time for dinner. Pack casual and warm. It's still very cool that high up, and the accommodations are quite rustic. Oh, I must take Emily and Sir Gaylord. We'll have a party all weekend." She quickly became distracted. "There's Patrice. Come along, Evelyn. I did promise to introduce you to the cream of society."

She flittered off with Evelyn behind. Edward followed only after a slow appraising look at Steven.

Somewhat dazed, Robert murmured, "This is only Wed."

"Since they don't work for a living, all week is a weekend," Steven answered thoughtfully.

Robert leaned close and whispered in Steven's ear, "But it could be millions. That was neatly done, partner."

Chapter One

A twisted, narrow road of switch backs, steep grades, and patches of the past winter's snow made reaching Morning Meadow a challenge to nerves and driving ability. The journey was well worth the trouble for Steven when the dirt track broke free of the dense forest. The sight nearly took his breath away. He stopped his car just to look.

With a backdrop of the Rocky Mountains and thick forest, the natural clearing, nearly free of snow, showed the early stages of spring green. The mansion stood to the far side, dominating the meadow and in turn being dominated by the towering snow capped mountains surrounding it. From that angle the house appeared to be nearly square, with a wide veranda covered by steep sloping roofs wrapped around the three sides he could see. It was three stories—four if you counted the attic rooms tucked under the high peaks of the multi-gabled roof—all on a raised basement. A simplistic Victorian was the best general description he could give to it. The flavor of the era was carried through in the ornate designs of the drip moldings over the second and third floor windows, the spindles, posts, brackets, balusters, and balustrades of the verandas. Carved and scrolled gingerbread bargeboards were tucked into the peaks of each gable as well. He could have sat there for hours, just looking, but since his hostess and company were already parked and out of the car, he pulled forward only to discover they were locked out.

* * * *

Caroleigh paced a length of the wide veranda to show her agitation. Her idea of warm and casual was wool slacks, silk blouse, and a knee length mink. Evelyn's attire was similar, except her mink was a waist length jacket. Edward wore slacks, sports jacket, and a silk scarf at his throat tucked into a cashmere sweater. Steven, understandably, felt underdressed. He wore Levis, a sweater over a shirt, and running shoes. The only one near to his interpretation of casual was the maid, Emily, in a plain cotton dress and cardigan sweater.

"She never locks the door," Caroleigh complained for about the tenth time.

"You have told her repeatedly she should," Edward said languidly. "Perhaps she has taken your advice."

She gave an unladylike snort. "That would be a first, wouldn't it? Are you sure it's locked?"

"You watched me try. The door won't budge. Certainly suggests to me that it is indeed locked. You may, of course, try for yourself." He raised one finger as if an idea occurred to him and said brightly, "Or, perhaps, Grandfather doesn't care for strange men just walking in. Haven't I heard he locks the doors at odd times?"

"I thought you said your grandfather is dead," Evelyn said.

"He is," Caroleigh answered.

"Quite," Edward said with a cocked brow.

Puzzled enough to stop her show of annoyance Evelyn asked, "Then how could he lock it?"

"He didn't," Caroleigh answered. "Kari did for some obscure reason."

"But why would he say he did?"

Both ignored her. Edward suggested, "An un-welcome message, perhaps?"

Caroleigh voice hardened. "If you can't say anything entertaining, do be still."

"Why would you say he locked the door if he's dead?" Evelyn persisted.

"They say he does still roam about," Edward told her, his eyebrow cocked again.

"Who says?"

"The locals have quite a few stories." He chose one of the wicker chairs scattered around the veranda and reclined lazily.

"Edward." Caroleigh warned at first only to shrug indifferently and explain. "Bored people amusing themselves, nothing more." She watched Steven as he studied the molding work around the windows. When he touched it relevantly and stroked the wood in a caress, she asked, "Impressed, Steven?"

"Absolutely," he told her with a grin. "The workmanship is superb, and the condition is unbelievable."

"Great Grandpa only hired the best and bought the best."

Steven peeked inside one of the tall, leaded glass lights along each side of the massive, nine foot tall door to look into the great hall. "Marble?" he asked of the floor beyond.

"Imported from Italy, as I said, the best."

"Why did he choose so remote a location?"

Edward gave a huge yawn, earning a look of irritation from Caroleigh before she answered. "Proximity to the source of his fortune. The mine, Morning Glory, is just over there." She pointed vaguely towards the east. "Totally worthless now, of course."

"Therefore uninteresting." Edward turned to Evelyn. "They also say Daddy does a bit of roaming about." He asked Caroleigh, "Has there ever been a butler, love?"

"In Great Grandpa's day, wife number two had the whole regime, butler, maids, nanny, cook and whatever else."

"But not in Daddy's day, so the butler couldn't have done it."

"Done what?" Evelyn asked.

"Sabotaged dear Daddy's car, of course. Clichés aside, who do you suppose it was? The wife? She did remarry very soon after."

"I suppose it was too much to drink, a stormy night, and a hideous road." Caroleigh dropped into a chair beside him. "There was never any question as to the cause of his death."

"Then why does he keep coming back?"

"He doesn't," she said with a scoff. "That's just one of the stories the villagers tell to amuse themselves. The house is not haunted."

Emily, a very young, petite woman, knew her place in the scheme of things. She sat off to the side, her hands folded in her lap and her feet flat on the floor. She listened quietly until that moment, then she forgot to be so proper. "Haunted?" she asked in alarm.

Edward was more than willing to go on. "Every stormy night—"

"Stop it, Edward," Caroleigh ordered.

"You did say to be entertaining."

"Entertaining, not frightening."

"Do be sure to teach me the difference." He moved gracefully to his feet. "I do believe she returns."

* * * *

Kari looked as out of place at the mansion as her battered old pick-up did parked behind Steven's Chevy parked behind Caroleigh's Mercedes. She was a few years younger than Caroleigh, as tall as her sister and probably as slim. Her actual size was hard to tell with her flannel shirt—several times too large—hanging almost to her knees and buttoned to the collar. Where Caroleigh's hair was dark, Kari's was chestnut brown, twisted in some kind of a knot on the back of her head and held in place with a pencil wedged through it. Behind too round and too large glasses that gave her the look of an owl, her amber eyes darted from one to the other of them and settled on Steven.

"Why have you locked the door?" Caroleigh asked tightly.

Kari spoke as she crawled out of the truck. "There's more than you said."

Since he had been included at the last minute, Steven spoke up quickly. "If it's a problem, I—"

Caroleigh cut him off. "It's not. She always has more food than we eat and with twelve bedrooms there's more than enough room."

Uncomfortable under Kari's intense stare, Steven opened his mouth to speak again just as Edward came off the porch.

"Kari, love." He went to her with his arms out. "You haven't even said hello."

She stiffened during Edward's embrace, stepped back as soon as he released her, and stated, "You're back."

"Like a bad penny." He draped an arm over her shoulders and started her to the door. "Now don't you worry about a thing, Caroleigh has brought sweet Emily. She'll see to cooking for us. You can just relax and visit." That rhetoric took them to the door. "If you will just be a dear and open the door."

He ended with a tip of his head towards the door. Kari's golden orbs looked from him to it and back to him before she twisted to look at the others.

"Open the door." Caroleigh ordered impatiently.

With her brows furrowed, Kari reached for the door knob.

"It's locked." Edward said and gasped.

Kari turned the knob and pushed the massive door in with one finger. "Anything else you need?" she asked blandly.

"Really, Edward," Caroleigh snapped.

He twisted to face her and exclaimed, "That door was locked. You saw. It wouldn't budge."

Caroleigh sighed in exasperation and went to her car.

Evelyn asked, "You mean we didn't need to sit out here all that time?"

"Are you Emmy?" Kari asked.

Evelyn puffed up indignantly. "Do I look like a servant?"

"Ah, Kari." Edward interceded quickly. "Allow me to make the introductions. This is Evelyn Goodman, Caroleigh's new friend. Emily is behind her, and..." He waved a languid hand towards Steven. "...that is Steven Chase."

Her intense gaze turned back on Steven, making him feel like squirming. He knew how out of place he looked compared to the others. "If it would be more convenient," he said quickly, "I can get a room in town."

Whatever her answer might have been, Caroleigh spoke first. "That's already been settled," she said firmly. "But you could be a darling and help with the bags. You too, Edward, and then move the cars into the carriage house. The weather up here is frightful for the paint."

"You know how I abhor anything physical," Edward complained, but he sauntered back down the steps to the trunk of her car.

Kari told them tonelessly, "I don't know what your arrangements are, but only two of the rooms are dusted. You'll have to put up with one or three not being, depending."

"We'll manage, thank you," Caroleigh told her coolly.

Kari looked back at Steven one last time before she climbed into her beat-up pickup and backed away.

"I really could stay in town," Steven repeated.

"Not to worry, old boy." Edward told him. He handed him two suitcases. "She's like that all the time with everyone. Once she gets us settled, we'll barely see her."

Evelyn took one small case from the trunk. "I did not care for her insinuation."

"She wasn't accusing you of being here for a tryst," Caroleigh explained patiently. "She simply said since she didn't know our arrangements. She's just blunt."

"Rude and insinuating," Evelyn corrected. "And to say we had to deal with the rooms being unprepared. There's no excuse for bad manners, no matter how strange she is."

"Hear, hear," Edward cried. He took two more suitcases from the trunk. "One must always remember good manners when dropping by on short notice. Shall we go on, Steven. I'm sure it will take at least two more trips for us to get this lot in. For myself, I shall be eternally grateful Evelyn packed light."

As the men walked up the veranda stairs with two suitcases each, Evelyn turned to Caroleigh and whispered, "Why do I feel like he's making fun of me?"

Leaning into the car for Sir Gaylord, her Maltese in his carrier, Carolyn answered with a bland, "I can't imagine."

* * * *

Steven had been an early riser all of his life from necessity, and the first morning he was anxious to see as much of the house as possible. He was up hours before the scheduled eleven o'clock brunch, though it took him nearly an hour to travel from his room to the veranda. The treasures of the u-shaped landing, hand craved banister, and elegance of the great hall were an architect's delight. Without Caroleigh hanging onto his arm, he was free to study the exquisite craftsmanship of masters in detail from crown molding at ceilings to inlayed paneled walls to the imported marble floor of the great hall. He examined every facet of construction, texture, color, and materials, admired the beauty, and appreciated the painstaking preservation.

Once outside he planned to walk the perimeter to see it all up close and then walk out away from the structure, beyond the drive surrounding it, to view it from every angle. He changed his mind when a sensation of being watched caused him to look up to see a shadowy figure behind sheer curtains in a third story window. He couldn't see the features clearly, but reasoned the only person it could be was Caroleigh's remote, younger sister. Everyone else, including Emily, was on the second floor, the last much to Evelyn's chagrin. To have a servant sleeping just down the hall with equal accommodations seemed inappropriate to her. She did accept it, grudgingly, when Caroleigh told her she would appreciate it should the need arise to call for a servant during the night.

For Kari to be up so soon before the others didn't surprise him. He could only wonder as to why she was up there, but whatever her reason, he did not want to offend her. That Caroleigh was in control of the estate had little bearing on the fact it was Kari's home. Little doubt remained as well as to who cared for property, making him wonder if Kari could possibly be as simple-minded as Caroleigh hinted. He didn't believe anyone who could keep so vast a house and grounds in such immaculate condition could be. After watching her the previous evening, he was sure her remoteness was more of indifference than mental ability, and he was curious as to what kind of personality lurked behind those oversize glasses.

She joined them for dinner the night before, obviously to Caroleigh and Edward's surprise. However, she barely spoke. She did watch them intently for some time, without comments or questions about their conversations. To him it seemed she just lost interest when she looked away. The few times he had spoken directly to her in an effort to engage her in a conversation, someone, usually Caroleigh, interrupted, driving her back into silence. After the meal, she drifted away and did not reappear for the remainder of the evening. There was not so much as a glimpse of her during the short tour Caroleigh gave them of the house, making him feel they were tolerated, not welcomed. Not wanting to add unfavorably to the situation by possibly trespassing in some way, he waved uncertainly and went back in the house.

As soon as he opened the door the smell of fresh coffee hit him, making his mouth water. The kitchen had not been included in their tour, but the room was not difficult to find by following the back, servant hall. As immaculately clean and updated to fixtures of the fifties as the bathroom off his bedroom, it was not where the coffee brewed. He thought Emily must be using a butler's pantry or a servant's kitchen for the small chore, which he could understand. The size of the kitchen could be intimidating. The problem was all three doors directly off the kitchen were closed. A hall ran from the kitchen to the back of the house lined with closed doors as well, and he didn't want to appear to be a snoop by opening and closing doors in a search for her. A soft thud behind one of the doors seemed the answer to his dilemma until he opened it.

"Emily could—?"

He did not find not a servant's kitchen, a butler's pantry, or Emily. The words choked off as his mouth dropped open. He recovered quicker than the woman even if he tripped over his own feet to back out. The momentum of his near-fall pulled the door shut with a slam.

"I am so sorry," he called out. "I—"

"I can't understand you through the door. Wait until I come out," she called back.

Steven grimaced at the prospect of what awaited him. Puzzlement followed. Next came recognition, and he groaned. Whoever he had waved at in the window had not been Kari, and did she ever look different, stark naked, dripping wet, fresh from the shower with only a towel in her hand.

He didn't wait long. She hurried. Her wet hair hung halfway down her back, soaking the dark blue, knit turtle neck shirt. She finished the top button on her jeans as she rushed out. Her feet were bare, and no glasses hid those amber colored eyes to give her the appearance of an owl.

"What's wrong?"

"Huh?" he asked dumbly, staring at the change in her.

"What's the emergency? What did you need?"

"Coffee," he answered with a grimace. "I was looking for coffee."

Her chin went up, and her voice sharpened. "In a bathroom?"

"I didn't know it was a bathroom or that you were down here. I thought I just saw you in an upstairs window. I thought Emily—"

"You're talking too fast," she told him curtly. "There's nothing wrong?"

"There wasn't until I opened that door," he told her glumly.

She stared at him a moment longer before shaking her head. "Coffee?" The corner of her mouth twitched as she turned away and pointed to the next door. "Help yourself."

"Can I fix you a cup?" he asked before she could disappear back in the bathroom.

She turned back to face him. "What?"

"Can I fix you a cup?"

"Sure. I'll be out in a few minutes."

As she turned away again, he told her, "I'm really sorry about…" He paused, unsure of how to phrase his invasion of her privacy.

She answered with, "One sugar and no cream," and shut the door.

"Does that mean I'm forgiven?" he asked hopefully.

"Can't understand you, and I don't feel like yelling."

He still didn't find a butler's pantry or a servant's kitchen. The door she pointed to opened into a complete kitchen, part of a complete apartment. Kari obviously did not sleep in the sixth bedroom on the second floor or any other of the upstairs rooms. There was a living room, and small dining area. Off to the side of a bedroom had to be the bath door, with a second door opening to the hall where he had blundered in. One corner of the living room held a computer center and phone. The opposite corner held a free standing fireplace. The furnishings were modern, easy care, and comfortable but in a style to match the era of the house. All of it was designed and arranged to leave the outside wall free. That wall was nearly all glass in French doors and windows. The arrangement made it possible to look out at a breathtaking view from every location in the apartment.

An open park surrounded the back of house and reached to the forest with the majestic mountains towering into the sky behind it. To add to the panorama, dark storm clouds were coming in with rumbles and flashes. He stood in front of the glass when she came out of the bedroom and joined him, silently taking the cup he held out. She had partially dried her hair and plaited it to hang down her back. An over shirt, not quite as oversized as the day before, hung open over the knit shirt. Socks covered her feet.

"It's beautiful," he said to break the silence.

"You sound like you actually like it."

Puzzled he answered with, "I do."

"How odd."

"Odd?" he asked with a quizzical smile. "In what way?"

"Most of the people Caroleigh brings up here can barely tolerate it."

He turned his head to look at her and found her staring at him. "I can't speak for most people, but this house is unbelievable, and the setting is beautiful." The intense way she stared at him prompted him to ask, "Was that odd too?"

"You certainly don't seem the norm for Caroleigh. Have you slept with her yet?"

"No and I'm not likely to either," he answered crisply.

"That's her intention," she said bluntly. "It might help you to know that."

"Help? In what way?"

"Depends on your intentions."

"Not to sleep with her." He remembered he talked to Caroleigh's sister before he said more to insult Caroleigh. He had no interest in sleeping with the woman.

Before he could think of what to say instead, she said, "Definitely odd." She half-smiled at him. "Since none of her previous guests have ever gotten up at this hour and the current ones don't, would you like some breakfast to go with that coffee?"

"I'd love it if—" He broke off, turned to listen, and then hurried to the kitchen door. In the main kitchen he could tell the yelps and cries he heard came from the dining room. He pushed that door open, and a white cloud of fur streaked through, slid on the smooth floor, and collided with the center bar in a thud.

"What the hell is that?" Kari asked from behind him.

"Caroleigh's dog."

The Maltese no longer yelped, but it was terrified. Every time Steven reached for it, it scrambled away. He made three tries before Kari pulled at him from behind.

"Get out of the way," she told him quietly and knelt down several feet from the dog. "Shhh, baby, it's okay, shhh. Come to me. It's okay."

Steven backed off and watched in silence until she coaxed the frightened dog to her. Even after she had it in her arms she crooned softly and stroked its silky fur. She also carefully checked for injuries with a light, gentle touch.

"Maybe the thunder is scaring him," he suggested.

"What is she doing with an animal like this?" She headed back for the apartment. He followed. "Little dogs like this need constant attention." She looked out the window as she closed the door behind them. "It must be the storm."

"They can't understand where the sound is coming from," he said in agreement.

"Too bad I can't make him earplugs. Waffles?"

"For earplugs?" he asked with a start.

She looked at him blankly for a moment, then laughed, a light cheerfull sound. She laughed softly still looking at him as she pulled the refrigerator door open with the dog hung over one arm.

"You meant for breakfast," he said with a chuckle. "Love them."

"Good." She sat a bowl of eggs on the counter and attempted to hand him the dog. It fought against going to him until they nearly dropped it.

She took it back against her chest and asked, "Can you cook?"

"You'd be surprised."

"Over and over it seems," she said thoughtfully.

"Pleasantly?" He hoped.

"I haven't decided yet," she answered candidly and turned away. She shifted the dog back to one arm, opened and closed doors and drawers and set out ingredients and equipment. With the countertop full, she turned back to ask, "Do you want to try to hold him again or mix?"

"Mix. I can only tolerate so much rejection." He looked at the full countertop in a degree of dismay. "Since I don't see a bag of just add water mix, I need directions though."

"Flour's in the big canister," she told him with a smile. "You need to start the waffle iron first. It's ready when the light goes out."

"Did the beeper break?" he asked, looking down at the top of the small appliance.

"Excuse me?"

He pointed to the top of the waffle iron. "It says it beeps when it's ready."

"Oh, I forgot it does that," she said with a shrug. "I can handle bacon with one hand. How does that sound?"

"Delicious."

"And eggs?"

"Over easy?" he asked with a grin.

"Considering the circumstances you'll be lucky if they aren't scrambled.”

“I’ll suffer,” Steven teased, amazed at how quickly she adapted to having the little dog draped over one arm.

While she gave directions she fried bacon and eggs. The dog still hung on her arm, quite content to be there. When they sat down at the small table to eat, she lifted her arm to look the little dog in the face.

"You are a demanding little rascal. Are you going to at least lie in my lap so I can eat?" It whimpered at her. “I suppose I have to share my food with you, too?"

"Maybe that's the way to his heart.” Steven broke off a piece of bacon and held it out to the dog. Its little nose wiggled, but as he moved the morsel closer, it pulled back. "Come on, Rascal, take it."

"Is that his name?"

"It fits him better than what I heard her call him. Sir Gaylord, I think."

Kari took the bacon from Steven. Rascal didn't even wait for her to get it to his nose. He reached out for it greedily.

"Rejected again. Do you usually have this effect on animals?" she asked.

"Usually they like me."

With a raised eyebrow, Kari asked, "Have you been mean to him?"

"I just met him."

"Really? How long have you known Caroleigh?"

"Not long enough to make friends with her dog," he answered evasively.

She studied Steven with that intense gaze of hers, making him shift uneasily and confess. "The truth is I never saw the dog until Caroleigh carried him in yesterday. I'm embarrassed to say I've only known your sister and the others a day longer than that."

"Oh? Why is that, embarrassed, I mean?"

"I wanted to see the house." He smiled self-consciously. "This is one of the few DeBains left. Most of his were built in San Francisco and lost in the 1906 earthquake and fires. Those were pretty typical for the times, but this one, the way he adapted the combination of styles for the environment, is genius. He created the look without the garish and superficial fancy work and the roof lines—even the veranda roofs—high pitched, flowing into one another to keep the snow from building up.”

"Let me guess, you're an architect."

"Guilty," he admitted with a chuckle. "Only part-time now though."

"But it's your passion?"

"Used to be. Work got in the way."

Kari studied him intently again. "You work?"

"Everyday."

"You aren't rich?"

"I work," Steven answered defensively. "That's why I got an invitation."

"Ha!" she said, surprising him.

"Are you back to that seducing thing?" he asked uncomfortably.

"Yes."

"Okay, I'm not completely naive. I thought maybe she was one of those women that flirt with any man, but just in case, I brought my own car. If she starts coming on too strong I can leave."

"And not study the house to your heart's content?"

"My punishment for being greedy." A new, appealing idea occurred to him. "You could take pity on me and show me around."

"I work at not getting between Caroleigh and her interests."

Taking a turn, he studied her. "I guess that explains the way you looked yesterday and the way you look now."

"Since you were early I had to improvise yesterday with one of Grandpa's shirts still in the pickup, but it is the way I'll look the next time you see me. And I would appreciate you not mentioning the difference."

"I won't, but—"

She shook her head. "No buts. I won't fight with her." She quickly changed subjects. "What are the plans for today?"

"A drive around the property and a look at the Morning Glory. She says it was a huge operation in its heyday."

"It was, but there hasn't been any activity in the shafts since the fifties, Grandpa's last attempt to find the lost mother lode Great Gramps was sure was there. They found some low grade stuff, but nothing to warrant mining. With mining and hauling expenses, it wouldn't be cost productive."

"Maybe the price of silver will go up."

"Gold," she corrected.

"I thought Caroleigh said silver."

"It was silver originally, during the boom, but they were fortunate in there being a large amount of gold as well when they devalued silver in 1893. Along with solid investments, diversity in iron and coal, and plain old frugalness, Great Grandpa stayed on top when so many suddenly became bankrupt and destitute when they switched to a gold standard."

"This house was frugal?"

"This house was his one exception, part of the package to attempt what so many of the new millionaires were doing, propelling themselves into acceptance in society, although he didn't do it for himself. He didn't care anything about that, but he wanted more than what he had for his children. He wanted a huge family; hence a huge house, but he also wanted what went along with it for them, more than he had been able to give his first wife and child. They both died in childbirth. He blamed that on the hardships she had to endure, and he set out to make money to keep it from happening again."

She smiled slightly. "I don't think he dreamed of making as much as he did. He went through hell to get it though. He worked his way out here from the East, nearly starving more than once. The first winter, while he waited with hundreds of others for the snow to clear enough to get to the newest fields, he was smart enough to read mining books. Because of that he was far ahead of the other placer miners. When they were giving up or selling their claims because of the blue-black sand that kept gumming up their boxes, he was buying them."

"Sand, which was?"

"Silver."

"Ah."

"Ah, indeed and unlike so many of the average, footloose, and fancy free prospectors who worked a placer only long enough to prove it was worth something to sell and move on, he started investing in development. That's where the real money was made. He also did a lot of grubstaking. He never made as much on one as Horace Taber's famous start, but he made at least that much combined."

Uncertain if he remembered the Taber story correctly, Steven asked, "A couple of million for a few bucks, wasn't it?

"He supplied seventeen dollars in goods in a grubstake—Taber had a store—for a share that netted him a million in a year."

"Unbelievable."

"A millionaire and famous literally overnight, he and several others in that time period. Great Grandpa's came a little slower, but he was a lot more cautious." She gave a wry smile. "And methodical, he could see that money alone wouldn't buy a rise in station for his heirs by watching how the Tabers and Browns—"

"Molly Brown?"

"He called her Maggie, but yeah, the same one."

"Go on."

"Are you really interested?" she asked dubiously.

"Don't tell me I'm odd again. He could tell by watching the Tabers and Browns…?" he urged.

"You asked for it," she warned. "They were his contemporaries, but he never really socialized with them. What they wanted and what he wanted were two different things. They wanted it for themselves, then. What he wanted was for his children's future, so he went to Europe and found himself a titled wife he could buy."

"That sounds cold-blooded."

Kari shrugged. "He had married once for love. That wasn't what he wanted again. To him it was a business deal, right down to a contract. He promised her a mansion and the funds to entertain to her heart's desire. She was to provide him with children and educate them properly, taking them into society and acceptance. His mistake was in believing she was sincere. Hers was in believing she could control him. In her opinion he was no more than a dumb Irishman who got lucky. I don't believe he ever voiced his of her, but she began to realize her mistake when he had the mansion built here."

"Definitely out of any social mainstream. The only one I've ever heard of more out of the way and remote was Vanderbilt's Biltmore in North Carolina."

"Have you seen it?" she asked in a teasing tone.

"I paid for a tour just like everyone else," he admitted freely. "They opened it for the public in the nineteen-thirties. I've also seen some castles built on the same scale."

"Great Grandpa never wanted a castle. He wanted a home. He also liked to be near his business. He did give into her on some details, like furnishings. He also agreed that none of the vulgar outbuildings needed to support so isolated a home would be visible from the house."

"I wondered about that. I thought they'd been torn down."

"Never were, just the carriage house, now a garage. She allowed that for convenience. There were never any formal gardens either. Aside from the soil and climate not being the best for them, he preferred the park look." Kari pointed out the window to the thick forest behind the house. "He planted native trees to thicken that up so she wouldn't accidentally see an even more vulgar mine. Originally the meadow went all the way to the edge."

"Edge?"

"That stripe is about half a mile deep. On the other side it drops off in a steep bluff. The mine is in the face of it." She pointed again, towards the east. "To get to it you have to drive by the Meadow drive a quarter of a mile, drive around the low end of the bluff and come back up. Or you can turn half a mile before the Meadow drive and take the high section of a loop that goes around the bluff. One way is a little longer. The other is a little better condition. If you don't want to drive you can climb down the bluff and walk over. There are stairs for that." She gave him a teasing grin. "Or you can use the Indian Ladder."

"Which is?"

"Toe and fingertip holes chisled into the rock face."

"I'll pass that," he told her with a chuckle. "But the rest sounds fascinating. I'd like to see it and the mine."

"You'd be disappointed. None of the town is left. It's just a ranch over there now."

"I didn't know there was a town. All I'd heard of was the mine."

"Morning Glory is still there, but the entrance is fenced off for safety to keep would-be prospectors and explorers out. Most of the shafts aren't safe anymore, and they aren't anything but dark, gloomy tunnels anyway."

"With the mother lode hidden just out of sight?" he teased.

"Now there's a dream that drove many a man to insanity and financial ruin. Or woman. You've heard of Tabor so you know how his mine, The Matchless, and his wife Baby Doe ended." He nodded for answer. "Personally, I don't think freezing to death in a shack, going weeks before my body was even found, justifies the dream of striking it rich again."

"Rags to riches to rags again. I always thought Baby Doe was a sad story, dying alone like that. I never understood why it took so long for people to know she was in trouble. Weren't there other people, a town like there was here?"

"No town. The Matchless wasn't as remote from a large city nor was the road as long and dangerous to reach it, and it was after the big booms. There just weren't many people around there anymore."

Kari shifted to lean back more comfortably in her chair. "Morning Town wasn't typical of boom towns either. Once the placer plots played out, the boomers moved on. Great Grandpa went to hard rock mining.

There wasn't a town site where anyone could put up whatever they wanted. He made sure he owned the land. The town was what he built for the men who worked for him and their families. There were no saloons, gambling houses, or brothels, but they had a church, school, general store, barber and bath house, eating houses, boarding houses, and barracks for the single men. He built homes for the families of the teamsters and miners. Even for the families of the servants who worked here. There was also a huge barn and corral for the mule teams, a wagon yard, and smithy. As production fell off, everything was dismantled bit by bit. There are pictures, old photo albums and some books on the silver barons in the library if you're really interested."

"I am. Caroleigh's idea of a tour was to stand in the doorway saying 'That's the library, that's the game room,' et cetera. She didn't include any history."

"History doesn't interest her much, but I can see why you asked for a tour."

She stood, little dog still draped over her left arm and started stacking dishes with one hand.

"Let me help."

"I can manage, and I'm sure you would like to get on with your exploring."

"Oh, you're throwing me out."

"Evan, I—"

"Steven," he corrected in a tease. "If you're going to throw me out, at least get the name right."

"Steven," she said precisely. "I wasn't throwing you out, but I do have things to do."

He pointed to Rascal. "Looks like you could use a hand."

"You might regret the offer."

"I won't."

She watched as he gathered up dirty dishes and walked to the kitchen.

"You actually do dishes?" she asked.

"I'm not odd. I'm a bachelor." That was something he wanted to be sure she knew.

She followed with her free hand full of more dishes. "Edward is a bachelor, but I doubt he's ever washed a dish in his life."

"Not a fair comparison. Even if I had the means, I wouldn't live the way he does."

"Edward is okay. When I can understand the sort of English-slur-accent he uses, he's funny."

"In a sardonic kind of way. I get the feeling he's mocking everyone, Evelyn anyway. His words say he's agreeing, but I think he's making fun of her instead."

"She's young and probably new rich. They have a tendency to over do in an effort to out snob the snobs."

"Bigotry among the rich?"

"Oh, my yes—soap's under there." She finished clearing the table while she talked, and Steven filled the sink with soapy water. "Edward is accepted even though he doesn't seem to have the money needed to travel their circuit fully. He's old family. They titter behind their hands about his sad misfortune, but they let him in. Caroleigh has generations of what is considered good blood and enough money to put up a good show, so she is too."

"And you?" She stopped to stare at him. "The title your great grandfather bought?"

"She only had one child for him. She made the mistake of thinking holding out would get her the things she wanted. He sent her home after he divorced her and kept the child." She answered his questioning look. "She didn't want her, inferior blood and all that, an embarrassment."

"She was still her child."

"Yeah, well some women aren't meant to be mothers," she said tightly and shrugged. "That child died anyway, along with three from his third marriage in a wagon accident. The only one who survived was my grandfather. He was the youngest, and had been left home with the nanny that day."

"Your great grandfather must have been heartbroken."

"They say he was. He'd married her when he was forty-five. She was only twenty-five, but they say they really loved each other. He never married again, either because he was too heartbroken or just getting too old. Grandpa never married again after his wife and six of their children died in an influenza epidemic. My father was the youngest and barely survived. The loss did nearly break Grandpa. He decided the curse was just too strong."

"Curse?"

"The Morning Meadow curse," she said soberly. "The original translation from the Indian name for the meadow was mourning, as in grief, not morning as in dawn. It's a very tragic story."

"Uh-huh," he said skeptically.

"Very tragic," she repeated. "The medicine man's son was in love with the chief's daughter, but the chief turned down his offer of marriage, saying the boy didn't have enough to pay. They had to buy their wives, you know. The boy went off to acquire more and had nearly accumulated enough when he received word the chief had already married her off. He charged into a band of enemies, committing an honorable suicide. The medicine man, blaming the chief's greed, laid a curse on the meadow, the tribe's summer home. The chief and any who stayed at the meadow would lose all their children save one through eternity."

"You made that up," he accused.

"No, I didn't."

"Do you believe it?"

"No," she drawled out. "Influenza took whole families by the thousands, and you've seen how bad the grade coming up here is now. You can imagine how bad it was then in a wagon. The locals sure made a big deal out of it though. It's no wonder Grandpa got spooked. He figured since there was only one child left, my father was safe."

Steven pointed out what he thought was a contradiction in her story. "Your father had two."

"One—me."

"If you're an only child, how is Caroleigh your sister?" he asked in confusion.

"Step-sister, sort of. My step-mother married her father, after my father died."

"Then how—well, it's probably none of my business, but if your great grandfather built this place, how did she become the owner?"

Stunned, then amused, Kari chuckled. "Just what business are you in?"

"Development."

"And you're here to?"

Confused, Steven answered, "Advise her as to whether she should sell or develop."

"What? Condos in the front yard?"

"More hotel/resort."

"Never happen."

Steven scratched his head with one finger while soap suds ran down his arm. "Okay, I'm lost."

"Oh, you've never had a woman use a come on before? She does not own the Meadow. She lied to you."

"You're back to that seducing thing," Steven stated with a sigh.

"If you're not interested, you better keep your door locked and not answer any light tapping."

"I shall become an incredibly heavy sleeper. Any other advice?"

Before she could answer, terrified shrieks echoed through the house.

* * * *

Emily huddled in a ball at the foot of the stairs. Between shrieks, she sobbed hysterically and pointed at the door. Kari took time enough to leave Rascal safely in the apartment before she followed Steven although she stopped several feet away with a grimace on her face and winced each time Emily shrieked. Just as they reached her, Edward, still in his pajamas, reached the head of the stairs.

Edward had to shout to be heard over Emily's screams. "What is wrong?"

Steven shook his head and knelt in front of her. "Did you fall?" he asked gently.

"Shake her and stop that horrid noise," Edward shouted as he jogged down the stairs.

Caroleigh arrived at the head of the stairs with a different idea. "Slap her," she ordered. She followed Edward with a cloud of purple chignon floating around her. "And stop that awful racket."

Steven did neither. He took Emily firmly by the shoulders. "Emily, look at me and tell me what happened."

"Man," Emily screamed, pointing again at the door.

"There was someone here?"

"Bloody," she wailed between sobs. "And…and his…his arm was missing."

Steven twisted to look at the door. He looked at the spotless marble floor. Last he looked at Edward. Edward shrugged. He'd looked the same places and didn't see anything either.

Edward asked of Caroleigh, "Does she see things, love?"

"Obviously she has," she answered indifferently. "The last time she behaved this way it was a spider."

"Did it have missing limbs as well?"

Caroleigh shot him a look of annoyance and moved closer. "Emily, stand up and stop this nonsense."

The simple maneuver was accomplished only with Steven and Edward's help. Emily shook and gasped.

Evelyn, the last to arrive at the head of the stairs, stayed there to ask, "Whatever has happened?"

"It would seem," Edward answered, "Emily has seen a spook." He turned to Kari who still stood off to the side. "Do you have spooks, love?" Since she still stared intently at Emily without answering, he added, "Ghosts, specters—?"

"Stop explaining everything to her," Caroleigh snapped. "Kari, go fix some tea."

"Ah, the famous cure all. Personally, I would rather have a valium."

"I have some," Evelyn told them. "I could use one myself. All that screaming simply shattered my nerves."

"Oh, goody, drugs, pass them out."

"Edward," Caroleigh said in a warning tone. She turned on Kari. "Tea. Now."

Only Steven watched Kari walk away.

The only one who benefited from a valium was Emily, putting her to sleep immediately, leaving, or should have left, the others to fend for themselves. However, at eleven o'clock Caroleigh announced it was time for brunch—she was famished after all the dramatics—and led the way to the dining room. Food awaited, though from the behavior of some it was expected, not appreciated. A buffet with soup, an array of fresh vegetables, and a wide variety of sandwich makings with thick slices of homemade bread covered a sideboard.

"What kind of a brunch is this?" Evelyn asked tersely.

"The kind for beggars," Edward answered absently, filling a bowl with soup.

Evelyn looked over the choices. "It isn't even a proper breakfast," she sniffed.

"I believe its called lunch," Edward told her. "Casual style. Caroleigh did warn you we had to rough it."

"She also promised a cook, not some hysterical little girl."

Edward moved on to fill his plate. "We all hope and pray she recovers quickly so we needn't suffer needlessly."

"Are you—?"

Caroleigh spoke quickly, interrupting her. "We should have a séance."

"Whatever for?" Edward asked lazily. Kari came in with a tea pot, distracting him. "Oh, love, you've made tea."

Kari, her hair again drawn to a knot, glasses, and oversized shirt buttoned to her throat, stared at him without comment.

"Put it on the table," Caroleigh ordered.

"I've never been to a séance." Evelyn picked through the buffet to find something she considered suitable. "Are they fun?"

"Marvelous," Edward told her. "Tables rattle, lights flicker." He wiggled his fingers in her face for emphasize. "Strange winds blow and horrid sounds float through the air."

"Are they safe?"

"Of course they are or Caroleigh wouldn't suggest having one."

"One what?" Kari asked.

As Caroleigh gave her a look of exasperation, Edward answered. "A séance. Doesn't it sound like fun?"

"No."

"Are you afraid of ghosts?"

"No and there are no one-armed, bloody ghosts in this house."

"Emily saw something, all bloody, missing a limb, and presumably very dead since he exited by walking through the door."

Kari stared at him the entire time he spoke. When he finished, she stared a moment longer before she walked out with a shake of her head.

"She probably had breakfast with him and thought nothing of it," Evelyn whispered.

"He wouldn't dare," Edward gasped.

"She probably…" she went on, "…communicates easier with the dead than the living."

Steven had heard all he wanted and started for the kitchen door.

"Do you need something?" Caroleigh asked to halt him and reached for the bell beside her.

"Just water." He put his hand over the bell to keep her from ringing it. "And I'm already up."

To enforce his intention, he walked off before she could say more.

Kari was on the far side of the center work bar. Lost in thought, she stared at something without seeing it. He was nearly to her before she realized he was there and startled slightly.

"I see you've lost your fur piece," he told her.

"Not hardly." She pointed to the floor. "He's become a slipper."

Steven leaned over the counter and chuckled. Rascal was draped across her feet with his black eyes peering up at Steven from under his long bangs. Kari sighed and looked down at her feet. "Poor little orphan. He’s been with me all day, and she hasn't even asked about him."

“Her day didn’t start until about an hour ago,” he told her as he straightened to find her gaze locked on his face. "Thanks for lunch."

"You're welcome."

He tipped his head towards the carrots she was slicing. "Is that for dinner?"

"With roast and potatoes in a crock pot so I can cook and still get things done."

"Sounds practical and good."

"You sound easy to please." Before he could comment, she asked, "Did you come in for something in particular?"

He shook his head. Steven wasn’t going to tell her he was sick of hearing the others make fun of her. "Not really, but I said water before she could start ringing that bell."

"It wouldn't have done her any good," she said dryly.

He assumed she meant she wouldn't have answered and with the implied hostility, Steven didn't comment. His eyes dropped, and he noticed green carrot tops and dirt in the sink. "Did you grow those?” he asked, looked back up and found her gaze still on his face.

"Yes."

"How, this time of the year?”

"In a greenhouse, it's in the valley."

"Where's that?"

"At the bottom of the bluff."

"Ah,” Steven said with a grin, “that's where the out buildings are. Inconvenient, isn't it?"

"Very. It's a three mile walk or nearly a ten mile drive just to feed the chickens."

"That's why your eggs were in a bowl, not a carton."

"Fresh from the chicken."

"Something tells me your great grandpa didn't do that himself," he mused.

"They say he did it twice a day, every day, until a week before he died."

"Twice?"

“He had to milk the cow. I don't have a cow."

"Smart girl," he said with a chuckle.

Caroleigh walked in. Her smile froze in place, and her eyes darted from one to the other of them. There was frost in her voice when she asked, "Did you have trouble finding the water?"

Kari told her, "I'll get it as soon as I finish here."

"Whatever that is, I'm sure it can wait a few minutes."

"It's your dinner since Emily isn't feeling well."

Without a thank you for the consideration and work on her behalf, Caroleigh said instead, "It can wait."

Kari pointed to a section of cupboard with the large knife in her hand. "The pitchers are over there."

"I'll do it," Steven said and moved to do so.

Caroleigh caught him by the arm and turned her touch into a caress. "Don't be silly. Go finish your lunch. I'll be right there."

"Thanks," he murmured with a brief glance at Kari.

Though Steven was through the door, he was close enough to hear Caroleigh turn on Kari. "What do you think you're doing?" she hissed.

"How long are you going to be here?" Kari asked instead of answering.

"Until I get damned good and ready to leave," she retorted and flounced out—without any water.

Steven barely made it to the buffet table before she shoved through the door.

* * * *

Caroleigh smoothed her napkin in her lap and spoke to Kari as she came from the kitchen with a bowl in each hand for their dinner. "What was the name of Grandpa's nanny?"

Kari didn't answer. As she leaned forward to set the bowls down Caroleigh shouted at her. "Kari, answer me!"

After a violent start nearly spilled the contents of those bowls, Kari set them down with thuds. "I thought you were talking to them," she said in irritation.

"Do you not listen at all?"

"Not if I don't know you're talking to me."

Edward leaned forward, elbows on the table. "We were wondering, love, what the name of that nanny was."

"Nanny?"

He tipped his head to urge her to go on. When she didn't, he did. "The one who is supposed to haunt the nursery?"

"Haunt the nursery?"

"Never mind," Caroleigh snapped. "She's heard the story all of her life. Now she acts like it's a total mystery to her."

Kari waited until Caroleigh finished, then told Edward, "Amilee. Some say she sits in the window watching for the children to come home. She never recovered from the shock of losing all her charges so suddenly in that horrible wagon accident. They say she just sat there, rocking the only one left, a wee babe, clutching it to her breast, until she starved herself to death. They buried her next to the children."

"That gave me the chills," Evelyn exclaimed. "Did they have to pry the poor thing from her dead arms?"

"That was my grandfather. He said she lived to be in her nineties, married with six children of her own and twenty-four grandchildren. It isn't her in the window. The middle window on the third floor was Great Grandma Kari Anne's favorite place to sit to watch the children play on the lawn while she nursed the baby. They say she still sits there, and the children still play on the lawn."

Evelyn leaned forward to listen to her and asked breathlessly, "Why?"

Edward leaned back to watch Kari speculatively. Steven, despite himself, was drawn in after seeing what he thought was someone in that window. Caroleigh gave her a look of heavy study.

"They died so suddenly and violently they can't accept that they're dead. Their wagon went over the side going down the grade to town one day. Only my grandfather survived because he was at home with the nanny. Great Grandmother came back to watch over him, and she keeps the other children with her. Many say they've seen her, that she wanders the house, taking care of things the same as she did when she was alive. Grandpa stays because she is still here, and she'll stay as long as her descendants are here. The third floor has been closed since her children died. Great Grandpa had the nursery with Grandpa moved to the room next to his when Great Grandma died. Grandpa and his wife never used it."

She had all their attention when she shrugged slightly. "I keep meaning to move that lamp, but I don't get up there too often."

"What lamp?" Edward asked.

"The one that sits in front of that window."

The two men smiled over being sucked in then dropped with reality. Evelyn, pettishly, dismissed Kari and turned to Caroleigh. Caroleigh had to pull herself away from a very thoughtful study of Kari to switch her attention.

"It's amazing how stories will grow out of the simplest occurrences," Evelyn said, as if she hadn't believed a single word of it for a second.

Edward leaned towards Kari. "Will you join us for our séance?"

With a slight twist of her lips, she answered with a flat, "No."

Steven asked quickly before she could leave again, "Could we talk you into a tour of the third floor?"

Caroleigh answered for her. "It's dirty and dreary up there."

Kari told him, "The lighting is bad. If you want to see detail, daytime is the best."

"Tomorrow?" he asked hopefully.

Again, Caroleigh answered. "If you really want to see it, I'll take you, the attics too, spider webs and all. Oh, we'll need candles, Kari."

"Candles?"

"Yes, candles," she answered in irritation. "For our séance."

"I don't think—"

"I believe we can handle a few candles."

"I'm not—" Kari shut the words off and just abruptly walked out.

"If the idea of candles makes her nervous," Edward said in a whisper, "we could just turn the lights down."

Caroleigh scoffed. "We're perfectly capable of burning a few candles without setting the house on fire."

As usual, it wasn't Caroleigh who did anything. The group moved from the dinning room to the parlor. Candles lit the room and a fire was built, again courtesy of Kari and with the same degree of appreciation shown as there had been for the two meals she provided for them. The four sat at a small table, Steven reluctantly. Kari's single refusal to join them had been accepted. His four attempts to refuse had been rejected. Even when Kari came in and took a seat off to the side on a delicate settee to watch in that intent way of hers, no invitations were made for her to join them at the table.

Caroleigh took charge. "We start by calling forth the spirit."

"How does one do that?" Evelyn asked.

"Here ghosty, ghosty," Edward teased, drawing a nervous giggle from Evelyn and a scowl from Caroleigh.

"Be serious or it won't work," Caroleigh ordered.

"I must say I'm not sure I want it to," Edward drawled. "He did give Emily rather a nasty start."

"Because she wasn't expecting it. It would help if we knew his name."

"I don't believe introductions were made, but one would assume it was Daddy."

"One must never assume. Now join hands, close your eyes, and concentrate." She waited long enough for her orders to be obeyed. "Oh, spirit of the house, speak to us. Speak to us now."

They all fell into silence with the only other sound being the abnormally loud ticking of a mantle clock.

“Oh, spirit, speak to—”

A noise started. Low at first, gaining volume as it drew nearer them. A sharp, irregular wail pierced their ears, and a chilled cold swept over them.

"Oh," Evelyn gasped.

"Whatever…?” Edward began and strangled off with a gasp of his own.

The sound of a crash reverberated off the walls, followed by a violent buck of the table beneath their hands. Edward jumped to his feet. Another crash slammed their senses. Evelyn screamed, jumped to her feet, and started to run. A split second later, she screamed again, falling with a thud to the floor. Before one scream faded, she screamed a third time when the room blazed into bright light.

"Stop that," Caroleigh ordered curtly from the light switch.

"It grabbed me," Evelyn cried in horror.

Steven started to chuckle. He choked back full laughter while he moved to help Evelyn to her feet since Edward, a look of total confusion on his face, couldn’t seem to move.

"It isn't funny!” Evelyn cried. “It grabbed me! And there was that awful cold, and the horrible noise and the crashes. The table nearly flew into the air, and the noise, that unearthly noise.”

Steven couldn't talk then for laughing. He pointed at Rascal cuddled in Kari’s arms.

All Caroleigh saw was Kari. "What did you do?" she demanded furiously.

Steven sobered quickly. "She didn't do anything. The dog did. He howled and bumped the table when he jumped to her lap."

"Oh, thank God," Edward said in reverence.

"The dog?” Evelyn asked in confusion.

"The noise you heard was him," Steven explained patiently. "Then he knocked over the lamp when he jumped into her lap. That was the first crash. Edward bumped the table getting up and knocked his chair over, the second crash and what grabbed you. You tripped over it.”

"Oh.” She stared at him for a moment then. "But he didn't cause the cold. I felt it. Didn't you feel it?" She looked at Edward who nodded. "It was like death or…or evil, but it's warm now. Yes, yes, just like someone good and loving pushed away the evil."

"I turned the heater on," Kari stated.

"Can you not stay with the simplest of conversations?" Caroleigh demanded tersely.

Kari sighed. "I'm going to bed," she stated and walked away with Rascal in her arms.

Evelyn grew more excited. "Don't they say dogs are sensitive to spirits? That must be what frightened him. He felt it just before we did. The house has a guardian. When the evil tried to come in, the guardian pushed it right out. It was fantastic! I never believed in any of this before, but now—My God, Caroleigh, that was fantastic!"

"Definitely entertaining," Edward agreed. "Whatever will we do to follow that up?"

Chapter Two

By his second cup of coffee Steven decided Kari was not coming out. She'd made coffee in the main kitchen and left it for him to find, but she had not answered his knock on her apartment door. At seven he put the cup in the sink, turned off the coffee maker, and picked up his coat. His intention was to take the outside tour he had planned the day before. He almost got to the kitchen hall before his plans were altered by Caroleigh, in a cloud of rose chiffon.

"Oh," he said in genuine surprise, "you're up early."

"Is she?" she asked coolly.

"Excuse me?"

"Is Kari here?"

"I haven't seen her," he answered truthfully. "Would you like some coffee? It's still hot."

In the time it took him to speak, she drifted close enough to lay her hand on his arm. "I haven't been a very good hostess, leaving you to make your own coffee. What time do you get up so I can have it made for you?"

He didn't miss that she would *have* it made or correct her mistaken assumption that he'd made his own. "There's no reason for anyone to get up especially for me."

"Kari is always up early, probably earlier than you. Sometimes I don't think she sleeps at all." She hesitated and glanced at the door to Kari's apartment. "This is awkward, Steven, but I really must speak to you about Kari. I'm sure you've observed that she's…well, she isn't…or rather she has difficulty…" She broke off with a faint laugh. "This is embarrassing for me. I love her dearly, but I have to admit she has a very difficult time interacting socially in a normal manner. There are medical terms for her condition, but basically she just does not relate well to others. She perceives things quite differently, misunderstands even the simplest of good intentions."

Steve leaned back against the bar, his arms crossed over his chest. "Such as?"

"Your kindness to her. You are so kind, just as you were to Emily. Emily understands you're just being kind. Kari…well, she…" She pressed her lips together and sighed heavily. "She perceives things differently."

"So you want me to be mean to her?"

"No, of course not, but please, be careful about being alone with her and defending her when you feel I'm being too stern." She stepped close, both of her hands on his folded arms. "I've dealt with this for years now. I really do know what is best for her."

When a door opened somewhere down the back hall, Steven knew who it was. He straightened and tried to step back. Caroleigh moved into him as she turned to face the hall and smiled sweetly as Kari came into the kitchen

"Where have you been so early already this morning?" she asked just as sweetly.

"Just checking the livestock," Kari returned blandly. The bundle she held under her jacket wiggled. "Sick rabbit, want to hold it?"

"No," Caroleigh cried as Kari started towards her. She held up her hand to ward her off and turned to Steven. "Quite the little farmer, isn't she?"

She turned just her head to let her gaze travel over Kari and come to rest on her muddy boots and pant legs. She didn't seem to notice there were no glasses perched on Kari's nose as she lifted her eyebrows to suggest Kari was hopeless. With a touch on his arm that turned into a light caress, she also seemed to forget her warning about being alone with Kari. She kissed him lightly on the cheek and purred, "See you at breakfast."

Steven stood where he was until he was sure she was gone. "That wasn't what it looked like."

"Seldom is with her," Kari answered indifferently.

With a smile of relief, he asked, "Sick rabbit?"

"The rabbit is fine." She folded back the edge of her jacket. "This never got close to it."

Two little black eyes peered out of muddy, burr encrusted hair. Rascal trembled and squirmed to get back under cover.

"What a mess," Steven said with a grimace.

"I don't suppose you know anything about grooming one of these things."

"I don't think you can just let them drip dry."

"Of course not." She turned to a wall-mounted phone, set the hand piece on her shoulder under her chin, and punched in the code for a speed dial.

"You're getting pretty good at that one-handed thing."

"Not by choice—oh, hi." The last was said into the phone. "I'm fine. I need to know how to groom a ten pound dog with hair longer than he is, full of mud and burrs." She listened with a frown. "He's shivering like crazy, like…you're sure…okay."

She hung up and walked down the hall at a rapid pace. Steven followed into a room he hadn't seen before, a laundry area big enough for a family to live in.

"Need some help?" he asked watching her open and close cupboards.

"God, yes. It has to be dog—there it is—shampoo, lots of creme rinse…" She started back out at a speed that had him do a quick side-step to get out of the way. "…of any kind and a blow dryer. No drip dry."

By then they had reached her apartment. She walked through the kitchen and livingroom to the bedroom. "I keep the outside door locked now," she told him from the bathroom.

"I'm not going to make that mistake again," he said in embarrassment, not that she noticed as she shoved towels, a blow dryer, creme rinse, and a brush at him.

"Kitchen?" she asked with a smile.

"Huh?"

Back on the move she said, "The sink is bigger in there."

"Oh, for him. You do have a way of changing subjects abruptly," he told her at her heels.

"Can't you keep more than one in mind at a time?"

"Guess I'll have to learn how," he murmured.

"Did you mean for me not to hear that?"

"Yes," he admitted. He dumped the load in his arms on the counter as she unzipped her coat for the squirming mud ball. "Oh, man."

"Just remember, you volunteered."

They stood shoulder to shoulder working as quickly as possible. Rascal, between unexpected attempts to jump out, huddled in a trembling ball in the bottom of the big sink making anything they tried to do more difficult. He fought all their efforts. They settled into a system with Steven holding while Kari worked out burrs.

"He looks like a rat," Steven commented.

"He does, poor thing. Think we have them all?"

He ran his hands over the shivering body. "I think so."

"I hope so." She leaned against him briefly to reach the bottle of creme rinse. "The water did warm him up a little, but…" The overhead light flashed. "Oh, sure."

"What is it?"

"Phone," she told him with a look over her shoulder at the phone on the far wall.

"Why doesn't it ring?"

She shook water from her hands to go answer it. "Grandpa didn't like to hear it, and I've never—"

Rascal went into a new fit. The only way Steven could catch him was to hold him in the air with both hands. Water sprayed every direction from his struggle to get free. "You hold. I'll get it," he said quickly.

The transfer ended with Rascal in her arms, up against her chest. "No you don't, you little stinker," Kari told him and plopped him back in the sink.

The battle was on to keep him there while Steven hurried to the phone. He grabbed it up, said hello, and twisted to watch.

After a pause on the other end, a deep, curt, male voice ordered, "Put Kari on."

"She's busy right now," Steven said, watching Kari hold Rascal against the side of the sink with one hand and squeezed creme rinse from the bottle over him with the other. "Can I take a message?" Rascal slipped from under her hand, and Kari scrambled to catch him one handedly. "Quickly."

"I want to talk to her now."

Rascal's front feet and head came up over the sink edge. Kari dropped the bottle to use both hands. "She's busy."

"Tell her it's Dell. She'll talk to me."

Rascal got away from her again. Kari caught him in mid-air. "Call back." Steven hung up and hurried back to help. It took both of them to work the rinse through the dog's hair, both again to hold him under the faucet to wash it out, and still both to swaddle him in a towel. It even took both of them to get him back safely up against Kari's chest where he finally quit his struggles. The light started flashing again.

"Who was it?" Kari asked.

"Someone named Dell."

"I'm going to sit down for the next part," she told Steven. "Want to get those?" She pointed to the blow dryer and brush as she went to the phone. She didn't bother to say hello. "What did you forget…You told me that already…okay…what?…a friend." She hung up abruptly. "He has to be brushed until he's dry. What a pain. Oh, God, what a mess."

The last referred to the counter and floor. Water had splashed all over both and on the floor it mixed with the mud from her boots to make a puddle of brown water. As well as a large area in front of the cabinet, a trail of muddy prints led to the phone. She leaned down for the laces on one boot, and Rascal whimpered with renewed squirms.

"Let me," Steven said quickly.

He squatted down in front of her. After he had loosened the laces on the first boot, she put her hand on his back to keep her balance while he held the boot for her to pull her foot free. Her hand was still on his back for the second boot when the back hall kitchen door opened.

"Uh-oh," He stood slowly with the last boot still in his hand. "We're busted."

Emily stood still with the door held open. "Has there been an accident?" she asked as her gaze flickered over the scene.

"Rascal got out," Steven explained. "We had to bath him."

"Oh." She stepped inside, allowing the door to swing shut. "Miss Caroleigh sent me down to fix breakfast. She'll be down as soon as she's ready."

"You're on your own," Kari said and snatched the blow dryer and brush from him.

He stayed right at her heels. "Oh, no you don't," he told her, but he hesitated at the apartment door to look back at the mess.

"I'll take care of it, Mr. Chase," Emily told him.

"You're a sweetheart," he told her, ducking through the door. With it safely closed, he fell back against the wood panel and gave an exaggerated swipe of his brow.

"Coward," Kari teased with a smile.

"Yep and not alone I notice."

"Not in the least even if it will take Caroleigh at least an hour to get dressed." She handed him the blow dryer and pointed to a socket in the living room floor by the couch. "As long as Emily doesn't snitch on us, we should be safe from the wrath of Caroleigh."

"Why would she?"

"Why not?" she countered with a shrug. She uncovered Rascal and held him up to look in his face. "Cleaning up your messes is a lot easier than cleaning you. No more going out without a leash."

The dog responded with squirms and whimpers. Hè really began to fight and even howled when the blow dryer started. Drying and brushing was as much a wrestling match as the bath had been. Once he was reasonably dry and only a little brushing remained, Kari called a break. She set him on the floor, and he immediately disappeared under the computer desk.

"Somehow," she stated tonelessly, "I don't think he's going to be saying thank you."

"Don't want to go buy a dozen of him?"

There was a slight pause before she answered. "A dozen? Of him?" Steven smiled in answer. "Sure and a hole drilled in my head." She looked down at herself, muddy and wet from neck to ankles. "I never worked that hard bathing my shepherds."

"You have shepherds?"

"Did. I lost them a couple of weeks ago," she answered softly.

"What happened?"

"Coyotes, I think. The pack probably took them down. In their prime, they wouldn't have messed with them as a pair, but they were both getting old. I haven't had the heart to replace them yet."

"I would imagine they were a lot of company for you," Steven said in sympathy.

"They were."

"You miss them."

"Terribly," she admitted before she changed the subject abruptly. "I'm going to change. Be right back."

True to her word, Kari retuned in barely ten minutes to crawl on her hands and knees to retrieve the dog from under the desk. Returning to the couch, Kari wrestled the dog and brushed.

"Every new experience makes life interesting," Kari observed and gave Rascal's bangs a final brush with her fingertips.

She referred to their morning spent with Rascal. It reminded Steven of the night before. He watched Rascal race back to his refuge under the computer desk and said, "I figured out the cold wind thing. When the heater fan comes on, it pushes the cold air in the duct work out ahead of the warm air." He knew he was right when she grinned.

"Have you spoiled their fun yet?" she asked.

Steven chuckled. "I don't think you could talk Evelyn out of it. She thinks she's had a religious experience or something."

"She'd probably turn inside out if she ever saw a real ghost."

"If there were any such thing, though it makes me really wonder what Emily saw."

"Nothing to do with a heater." She looked at her watch. "Since you didn't get to see the mine yesterday, if you still want to, we could go now and be back before the storm gets here."

"I'm glad you changed your mind, but what makes you think it's going to storm?"

With a perfectly straight face, she said, "Grandpa told me after he stepped on Rascal's tail last night. He's the one that locks the door, too."

Steven's first thought, after the story she'd told the night before, was that she was joking, but she didn't smile. His second thought was that the door had seemed to be locked and how easily it had opened for her, and something had frightened Rascal twice that he knew of.

Kari suddenly batted her eyes. "National Weather Bureau," she told him as she stood.

"Funny," he retorted and stood with her.

"But I had you going."

"Did not."

"Did."

The smile started at the corner of her mouth and spread slowly over her lips. Just as slowly Steven leaned towards her as if drawn by a magnet. He sighed and turned his head when someone knocked on the door. "Want me to get it?"

She walked by him to get it herself. Emily stood there, her head turned to watch behind her. Her eyes quickly flickered over Kari's change of clothes and Steven's still damp ones and spoke to him. "Breakfast is ready. Miss Caroleigh is waiting. I didn't tell her where you were, just that I would find you."

"Thank you. Tell her I'll be there soon. I want to change first."

She smiled faintly and told Kari, "There's more than enough if you would like to join them."

"Thank you, but I've already eaten."

Emily nodded and backed away. Steven moved by Kari enough to shut the door for privacy. "It would be rude to refuse after she went to the trouble of fixing it," he told her with regret.

"Enjoy."

"We can go after I eat."

"Dreamer, Caro didn't get up this early to spend the day alone. She did promise to give you a tour of the third floor."

"I'd rather you show me."

"Just make her slow down. Walk off if there's something you want to see," she advised.

"That isn't why," Steven told her frankly.

"I really didn't think so," she answered without any coy pretense.

He took her words as encouragement. "Later today?"

She shook her head. "There are some things I need to get done."

"That you had forgotten," he said in disappointment.

"That I was going to put off. I'll get them done today and have tomorrow free."

He smiled broadly. "Seven too early?"

"No, but you'd better leave a note telling them you won't be back until dinner. I'll pack us a lunch."

* * * *

When Kari came in for dinner, Steven gave no particular attention to her simply because she gave him none. She didn't give any of them much attention. She looked tired and preoccupied. After a brief greeting, they ignored her. Ignoring them, she took food as it was handed to her and took no part in the conversation. She occupied herself instead taking bits of meat from her plate to hold under the edge of the table.

"I hate thunder and lightning," Evelyn said.

"It's still very far off," Edward told her.

"But it's coming very fast and sounds like some giant monster. It's so much louder and brighter here."

"Closer to it," Steven commented while he watched Kari out of the corner of his eye.

"It sounds as if it's going to come right through the roof at you. I suppose some people could get used to it living here, but I certainly wouldn't."

The only person who did live there offered nothing on the subject. She slipped another bit of meat under the table.

Caroleigh looked under the table. "Don't feed him, Kari. I don't want him to learn to beg."

Kari looked up, but didn't answer. When Caroleigh didn't say more, she took another bite of food with her gaze going to the windows. "There's a storm coming," she commented.

"Yes, dear," Caroleigh said with a roll of her eyes. At that moment, a loud clap of thunder prompted Rascal to vault into Kari's lap. "Put him down. We don't need a dog at the table."

Rascal squirmed around until he was comfortable, draped over Kari's arm. He stretched his neck out towards her plate, and Kari, instead of putting him down, handed him a piece of meat.

"Kari!" Caroleigh shouted.

Rascal cowered, and Kari jumped. "What?" she asked in annoyance.

"I already told you."

Steven told Caroleigh, "I've never met a dog that had to be taught to beg."

"He never has before," she retorted and snapped at Kari. "Put him down."

"He's afraid of the storm," Kari told her.

"I don't care. I will not have him babied or spoiled." She twisted in her chair and rang the bell for Emily. As soon as Emily appeared at the door, she told her, "Put Sir Gaylord in his carrier."

To bridge an uncomfortable silence while Emily struggled to take the squirming, growling dog, Edward asked Steven, "So what do you think of the Meadow?"

"It's beautiful," he answered briefly, watching Kari, Emily, and the dog.

Kari told her sister. "It's mean to lock him up when he's frightened."

"Unless you—" Caroleigh began hatefully.

A boom loud enough to rattle the windows drew a yelp from Rascal and a scream from Evelyn. While everyone looked at Evelyn, Rascal took advantage of the distraction. He leaped from Emily's insecure hold and hit the floor in a run. Emily took off after him. Kari went to her feet glaring at Caroleigh in a ready-to-do-battle stance that had them all staring expectantly. When she spun to follow Emily, Edward blew out a breath only to suck it in again when Emily screamed.

Kari was the first one Emily collided with on her frantic run back to the dining room, still in full scream. She ran by Kari and didn't stop until she ran into the others, all in a dead run toward her. Her only coherent response to multiple questions was to point to the great hall. As a group, Emily supported by Edward, they joined Kari in her silent—though distant—examination of the dark puddle in front of the door.

"Is that blood?" Evelyn gasped.

"Looks to be," Edward answered as they formed a semi-circle around it, each careful not to touch it or the bloody prints leading from the door to it, though none led away.

"You see, the dark spirit came in this far before the light spirit blocked his way," Evelyn said excitedly.

"That better not stain," Kari said to no one in particular.

"The spirits are trying to tell us something," Evelyn went on. "Someone died a violent death or was murdered."

"Driving over a cliff seems rather violent to me," Edward drawled.

"Maybe someone caused it. That would explain it. Maybe he's come back for revenge."

"That was twenty years ago," Caroleigh said tersely. "There's no one here who could have caused it. Emily, clean up that mess."

Emily shook her head and backed away.

"Oh, brother," Kari muttered and walked off.

"Don't look at me," Evelyn said quickly.

"Let him," Edward suggested. He pointed to Rascal who sniffed at the edge of the pool.

"No!" Caroleigh shrieked. Understandably, she startled the dog into a panicked run. "Get him."

The last was directed at Emily. The chase went back through the dining room. He might have been cornered if Kari hadn't pushed open the kitchen door, mop and pail in hand. Rascal jumped quickly at her leg twice in an effort to get her to pick him up before he darted through the door Kari held open just as Emily reached for him.

"Move, Kari," Caroleigh ordered.

Kari stared at her, side-stepping slowly into Emily and let the door swing shut. She looked blankly at Emily as the other woman dodged by her to push the door open.

"You did that deliberately," Caroleigh growled.

Her expression blank, Kari asked, "What?"

Caroleigh threw her hands in the air and stalked off. Evelyn and Edward followed with Evelyn back on the subject of possible messages. Only Steven stayed to watch Kari until she batted her eyeslashes at him. Smiligng, he joined the others, reluctantly.

Caroleigh whispered and looked repeatedly toward the great hall where Kari cleaned the blood away. "A change of any kind upsets her. I don't say anything until plans are definite, then I ease into it gently."

"Is she autistic?" Evelyn asked.

"No, that isn't what it is. Sometimes she's even quite rational." The last was said directly to Steven.

"I haven't seen that," Evelyn whispered. "The way she stares at people gives me the willies. The rest of the time she doesn't seem to know anyone is even there, and she has the personality of a cardboard box."

"It is best not to upset her," Caroleigh repeated. "Just don't discuss the possibility of a sale or development in front of her. It isn't even definite, and she would just be upset unnecessarily if nothing materializes."

"You have the patience of a saint."

"Ah, yes," Edward said drolly, "St. Caroleigh."

Caroleigh smiled faintly. "She is my sister. I can't just lock her up."

"Where would she go if you do develop?" Evelyn asked.

"I have other, smaller properties and not so isolated." She sighed heavily. "I'm afraid I'm going to have to move her soon anyway. She withdraws more and more each time I come for a visit."

"Really?" Edward mocked. "I thought she was much chattier this time."

"That's chatty?" Evelyn asked in disbelief.

"She does do better in a one to one situation," Caroleigh went on, again directing her remarks to Steven. "She can cope better, but when there's more than one person, she gets overwhelmed, so lost and confused, and draws into herself, shuts people out."

Evelyn was still the only one to ask questions. "Is it safe for her to be alone?"

"So far."

The object of their conversation wrung the mop out one last time. She looked their way, watched them for a moment, then picked up the bucket and left.

Steven got to his feet. "Excuse me."

"Where are you going?" Caroleigh asked sweetly.

"For some air."

"It's raining," Evelyn said.

"Not on the veranda," Caroleigh pointed out as she stood to go with him. "Some fresh air would be nice. The air is so wonderfully brisk in the spring."

"Would you like to join us?" Steven asked quickly of Evelyn and Edward when he saw which direction things were going.

"Hardly," Edward said. He slipped down in his seat. "What she calls brisk, I call cold and damp."

"Me too," Evelyn agreed and then asked Edward, "Would you care for a game of gin?"

"I'll just get my coat," Caroleigh said and hurried off.

"Do have a good time," Edward told Steven, one eyebrow cocked knowingly.

"Such a nice night to cuddle," Evelyn said with a smirk.

Kari walked in as far as the doorway and announced tonelessly, "The carriage house is on fire."

Edward and Evelyn just stared at her. Steven went to her, asking, "What's the quickest way out there?"

"Out where?" Caroleigh asked, returning with a mink over her arm.

"She said…" Evelyn said with a half-laugh, "…that the carriage house is on fire."

"Really, Kari," Caroleigh retorted.

Edward moved up behind Steven. "Shouldn't we do something?"

Steven didn't wait for Kari to show him the way. He started toward the dining room to find the back entrance. When she came up beside him he broke into a run.

"It's too late to get your cars out," she told him.

She was right. Steven stopped as soon as he could see the fire. Flames shot out the windows on both ends and through the roof in several places. Everything in-between was fully engulfed.

Kari told him, "I hope you didn't have anything important in there."

Steven shook his head. "Nothing I can't replace."

She stared at him, and her expression was not bland or indifferent. "You?" he asked gently.

"There's over hundred years of history in that building," she answered softly. "Great Grandpa—" She broke off with a jerk when Caroleigh shouted behind her.

"Don't just stand there! Do something!"

"It's too late," Steven told her. He turned to Kari. "Do you think it will spread to the house?"

Caroleigh retorted, "What are you asking her for? Why do you think she would know?" She shouted at Kari. "Call the fire department. Get some help. Where's the phone?"

Her ravings took her back in the house. Then Kari answered. "I think it's wet enough it won't spread to the house, but I am concerned about what might happen if the gas tanks explode. It sits closer to the strip than the house. If the heat dries it out enough, it might ignite."

"What can we do?"

"Wait. The others will be here soon."

With his brows furrowed in puzzlement, he asked, "Why didn't you tell her you already called for help?"

"She knows how things work up here."

Help was not the fire department. The nearest of those was twenty-five miles away over switch-backs and dangerous grades. Help came instead from neighboring ranches. The owners and their employees arrived by pickup loads. After their initial conversation with Kari, they all settled down in their trucks and on the veranda to watch from various vantage points for any indication of spreading. Disgusted by the lack of action, Caroleigh went in the house. Evelyn and Edward soon followed—it was just too cold. In a show of her appreciation for the men who gave up sleep on a cold, damp night on her behalf, Kari went to the kitchen. She made soup, sandwiches, and lots of coffee. Steven tried to help, only to be told bluntly his help wasn't needed. He joined the men outside.

Steven heard more than once how strange lightning was and the weird things it could do while he visited with the neighbors on the veranda and walked the perimeter of the fire with a shovel in hand. Fortunately the explosions Kari worried over had either taken place before she discovered the fire, mistaken for thunder, or simply did not happen. By dawn everyone was satisfied any potential ember had been found and smothered and the fire was safely burnt out. They loaded back up in their pickups with Kari thanking each man personally. When the last of them drove out, a sheriff's car drove in.

"A little late, isn't he?" Steven asked.

"He doesn't fight fires. He just writes reports on them. Would you mind getting him a cup of coffee?"

"Sure," he said though he didn't miss the way the man smiled at her and scowled at him as Kari walked out to meet him. The scowl puzzled him. The neighbors had all been friendly, though reserved. None of them had exhibited any open hostility, but the sheriff did. Steven was curious as to how a cup of coffee was going to be accepted, but he never found out. Kari was back on the veranda as he went out and the sheriff drove away.

"He didn't stay long."

"There wasn't much to see," she told him tonelessly.

"Everyone figured it was lightning."

"That seems reasonable."

Her tone was so abrupt, Steven backed up a step. "Guess you'd like to get some rest."

"Sounds like a good idea."

Confused, he asked, "Are you mad at me over something?"

"No."

He backed another step. "Guess I'll see you later then."

"Later."

At a loss, he nodded and turned away. She let him get two steps. "Evan, thank you."

He still didn't understand her mood, but he smiled. "Anytime, Terri," he teased back.

Chapter Three

After a couple of hours sleep, Steven was up and headed out. He recoiled in surprise when he nearly collided with Caroleigh in the hall. Not only was she up, she was dressed and hooked an arm through his possessively. She hung on his arm all the way to the dining room. Evelyn, Edward, and Kari waited for them. Kari glanced up, her face lined with fatigue, and back down at her plate with disinterest.

"What a ghastly night." Caroleigh waited for Steven to pull her chair out for her. She continued while she settled. "Such clamoring and carrying on I could barely sleep. Have you called the insurance company yet?"

Everyone knew the last was directed at Kari, except Kari. She sat with her head down and her fork motionless.

Caroleigh leaned forward and slammed her hand down on the table. Everyone jumped, even those who saw it coming. Kari nearly startled out of her chair.

"It would really be nice if you would answer me when I speak to you," Caroleigh told her.

"I didn't hear you," Kari retorted.

"Then focus. I don't believe that's too much to ask." She yawned and looked down briefly to lay her napkin in her lap. "Have you called the insurance company yet?"

"Insurance?"

"Don't parrot me like an idiot. Just answer the question. My car will have to be replaced; Steven's as well."

"And my laptop," Evelyn put in. "And my cell phone and mink jacket."

Caroleigh rang the bell for Emily. "I don't expect it to take forever, either." She looked over her shoulder as Emily came in. "I would like tea this morning."

Edward had an eyebrow raised over the mink jacket Evelyn had worn into the house, not left in the car. "Poor Ester," Edward said drolly, "had to wait months after her car caught fire, and then they denied several of the items she claimed were in it. They said there was no proof they were actually in the car. They as much as called her a liar."

Caroleigh said in a bored tone, "Knowing Ester, she was."

Kari eyes shifted from one to the other of them as they talked, her expression one of intense concentration. When they snickered, she closed her eyes. She sighed before she opened them again and stood up slowly.

"Did you find Rascal?" she asked.

"Did I what?" Caroleigh asked.

"Your little dog, did you find him?"

"No," she answered, dismissing the subject.

"You need to make sure he didn't get out last night."

"You should answer me about the insurance," she countered hatefully.

"I'll get you the number. You can make your own claim."

Head down to fuss with the front of her blouse, Evelyn asked, "Should I make a separate one?"

Kari stared at her for a moment before she shrugged. "Whatever," she murmured.

"She seems particularly vague this morning," Edward whispered as she disappeared.

"Upset," Caroleigh corrected. "I told you she gets worse when she's upset." She sighed heavily and said to Steven. "I am so sorry about your car. The insurance company must pay for rentals until ours are replaced. I'll call today just as soon as we finish eating. They must be delivered. They will charge us, of course, and the insurance can pay for that, too."

"Don't let them talk you into one of those economy things either," Evelyn advised.

"Certainly not," Edward agreed. "Wherever would you put all your luggage?"

"Make light of it if you wish, but they do take outrageous advantage."

Steven ate. Two bites short of him leaving, Kari walked back in. She handed Caroleigh a slip of paper and sat back down. Evelyn immediately started off on another subject, complaining loudly to draw even Kari's attention,

"At least last night there weren't those awful animal sounds in the dark. I would have been able to sleep, but last night there was something in my closet. It was a rat, I know it was. I was so petrified I slept with the blanket over my head."

Steven leaned towards Kari with his hand stretched out. "Rascal?" he asked.

"Maybe."

They started off; Caroleigh right behind them. "Where are you going?" she demanded.

"To see how big a rat it is," Steven answered.

Evelyn shot to her feet. "You think it really was a rat?" she cried and struggled free of her chair to follow.

Edward sighed, laid his napkin on the table, and followed at a slower pace, the only reason he did not run into Evelyn. Evelyn did run into Caroleigh who ran into Kari when she and Steven suddenly stopped.

In front of them, the huge, heavy front door crept open slowly. No hand pushed it. At two feet, it stopped as abruptly as though it had hit a block wall, held still for a moment, and then slammed open with such velocity they all jumped. At full arch it rebounded halfway where it stopped again and quivered despite its weight. As they all stared at it, a little white ball of fur came from the back hall, Rascal making for the opening at a full run.

"No," Kari cried and dashed forward to head him off.

In an effort to stop and change direction, Rascal went into a slide, his paws clawing frantically at the slick floor. Ironically he didn't find any purchase until he slid into Kari's feet. She nearly had him when he pushed off her feet, clambered away, and disappeared into the drawing room. That was when the door slammed shut with a reverbrating boom, again without any hand to push it. The action set Evelyn off, taking Kari’s attention before she could start in pursuit of the dog.

"Did you see that?" she cried excitedly. "He tried to come in again. The guardian stopped him, just like before."

"More than likely…" Edward said in a bored tone, "…the door wasn't latched properly and the wind blew it open.”

“And shut?” Evelyn marched dramatically to the door. She pulled it open, just as dramatically, and stepped out on the veranda. "There is no wind," she announced and suddenly turned to Kari. "Do you have a video camera?"

"No, she doesn't," Caroleigh answered since Kari, staring up at the landing, had a vague, preoccupied look on her face. "Come in and shut the door." She turned to Kari. "You frightened Sir Gaylord. Don't do it again. He is a valuable champion."

Kari turned her eyes to Caroleigh but still seemed preoccupied as she said, "Don't let him get out. The coyotes would finish him off in about five minutes." She walked off only to turn back and ask, "When are you leaving?"

With a funny little start, Caroleigh stiffened. "I've already told you that."

"Do you want us to leave?" Steven asked, curious over what Kari had been looking at. It wasn't the way the dog had gone, and whatever it was, it seemed to have disturbed her.

Caroleigh answered for her again. "We can't leave. She knows that. She's just being particularly difficult."

Steven hid his disappointment and persisted. "If she wants us to—"

"We aren't leaving," Caroleigh retorted. "We can't anyway until the rentals get here?"

"Until what gets here?" Kari asked.

"Rentals," she answered nastily. "Rentals to replace our cars; we discussed it at breakfast."

Steven interrupted. "That was after she left," he said quietly.

Kari told her, "There are no rentals in town. The closest you'll get is to hire the shuttle to come after you."

"Fine, I'll call them."

"Fine, I'll get you the number."

After she walked away Evelyn asked in a whisper, "Is she throwing us out?"

"It would appear so," Edward said lazily.

"How can she throw you out of your own home?"

Caroleigh gave an exaggerated sigh. "Sometimes it's better to allow her fantasies than to…well, it's just easier to humor her." To Steven she said, "Have you seen enough?"

"I've seen enough," he answered as he walked away.

* * * *

Caroleigh had a very satisfied smile on her face. "The shuttle office is closed until Monday morning."

The three waited for her in the drawing room. Each reacted differently to the news. Edward merely slipped down further without much interest. Steven was concerned. Evelyn leaned forward anxiously.

"Will this cause her to do anything weird?"

"She's not dangerous," Edward answered.

"She's spooky," she whispered, then giggled. "She fits right in with the house, doesn't she?"

Edward told her with a cocked brow, ""Maybe the house is why. Ever think of that?"

"If they bothered her, wouldn't she leave?" Evelyn countered before she told Caroleigh, "And you said the house isn't haunted."

"Nothing like this has ever happened before," she answered indifferently.

"Really? Then one of us must be a catalyst."

"That would be you then, dear," Edward told her in a bored tone. "Caroleigh and I have been here several times before."

"Steven hasn’t. It could be him, or it could be a combination. I've seen that in a movie. People who never had a psychic experience before enter a zone or something or come in contact with a particular spirit, something to do with reincarnation or ancestry."

"Evelyn," Caroleigh pleaded.

"No, no," Edward cried. "Let her go on. It's fascinating. I belive I saw the same movie. Two women, one man, only he was trifling with both, wasn't it?"

"No, not that one,” Evelyn answered innocently. “This one was a reincarnation of a man who had been murdered in a past life. When he went to where the murder had taken place, the spirit of the murderer came after him."

"Sure it wasn't a woman out to kill a man who played with her affections?"

"Shut up, Edward," Caroleigh told him.

An undercurrent Evelyn didn’t seem aware of hung in the room. Steven was, even though he didn’t understand the cause of it. He did, however, have the uncomfortable feeling Edward’s remarks were being directed at him.

Evelyn answered. "No, but there was a woman involved, his lost love. He was murdered because of her."

"And did he get her in the end?" Edward asked.

"How could he if he was dead?” Caroleigh asked.

"The murderer, love, not the murdered."

"I think she died, and neither man got her, but that isn't important," Evelyn said.

"There have not been any murders here," Caroleigh stated flatly before Evelyn could say more.

"No?" Edward queried. "Just the usual infidelities? All discreetly done, of course?"

"Oh, well yes, that. It is said that Daddy was having a fling with his second wife before his first wife disappeared."

Evelyn gasped. "Disappeared?"

"Left him; fed up with his indiscreet infidelities. No murder," Caroleigh assured her.

Edward shrugged and yawned, suddenly bored with it all.

Evelyn wasn't in the least bored and continued. "There is a theory of unfinished business also. Maybe he's still trying to get home." No one commented on her latest speculations. "Or he was bludgeoned with an ax, and there was no accident at all."

Caroleigh laughed hollowly. "I can see we aren't going to talk you out of it, but I'm sure if there had been any chopped up ancestors at Morning Meadow, I would have heard about it."

"How far away is the mine?" Steven asked suddenly.

"Do you think it was a miner?" Evelyn asked, still on her subject.

"I just wondered how far away it is."

"Do you think it may be a deterrent for a resort?" Caroleigh asked.

"Why would it be?" Evelyn asked.

"Ugly, dear," Edward answered. "No doubt a dastardly scar on the beauty of nature."

"There's map on the wall in the library," Caroleigh told Steven. "I'll show it to you."

"I'm sure I can find it."

"What kind of a hostess would I be if I just sent you off alone?"

She was the kind that was all over him. She stood close to brush up against him. When he backed away, she followed. The second time he backed she hooked her arm through his and leaned close under the pretense of pointing out something on the map.

"Grandpa made this. You can see he wasn't an artist."

"Thank you for taking the time to show me." He pulled his arm free. "It looks like about four miles. If I leave now, I can be back before dark."

With her hand on his chest and a seductive smile on her face, she deliberately stepped closer. "There aren't any cars."

There was a pickup, which he didn't point out. Had she bothered to look at the ruins of the carriage house she would have known Kari's pickup had not been in there, not that he had any intentions of asking Kari for the use of it. "I'm going to walk," he told her.

"Four miles?" she asked in astonishment.

He grinned at her. "Eight, I have to walk back."

"You must really want to see it," she commented with an edge to her voice.

"Mines have always fascinated me, and I really need to see if it will impact the resort idea," he told her with satisfaction over using her lie against her.

He reached for the door knob. She slipped around him to lean back against the door. "We can drive by on the way—"

The door smacked her in the back. Caroleigh jerked it open a few inches, already annoyed. Then she saw who it was. "Don't you ever knock?"

There was a pause before Kari answered. "I didn't know anyone was in here."

"There is and…" She pushed the door open wide to show Steven. "…you are interrupting."

Steven mouthed thank you, and Kari's expression instantly went blank.

"I'm sure you can understand…" Caroleigh purred, "…how two people would enjoy having some privacy."

"Have you found your dog yet?"

Caroleigh threw her hands in the air. "Can you not follow the simplest of conversations?"

"I try, if it is a conversation. Have you found him?"

Emily appeared behind Kari. Her expression was one of puzzlement when Caroleigh answered.

"No and he isn't in here," she told Kari curtly. Just as curtly, she asked Emily, "What do you want?"

"There's a call for Mr. Chase."

"Tell them he will call back."

"I'll take it," Steven told her crisply.

"You have to go all the way to the kitchen," Caroleigh told him, oblivious to his irritation over her answering for him. She hooked her arm through his to walk with him through the back hall. "The house has never been wired for phones. It was built before telephones were common.There's just the one line into the kitchen."

Kari followed them. "Caroleigh, you need to find that dog."

Caroleigh flipped her hand over her shoulder in dismissal. She continued with, "It was built before electricity was common as well."

Steven pulled his arm free to push the back kitchen door open. "Excuse me."

"We'll just give you some privacy," Caroleigh said sweetly and spun as soon as the door swung shut to attack Kari, either not knowing or not caring how their voices carried. "You did that deliberately."

"He could starve to death."

"What do you care?"

"He has no access to water and—"

"Shut up about that stupid dog."

She forgot all about giving Steven privacy. She shoved the door open and stormed in, went to the oversized refrigerator and jerked the door open. Kari came in behind her, went straight through the kitchen by Steven at the phone and into the hall. Emily came in last and stopped in the middle of the floor in uncertainty.

Steven's gaze followed each as they came in and rested on Emily simply because she was the last. "No," he said into the phone.

"There's no water in here," Caroleigh complained. She slammed the door shut. "Where does she keep it?" She opened and closed cupboard doors, all with a slam.

"Is the deed encumbered?" Steven asked.

"Huh?" Robert grunted on the other end, understandably since they had not been talking about a deed.

"You're the one there. You'll have to do it," Steven said as he watched.

Kari returned with several plastic bowls of dog food stacked together. She stopped a few feet from Steven to ask Caroleigh, "What are you looking for?"

"Water."

"Try the sink."

"I get it," Robert said. "You can't talk, and you want the deed checked."

"Right," Steven said. Though he believed Kari, he wanted to be sure which one was a liar.

"I do not drink sink water!" Caroleigh retorted.

"Then do without," Kari snapped. "Your dog is."

"Wow, that doesn't sound like a happy group." Robert told him.

Steven confirmed that. "It isn't."

"Well, I can't do much—"

"Hello?" Steven held the phone out and looked at it when it went silent.

"Another fine convenience of this place," Caroleigh retorted. "The phone always goes out and cells won't even work." With a new thought, she turned on Kari. "Did you turn it off again?" Kari walked off, Caroleigh right behind her still talking. "It's an incoming call and not going to run up your precious phone bill."

"Since I was standing right there when it went off, it's not likely I did anything, and a four hundred dollar call to Brazil was…"

Their voices trailed off as they disappeared through the dining room.

“There's some in the pantry," Emily said softly.

"What?” Steven asked as he hung up the phone.

"Bottled water, there's some in the pantry. She must have forgotten."

Steven doubted that since Kari had just come from there.

* * * *

The path had been used for over a hundred years and was well defined cutting straight through the belt of forest and ending at the edge of a rock bluff. The rock wall dropped gradually for about ten feet to a sheer drop. A shallow, wide creek meandered around the base. Across the creek the area opened into a huge field filled with fenced pastures and outbuildings normally associated with so isolated a home. A three story barn dominated. Nearest to the creek stood a greenhouse, dwarfed by the barn but never the less large. A fenced garden was beside it. A chicken coop and yard with about a dozen chickens and a pig pen with four full grown pigs basking in the warm spring sun stretched out from there. The corral, adjacent to the barn, held a good dozen horses. One long narrow building looked to be a bunk house and other buildings of various sizes and shapes were scattered about. On the far side of the clearing a two story house stood.

"But no cow," Steven murmured to himself. It certainly had everything else.

The path followed the curve of the bluff to a new vantage point and new vista. Steven stopped on the first step of the set of stout stairs down the steepest portion of the bluff to stare in awe. The bluff turned out further down, exposing a portion of the mine and the top end of a colossal tailings pile that spilled down the side of the mountain.

"That is more than four miles and too far to walk this late," he said to himself. “Grandpa’s map is just a little out of proportion.”

He tied the sleeves of his coat around his waist and started down the stairs to explore the ranch instead. A loud creak sounded when he reached mid-point, and then a tremor vibrated the stairs. Steven froze to look down at the eight by eight timbers under his feet. The movement didn't seem to be a normal shifting. He saw and felt them shift more and grabbed for a hold of the thick hand rail. Everything seemed steady and solid for a moment; long enough to judge whether it would be quicker to go down or back up to get off of them. He took a careful step up just as everything tilted and fell from under him.

Hours later, he didn't hear her coming. He'd closed his eyes to rest a minute and opened them to see her a few feet from him. She studied the debris pinning him down, but those sharp, amber eyes shifted to him as soon as he moved.

"Didn't hear you coming," he told her with a slight smile.

"You were unconscious."

"Asleep," he corrected. Must have been since he didn't hear her come up. "I am a little tired."

"I imagine so after last night."

"You-ah, didn't happen to bring a chainsaw with you?"

"Left it home today," she answered absently. She went back to study the tangled mess. "It didn't match my blouse." Her eyes shifted back to him. "How long have you been here?"

"Don't know." He showed her the broken crystal on his watch. He was on his back, right leg at an upward angle, trapped between two boulders and held there from the knee down by a piece of timber. "I came out right after that thing in the kitchen. It seems like quite some time ago."

"I imagine so." She sat on her heels beside him. "You came out to make a twelve mile hike without water or a jacket?"

He corrected her defensively. "I decided it was too late to make that long a walk, and I did have a jacket with a bottle of water. I dropped them."

"Glad to hear you aren't stupid," she murmured, preoccupied again in an examination of the wreckage for his jacket.

"Don't pick on me. I feel dumb enough already," he told her in feigned lightness. "Do you think maybe you could bring me something to use for leverage. I can't get this timber to budge from here. It seems to be weighted down there." He pointed to the low end covered in a pile of tangled timbers. "And wedged in there." He pointed to the rock wall, a protrusion in particular that held the upper end bowed down.

"I noticed," she said as she stood. "Cover your head in case it goes flying."

"What are you—?”

He broke off in dread as she drove her heel into the high end of the timber. Her kick shifted the timber a fraction of an inch under the protrusion; just enough to destabilize it. Physics took over. That high end gouged out rocks, releasing the pressure stored in the bowed beam, gained momentum, and scraped away more until it slipped free. Like a mousetrap of giant proportions, the mass shot apart. The timber flipped, throwing rock and dust into the air at one end and landed with enough force it bounced end over end on the opposite, tossing wreckage and water in a wild scatter.

Steven covered his head with both arms, but before all the rocks spattered to the ground, he was up on his elbows and shouting. "Kari?"

"What?" she asked, stepping away from the rock face where she had huddled for protection. Just as calmly she brushed rocks from her hair and dust from her clothes.

He dropped back down flat in relief and shivered. "Well, that was fun, but let's not do it again, okay?" he joked weakly with his heart still feeling like it was lodged under his Adam’s apple.

"No more timbers."

He started up again with a smile that soon changed into a grimace. He also suddenly found her hand planted on his chest, holding him back down.

"I'm going to pull your leg up by your pants. Once it's free, see if you can lever yourself around so I can lay it flat."

"I can…” He groaned and gave up the effort to lift his leg free without help. “Maybe not.”

"And you shouldn't try. It may be fractured."

He smiled faintly behind a grimace of pain, reached for his leg, and shivered again. "It was numb."

"Circulation coming back, hurts like a bitch, right? Let's do it my way."

"Okay," he agreed with yet another shiver.

She patted him lightly and then climbed up on the rock next to his leg. With two handfuls of his pants, one at the knee and one at the ankle, she carefully pulled up. Steven clamped his jaw. Several seconds later he managed to get himself up to his elbows and several more passed before he was able to drag himself back far enough for her to slide off the rock and gently lower his leg to the ground. By that time the intermittent shivers had become chills to shake his body and made his teeth chatter.

She took off her coat and covered him from his chin down. "Hypothermia," she told him.

"Does…that mean…I'm cold," he joked bravely through clicking teeth.

"It does. I need to see if it's fractured."

He nodded and set his jaw, as much to keep his teeth still as against the pain. He stoically bore the quick, deft movements of her fingers down his shin and blew out a breath when she finished with her fingers resting on his ankle.

"I can't feel a break, but you shouldn't put any weight on it until it's x-rayed," Kari told him soberly.

"Splint?"

"Not unless you want to drag around an eight by eight. Great Grandpa built those stairs to stay."

"Didn't work," he quipped weakly. "Crutch?"

"Just me."

"Okay."

"Listen to me first. The sun is going down. The temperature is going to drop drastically, and you're already hypothermic. I don't think you should try to walk on that leg, but right now the most important thing is to get you warm. The greenhouse is closest, and it's heated."

"Okay," he agreed, not too proud to reach for her for support.

Kari caught and held his hand. "Let me finish. I think we can get to it in less time than it would take me to go back for the truck and drive around."

He shook his head while he used her arm to pull himself up. His speech was garbled from the chills when he told her, "You crutch…we go…warm."

"I want you to understand the risk. If it is fractured; putting weight on it could make it splinter." He pulled harder and folded his uninjured leg to get it under him. "Okay, we walk."

The first obstacle was the narrow foot bridge across the creek. Steven slipped off. Getting out of the creek and up the bank soaked them both. From there it was a stagger and fall, slow and painful journey. Before it was over, Kari shivered almost as badly as he did, and she was nearly as exhausted from supporting his weight. He hopped as much as he could to ease the burden on her, but with his violent shivering, his degree of coordination would have been handicapped even without the crippled leg. Every time he tried to put the slightest of weight on it, the pain caused it to buckle immediately. With one last hop through the glass door, he collapsed on the dirt floor, and despite the warm, humid air, he drew into a shaking ball.

Kari pushed the door shut and dropped to her knees beside him. "Up—sit up, we've got to get these wet clothes off of you."

It was harder than undressing a baby. Size aside, his mind told him what to do to help, but his body didn't respond correctly. It was a struggle just to sit, and he only accomplished that with her behind him, her legs on either side to hold him upright. She unbuttoned his shirt cuffs and enough buttons in the front to pull it and his T-shirt over his head at once. She held him there to briskly rub his chest and arms.

"Ba…Ba…Baby," he chattered.

"I can't understand you."

"Feel…stupid," he forced out clearly. He drew a deep breath for the next words. "Can't stop…"

"Your core temperature is too low." She slipped away from him and lowered him to the floor. "I need more."

"Don't…" He gave up what he wanted to say. She was already gone.

In a tight ball, his arms wrapped around his chest, his hands were in fists, rammed into his armpits in an automatic reflex to find warmth. He was also barely aware of what was going on. It seemed to him she was only gone a few seconds before she was back to push and pull on him.

"You can't sleep." She dropped a thin mattress behind him and knelt on it. "Come on, Steven. You have to move." He mumbled with no voluntary movement. "Just once more, I promise. Just roll over." She pushed, tugged, and rambled. “Damn I wish there were lights. The circuits went out last week, and the electrician won’t be here for a couple more days. Steven, move. This is hard enough without being able to see you.”

She got him to his back. Once she let go of him he rolled, again in reflex, to his side, back into a ball, but the pain of moving made him more alert. A thick blanket smelling of horse went over him, and she started on his shoes. Steven shook even harder. The mattress under him and the blanket over him did nothing to chase away the cold, no more than the heated greenhouse had. The only way he could help her was to deliberately not fight her assault on his modesty while she pulled his clothes off under the blanket.

"In…in…"

"I can't understand you."

With a deep breath, he got two words out. "Cold inside."

"I know."

With the Levis and briefs slipped off his feet, she hovered over him. Her hands moved rapidly to briskly rub through the blanket from his neck to his feet.

"Don't go to sleep." she ordered when he got quiet.

"Okay," he murmured.

"Do you feel warmer?"

"Li…lit…"

"Damn it."

"Don…n't." He tried to rise up when she stood up straight, but settled back down when she touched him. "St…st…st…"

"I'm not going anywhere."

Since his eyes were closed, he couldn't see what she did even if the dark hadn't settled in around them. A few moments later when a cold draft hit his back, he still didn't know. He did know an instant later that warmth replaced the draft, but it didn't really register it was her bare, warm body pressed against his.

His chills soon subsided to no more than infrequent tremors, and he was very aware of what warmed him. Her hands still rubbed his bare arms, chest, and down his thigh, and her body still pressed against his equally bare back. Though still chilled, at least his teeth no longer chattered.

"Question?" he asked.

"I didn't understand you," she whispered in his ear.

Steven rolled his head toward her. "Are you…responsible for…any of that…weird stuff?"

"Me?" she asked in surprise. "Whatever for?"

"Get even…maybe for…for the…the way they…treat you."

"It's your question. You answer it."

"No."

"Good answer, considering the circumstances."

He managed a light chuckle. "Biased though, I…I like…you."

"Ah, shucks, I was hoping for more than that."

"Too soon for…for love at…first sight, sounds like…like a line."

"Oh, I don't know. I read somewhere that men usually decide within the first ten minutes of meeting a woman if they want to marry her. Women, being more practical, of course, take longer."

"How long?"

"Don't remember that, just the ten minute thing," she said with a slight shrug. "I never could decide if I believed it."

"Man or woman?"

"Both. Can you straighten out a little?"

"Afraid to try," he admitted. He had earlier and gone into a fresh fit of shakes.

"Don't try then."

"Sleep now?"

"Still feel cold inside?" she asked in concern.

"Sleepy."

"Typical."

"Do better next time," he told her with a smile.

"Promises, promises."

He chuckled softly and rolled his head back with a sigh. As he drifted off, his hand went to the arm around him and closed to hold her. He drifted into sleep, but not deep or sound. When she tried to slip her arm from under his head, he woke, and his hand closed tight on the arm over his chest.

"I'm going to hang our clothes up to dry," she assured him.

"Don't leave," he murmured groggily.

She leaned over close. "Say it again."

"Don't leave."

"I'm just going a few feet away," she promised.

As she pulled her arm free, his hand slid down it to catch and hold her hand for just a moment before he released it. Even in that short a time, he started to shiver again.

Asleep before she returned, Steven woke when her warm body moved away from him again.

"I was just starting to feel like thinking about taking advantage of the situation," he told her as she slipped out from under the blanket.

She tucked it back close around him and told him, "You are such a liar."

"I did say thinking," he said lightly, but his hand shot out to find her arm in the dim moonlight coming through the glass walls and roof and hold her. "Where are you going?"

"To get dressed."

"Can't sleep or embarrassed?"

"In-bare-ass is not how I intend to climb the bluff."

She teased, but Steven was serious when he told her, "On that Indian Ladder thing? No way. You aren't going up that bluff in the dark."

"I know the way."

As she started to pull away, his grip tightened. "Don't leave."

"I'm going after my truck so I can take you to the hospital."

"I'm fine, I don't need a doctor, and we can walk back in the morning, in daylight."

She leaned over him. "I don't think you're fine."

"I'm sore and tired."

"Weak," she corrected. "And you were unconscious when I found you."

"Asleep."

"Unconscious, Steven, I know the difference. Any headache, dizziness, or nausea?"

"No, no, and no."

"As healthy as a horse." She moved the blanket to take both of his hands. "Squeeze my fingers."

"This is silly."

"Do it or I go right now and call for an air-lift."

"The phone—okay." The last was when she started to pull away. He caught her by her fingers and squeezed. "Anything else?"

"There would be if I had some light."

"I won't be running a race for a few days, but I'm fine."

"You have the chills again."

He couldn't deny it and didn't try. He didn't argue either when she slipped back under the blanket with him, pressed up against his back, and renewed the arm and chest rubbings.

She told him, "You're temperature is still too low."

"Maybe I just like being babied. You are awfully good at it." In just a few minutes he caught her hand to still it. "You might want to stop that now."

"You want me to stop?"

Her hand stilled, but her fingers stroked the hair on his chest. He closed his hand over hers, curled her fingers under his to still them and stop what she was doing to him with the light caress. Her fingertips were affecting him worse than the brisk rubbing.

"No," he told her with a wry smile, "that's why I said to stop."

"You're contradicting yourself."

"I'm a sick man, delirious or something."

"And I hoped you were warming to the core."

Steven rolled to his back. He was warming and faster still when she had to either lean against him or be pushed off the mattress. His voice was a trifle strained when he said, "I don't want to take a chance on giving the wrong impression and spoiling something I think is going to be very important."

"That old ten minute thing?" she teased.

"About that once I met the real you." He added quickly, "I know that sounds corny and—"

"Sweet." Her fingertips found his lips. Her lips soon followed to give him a light kiss. "I don't think one spoils the other."

Steven's arms went around her, and his mouth found hers. His kiss wasn't gentle as he rolled a bit more to face her and pull her even tighter against him.

"Whoa." She attempted to pull back. "I don't think you're in any condition to—"

He held her with one arm and pulled her head down with the other hand to meet his lips again. She had sparked a need in him all too evident in what grew between them. Kari didn't pull away, and in short order he proved his condition was not that much of a deterrent.

* * * *

She woke him easing away.

He missed his grab for her arm. "Don't leave," he told her urgently.

"I'm getting dressed," Kari told him firmly. "I shouldn't have let that happen. It was stupid."

"But—"

"I shouldn't have jeopardized your welfare with that kind of exertion after the trauma your body suffered."

"Huh?"

"I didn't expect it to be—I was just thinking the stimulation would—"

Totally perplexed, he exclaimed, "What the hell are you talking about?"

"I didn't expect it to be so explosive," she told him meekly.

"And you wish we hadn't?"

"We shouldn't have. How do you feel?"

"Confused," he admitted.

She rushed back to him. "Dizzy? Headache?

"No," he said with a laugh and wrapped his arms around her. "I feel fine, and I would really like it if—"

"No." She pushed his arms away and moved quickly out of reach. "I'm serious, Steven. You shouldn't be doing that. I shouldn’t have let you no matter how much I wanted it."

Placated over fearing she regretted what happened between them, but still confused, Steven rose up on his elbows to see where she had gone. In the pale gray of dawn all he could see was a shadow and hear the sound of her clothes being pulled on. She ran back in her jeans and knit shirt with her arms full of their clothes. Dropping to her knees, she deposited the clothes in the floor and leaned forward to feel his cheek.

"I'm fine," he repeated.

She gave him a quick kiss, chasing away his fear of morning after regrets and rejection. Dropping to her butt, she sorted through the clothes until she found a sock. With it halfway up her foot, she giggled and tossed it to his chest.

"That one's yours."

Steven closed his hand around the sock and sat up slowly, by necessity, favoring more than one bruised, aching, or stiff spot. He didn't miss how she watched him out of the corner of her eye while she put on her sock.

"You think I can't dress myself," he accused.

"I think how well you do will contribute a lot to whether or not I take you to the hospital," she told him frankly.

Determined to prove he didn't need a doctor, he pulled the blanket up to reach his feet. It was light enough then for him to see his leg for the first time. "Ouch," he muttered. The bruise reached from a few inches below his knee to a few inches above his ankle.

"Eight by eights landing on you have a tendency to do things like that."

"You've seen it already?"

"By match light one of the times you were asleep."

He ignored the twist she gave the last word. "I hope you didn't take unfair advantage."

"Every chance I got."

"You did not."

With a chuckle she laced up her first boot. "I had to check for injuries."

"I hope you liked what you saw.”

"And felt," she answered with a straight face and a mischievous look in her eyes. "Aside from your leg, the damage seems superficial."

"Told you."

"Seems," she repeated and laced her second boot.

He had only one sock on with the top rolled down to keep even a minor degree of pressure off his calf. "Don't you have something to do?" he asked in a rush of self-consciousness.

"No." She stood, brushing her hands against her pant legs. "But I'll find something. Just don't try to stand to get your pants on. Pull them up over your legs, and then lift your hips. Yell when you're decent."

After wrestling his pants on and with a lingering scent of horse on his person, Steven buttoned his shirt to finish the chore of dressing. He was more worn out from the effort than he wanted to admit and wouldn't to her.

"These are all vegetables," he said of the beds and tables around them.

"Flowers aren't my thing." She shrugged slightly and sat down in front of him. "The green house is here. I may as well make use of it. I get fresh vegetables all winter. In the summer I can grow things in here when the season is too short for outside."

"Is this where the town was?"

She nodded. "It isn't quite all gone. The house was a boarding house. Grandpa kept it for the foreman and his family along with some barracks for a bunkhouse and the barn when he started ranching. Some of the smaller buildings are leftovers too."

Going to her knees with a pair of pruning shears in her hand she told him, "I should have done this first."

She lapsed into silence, concentrating on cutting open his pant leg with the clumsy implement. He concentrated on not wincing at the slight bit of pressure the clumsy cuts caused. Then he concentrated on watching her. When she looked up and found his eyes on her face, she smiled and leaned forward for a kiss. She kept it from becoming more with a quick retreat when his arms started around her.

"You can't walk on that leg," she told him.

"Let's just stay here then."

"I want the doctor to look at it."

She started up, he pulled her back down, but with the light of early morning she could see the look on his face, and asked, "Are you afraid of something?"

"No," he answered too quickly.

"You're a horrible liar."

"That wasn't an insult," he teased with a move to kiss her.

“What are you afraid of?” A hand planted in his chest to hold him back. "Why don't you want me going after the pickup?"

"I want you to stay with me."

"Because?"

"Silly question.”

He leaned forward only to have her put her fingers over his mouth. "You're going to have to give me a reason or I'm going after the pickup," she told him with her brow furrowed in concern.

"I don't think it was an accident," he blurted out.

"The stairs?” When he nodded, she asked in alarm, "Why would someone want to hurt you?"

"Not me,” he exclaimed. “I'm not the one that uses them everyday."

She sat back on her heels. "That's silly, Steven. No one would want to hurt me. The high water from the storm last night probably undercut the anchor blocks."

"And lightning probably struck the carriage house, coyotes probably got your dogs, and the phones line just happened to go out one day after a fire that should have burnt up your truck and the next day the stairs collapse when you’re usually the one on them, leaving you hurt and with no way to call or go for help.” Or dead which he didn’t say. “I had a lot of time to think while I was trapped on my back."

"Under conditions perfect for breeding paranoia. I have a radio in my pickup, cell phones work if you take the time to find a spot, and my pickup wasn't in the carriage house."

"Does Caroleigh know all that?"

"Caro?" she asked in shock, and then laughed. "I know she can be a bitch at times, but not murderous. Why would she anyway?"

"Why lie about owning the Meadow?"

Kari still chuckled. "I thought we covered that." She scoffed. "Once she got you to bed, she'd just tell you she had changed her mind."

"What about this ghost business, and the things she tells people about you?"

"I'm sure the ghost business is someone's idea of a joke, and I don't care what she tells people about me."

"Do you know the things she says?"

"Pretty much. I usually just go along with it. You were different."

"Then why were you kicking us out?"

"I just asked when you were leaving. I wanted to know how long you would be here. Caro jumped to the wrong conclusion. I knew the shuttle office was closed. If I really wanted you to leave, I'd have given her Vern's home number."

"You didn't want us to leave?"

"Not you," she said frankly. She frowned slightly. "Maybe this would be a good time to tell you, this is not my usual behavior. You're, ah, with you it's just different."

"Me, too," he said softly and absently while he deliberately let the conversation move away from his concern. Gaze locked on her face, he wanted to take her in his arms but settled for brushing her hair with the backs of his fingers. "I've never found anyone I feel so comfortable with, or I could talk to like I do you. Nor anyone I wanted to touch since my wife died, either."

"You're a widower?" When he nodded, she asked, "How long?"

He smiled self-consciously. "Three years."

"No wonder it was so explosive."

Stunned for a moment, he recovered with a burst of laughter and did take her into his arms. She returned his kiss, but when he began to pull her up and twisted to lower her to the mattress, she pulled away from him.

"Oh, no you don't." She went to her feet quickly. "We are not doing that again until I know you're okay. I'm going after the pickup."

She would have too, only he held her by the hand. A wrestling match brewed when he turned his head to listen.

"Sounds like your pickup is coming to you," he told her glumly and let go of her hand.

Kari dropped to her knees to look out under one of the tables against the glass wall. "I'll be damned."

Steven scooted himself far enough to look out with her. "Looks like all three of them."

"And before brunch." She sat back on her heels, lower lip drawn between her teeth. "Caroleigh's going to be really nasty if she finds us together."

"You've got to tell her sometime."

"Just not yet." She dragged the mattress and blanket with her as she moved away on her hands and knees. "I have to think about how I'm going to handle this." She crawled quickly back, gave him a kiss, and scurried away. "I'll see you back at the house. Keep that leg up and don't put any weight on it."

After Kari disappeared around a bank of raised beds, Steven got to his feet—one foot actually—and it wasn't easy. He used the table along the wall for support to reach the door and only went out far enough to shut it behind him before he waved and shouted at the pickup cruising around the buildings. "Am I glad to see you," he called out as it pulled to a stop in front of him.

Edward climbed out from behind the wheel. Caroleigh and Evelyn came around from the passenger side.

"Where is she?" Caroleigh demanded, stalking straight by him into the greenhouse while Evelyn and Edward stopped in front of him.

Steven didn't bother to answer. Caroleigh had already disappeared inside. He turned on one foot and leaned against the building to watch through the door as she marched to the far end. He let out a light breath of relief when she started back and twisted to find Edward in a thoughtful study of his dirty, disheveled, shirttail hanging out, appearance.

"It would seem…" Edward said drolly, "…you and Kari went missing. We've been looking for you the full night." His tone changed slightly. "Are you…"

"The full night," Evelyn whined.

"Are you…" Edward began again.

Caroleigh stormed back out. "Where is she?" she demanded.

"If you mean Kari, I don't know," Steven answered truthfully.

"Are you going to stand there and tell me you…?"

"I suspect he would rather lie down," Edward said over her.

"…that you—what?"

"I believe he's injured, love." He tipped his head towards Steven's cut pant leg. "Can you walk on it?"

"Not really," Steven told him frankly. "I had a hell of a time getting this far."

"My God, Steven," Caroleigh exclaimed. She did a rapid mood shift. She hooked one arm through his and patted it with her other hand. "I'm so sorry I was short with you, but we were so worried. So many dreadful things can happen out here. Just like this."

"So it would appear Kari was justified in being concerned," Edward pointed out.

Caroleigh ignored Edward, telling Steven, "Let me help you."

"Thank you, but," Steven pushed her hands away firmly, "I'm afraid I really need help."

"I'm stronger than I look," she purred.

"And I'm heavier. Edward, if you would?"

"Of course, of course. Excuse me, love."

He stepped between them to take Steven's arm over his shoulders and grunted the first time Steven's weight shifted to him. Edward nearly staggered out from under his arm, and Steven had to hop clumsily to stay up.

"Maybe it would be better if I just hop," Steven suggested without much faith in Edward's help. Kari with her slighter size had done better, but then Kari had expected his weight.

"No, no, we'll manage." Edward assured him and took a firmer hold of Steven's wrist and waist. "All in the timing I believe, although I don't recall ever doing this before."

"No helping…" He tried to put more weight on his leg to spare Edward only to hop to stay up when pain shot up his leg and through his body. He nearly dragged them both down before he was balanced on one leg again.

Edward wasn't deterred and said lightly, "As I said, old boy, timing, and I am stronger than I appear."

Steven could tell the truth of his statement by the muscle he could feel under his arm, the wiry, stronger than it looks kind. He nodded, and they started again. He didn't stress his leg to save Edward, and Edward braced himself to support his weight in time with each step. It went better then.

"You were going to ask?" Edward quizzed lightly.

"No drunken friend?" Steven panted.

"No, none that I recall. I've always been of the opinion that if one got themselves into that condition they could take care of themselves. No sympathy for hangovers, either."

Steven smiled grimly. He gripped the side of the pickup when they reached it and leaned down. With his forehead on his hand he rested to catch his breath. Edward leaned down further, moved the pant leg for a clearer look and jerked up quickly.

"Should I take you into the doctor?"

With a blown out breath, Steven straightened and shook his head. "I just need to get off of it and get it elevated."

Edward's expression said he did not agree, but he didn't argue. "You may be more comfortable in the back than in the cab." He paused then added, "If you can get up there."

Evelyn said, "A doctor could give you some marvelous pills."

"It'll be fine once I can lie down," Steven said with a shake of his head.

"Stiff upper lip, grin and bear it type?" Edward asked casually as Steven hopped up on the running board to sit on the side, but he grimaced when Steven set his jaw and stifled a groan to lift his leg over the side with both hands.

"Not grinning," Steven gasped out after he lowered himself into the bed of the truck.

"I much prefer a drugged bliss," Evelyn commented before she walked around to the passenger side.

"You may wish to reconsider," Edward said softly to Steven.

"I'll let you know."

Edward turned to Caroleigh. "Are there blankets or something inside we can use for padding?"

"How would I know?" she asked pettishly.

"By looking, love," he told her dryly and went to do so himself. "Do give me a hand."

She did so grudgingly, leaving Steven alone with Evelyn.

"It's doubtful Kari's actually missing at all," Evelyn said softly. "After telling us we should look for you, she probably went off to do one of her things and didn't bother mentioning it. She's used to no one being around to tell."

"What kind of things?"

She shrugged with a look towards the greenhouse. "I can tell you though it isn't a good idea to get between those two. Before Kari got so strange, they had a regular contest going, which could get the guy. It got pretty vicious from what I hear."

"Really?"

She didn't hear the tartness of his question and continued. "From what I hear it's been going on since high school. Kari took one loss so badly she ended up over doing, if you know what I mean. That's what made her so weird. She dropped out—really dropped out—after that. Not too many know it though. Caroleigh does protect her. She tells people it was some disease."

"Are you talking about drugs," he asked even though he was sure of what she meant.

"Big time," she answered with a meaningful roll of her eyes. "Nearly killed herself. Maybe she wanted to."

She ended abruptly when Caroleigh and Edward came out of the greenhouse empty handed. "Not a thing," Edward told him. "Sorry."

"I'll be fine," he answered absently. Where had Kari, a mattress, and a blanket disappeared to and more importantly why?

The rough ride to the mansion had been torturous and left Steven exhausted. Once they arrived back at the house, Steven had no more desire to climb the stairs to the second floor than Edward had to support him up the climb. After the veranda stairs, which had been hard enough to manage, he quickly agreed to Edward's suggestion of the drawing room instead of the bedroom. One of the spindly, antique settees didn't sound particularly comfortable, but anywhere he could lie down instead of going up a flight of stairs was preferable. The first obstacle once they reached the porch was the front door. It was locked again, with Emily outside on the veranda, not inside to open it for them. The second was Kari. She opened the door before Caroleigh could send Emily around to the back, surprising Steven by her being there ahead of them.

"Move," Caroleigh ordered curtly as soon as she saw Kari.

Kari did but only as far as the drawing room entrance. She didn't move from there even though it was obvious that was where the two men were headed.

"We're just going to put him down on the sofa, love," Edward told her.

"On the sofa?" Kari questioned.

"Get out of the way," Caroleigh ordered impatiently.

Kari looked straight into Steven's eyes. "The library would be better."

"If we get the sofa dirty," Caroleigh told her with an unsuccessful attempt to push her aside. "I'll get it cleaned."

Steven understood what Kari wanted even if he didn't understand why and told them, "The library would be better. I wouldn't be in the middle of things there."

Edward shifted their direction. "Library it is."

Caroleigh couldn't budge Kari before. She couldn't stop her when Kari did move. She tried. Kari just pulled free when she grabbed her arm.

"Where were you all night?" Caroleigh shouted when Kari walked away.

"To get the library ready," Kari answered, but she disappeared into the dining room.

Edward stopped to watch Kari disappear and commented, "Seems to be one of her vague days."

"She does that just to aggravate me," Caroleigh retorted. No one offered a comment. "She disappears all night, worrying everyone as to whether she's dead or injured. Does she care? No. She won't even give you a straight answer when you ask where she's been."

"We thought she had gone looking for you," Edward told Steven. To Caroleigh he said, "In all fairness, love, from her point of view, we could have been the ones missing. We did take that wrong turn."

"You got lost?" Steven asked.

"Bloody poor showing for a rescue team, but it was dark, and I'd never been over that route before. We got off on a logging road or something. We'd have been there several hours sooner if not for that."

"I'm sorry I put you to so much trouble," he said, while grateful they hadn't gotten there any earlier.

"No trouble, darling," Caroleigh told him.

"Certainly not," Edward agreed cheerfully. "It has made us feel quite the heroes. Now let's see if we can't get you comfortable."

"I appr—" The words ended in a quick intake of breath when they took the first step.

"You're welcome," Edward told him quickly. To Caroleigh he said, "Do run ahead, love, and see—oh, you sweet girl."

The last was for Kari when she appeared again in the back hall. Edward made sure Steven was secure leaning against the wall before he rushed to her. To Kari's astonishment he gave her a vigorous hug despite the fact she held a good sized bundle in one arm and crutches in her other hand. He took the crutches, hugged her again, and hurried back to Steven. "That girl is an absolute life saver."

"You don't know where those came from," Caroleigh said pettishly, "or how old they are. They may be rotten."

"They're aluminum," Steven answered tightly. He deliberately leaned on them without testing.

During their exchange Kari disappeared into the library. She reappeared, arms empty, before he had gone more than a few steps, and disappeared back down the back hall, all without a word to any of them.

Caroleigh dashed ahead of Steven while Edward stayed cautiously close by. She fluffed a small decorative pillow and placed it flat on the couch. The couch was a massive overstuffed, comfortable looking and practical thing instead of the fragile furniture of the drawing room.

"Thank you," Steven told her with a weak smile.

"Anything else I can do? Get you a glass of water?"

He was tempted to ask if it was sink or bottled, but he let it pass. With a shake of his head he told her instead, "I just want to get some rest."

"Excellent idea," Edward told her. "Let's leave him to it then."

"I want to see he's settled first."

"Caroleigh, I'm sure—"

Kari came in the door with a double arm load of blankets, pillows, and linens. Edward sighed deeply even before Caroleigh shrieked, "What are you doing?"

Kari stutter stepped slightly, her only response to the question. She didn't answer and tossed the pillow Caroleigh had put there to a nearby chair.

"Kari, get out of here," Caroleigh ordered furiously.

"Can you make a bed?"

"He doesn't want a bed. He just wants to take a nap."

"I really think—" Edward began.

"Shut up," Caroleigh snapped. Edward's hand shot out to grip her firmly by the arm. "What do you think you're doing?"

Edward pulled her out of the room. Kari shook her head slightly while she stretched and tucked a sheet around the heavy cushions of the couch. She didn't look around at Steven or speak until she was sure Caroleigh was gone.

"There are towels and pajamas in the bathroom." She did look around then. "Are you okay?"

"Tired."

"Weak," she corrected.

He didn't argue. He felt weak, and he hadn't done enough to warrant it. "I'll get cleaned up."

"Never mind. Just come lie down."

"I'm filthy."

"It doesn't matter," she told him sharply. "Lie down before you fall."

"I'm not—" He dropped his head wearily. "Okay, I'm bushed."

"Come on." She moved the low table from in front of the couch to give him a clear path. While he covered the remaining distance she tossed one pillow to one end of the couch for his head and two to the other. The blanket draped over her arm, ready when he got there.

"I don't understand why…" He groaned despite his efforts not to when he lowered himself down. "…a bruise is…"

"It's not just a bruise."

She knelt in front of him to take off his shoes and knocked his hand away when he tried to stop her. Steven gave into practicality and leaned back. It wasn't the first time she'd taken them off. The left shoe and sock she pulled off together. For the right she loosened the laces to the maximum and eased the shoe off carefully, then the sock. "I'll lift, you turn."

Even though she lifted the leg and lowered it to the two pillows, it hurt. But then it hurt without moving. He flopped back, waiting for the pain to ease off. She took the time to fold back the edge of his pants to look at his leg.

"It doesn't look good, Steven," she told him seriously, her fingers resting on his ankle.

"Kind of swollen," he said casually, but casual was not how he felt. Not only did the black and blue shin have the abnormal shine of skin stretched too tight over the swelling, but his calf, ankle, knee, and foot were puffy.

"I'll be right back."

"So much for keeping me company," he complained to himself. She was already gone.

True to her word, she was right back. She carried a tray laden with a covered pitcher, a glass, several chemical ice packs, a thermometer, scissors, and a bottle of ibuprofen.

"Open," she ordered, thermometer in hand.

"I don't need that."

"In less than five minutes I can have an air-lift on the way."

"That's blackmail."

"Right. Open."

He opened his mouth, allowed her to put the thermometer under his tongue and propped himself up on his elbows enough to watch. While he fumed over what he thought was unnecessary attention, she cut his pants up further and laid a towel over his leg from above the knee to his ankle. The ice packs were next. He was pushed flat when she tucked the blanket around him from his chin down, leaving only his ice-packed leg free. After a glance at her watch, she took the thermometer.

"Well?"

"Ninety-nine point eight," she read to him.

"Barely worth mentioning."

"We'll see."

She poured him a glass of water and handed it to him. Shaking tablets out of the bottle, three were in her palm with another teetering on the bottle edge when Caroleigh walked back in.

"What are you doing?" Caroleigh demanded furiously.

Kari started so violently she missed her hand with the last tablet.

"You are not a doctor," Caroleigh shouted. She stopped a bare two feet away with her hands on her hips, hovering over her as Kari leaned down to find the spilled tablet. "You threw that all away."

Kari stood slowly and looked Caroleigh straight in the eyes. "Even for you that was particularly cruel."

Her mouth opened to retort, thought better of it, and snapped her jaw shut with a click of teeth. "I guess you don't need any help," she retorted as she disappeared.

With a tablet between her fingers, Kari told him, "Two is the recommended dosage on the bottle. If you…"

He took that tablet along with the other three and swallowed all four. "Want to talk about it?"

"Do I need to defend myself?" she asked tightly.

"No, but you seem upset."

Emily, speaking loudly from the door, provided a distraction from what was developing into an awkward moment. "Miss Caroleigh, thought you might be hungry."

Kari tipped her head to look at her quizzically.

Emily hustled in and dropped her voice. "She came in after you. I didn't mention that you had already asked me to fix something."

Steven looked at what was on the tray she carried and complained instantly. "Soup? I haven't eaten since breakfast yesterday."

"We'll keep it light for now," Kari told him in a way that told him it would do no good to argue.

After Emily left, they argued over whether she was going to feed him. That one he won. She propped him up with decorative pillows behind his back and left him alone. Her only explanation was that she would be back.

After an hour, wasted in an effort to sleep after soup that didn't settle well, he started to worry. The concern put sharpness in his voice when she drifted silently in the door.

"Where have you been?"

"It's time to take your temperature again," she said instead of answering.

"I don't need that."

The thermometer was in his mouth anyway, and she sat back on her heels. "I'm going to tell you something that is going to upset you."

Steven's mind jumped ahead of her, expecting her to say she had decided what happened between them the night before shouldn't have. He reached for the thermometer to argue. She caught his hand and held it with both of hers.

"First I'm going to explain something to you. The swelling is compromising the circulation in your foot."

Her words were so far from what he had expected, he stared at her.

"You could be clotting. If you are, you could throw a clot and be dead before we could even get you to the pickup."

He reached for the thermometer with the other hand. She caught and held it.

"I radioed for an air-lift. They'll be here in about fifteen minutes."

Steven spit out the glass rod. "I don't—"

Kari retrieved the thermometer with one hand and put the other lightly over his lips. "I know you're worried about me. I think it's silly, but I'm going with you. I want to anyway, but I'm going to stay until you can come back. Okay?"

"Okay," he agreed from under her fingers.

She replaced her fingers with her lips in a quick, light kiss. His arms went around her, and she didn't leave the circle of his arms. She leaned one arm on his chest, held the thermometer up with the other hand to read.

"The way you acted this morning, I was afraid you'd decided last night was a mistake," he confessed.

She smiled and shook her head. "I just haven't decided what to do about Caroleigh yet."

"Tell her."

"She is going to be pissed. It's going to make it unpleasant for everyone."

"Kari, she doesn't care anything about me," Steven told her.

"Maybe, sometimes it’s hard to tell. Either way, she had you staked out."

"Staked out?"

"You know what I mean. She’s after you."

"Edward," Steven stated.

Kari dismissed that. "He's to keep Evelyn occupied."

"No, I think he's coming."

He tipped his head towards the hall. His impulse when she sat back quickly on her heels was to hold her, not caring who saw, but he let her slip away and laid his arm across his belly.

Edward reached the open doorway and paused while his eyes swept over the scene quickly. "Kari, love, I've been watching for your return."

"Return?” Steven questioned.

"I had to feed the animals."

Edward waited for the brief exchange before he continued. "I wondered if I might speak to you."

"Okay."

Since she made no move to get up, he added, "Privately."

"I don't think we have anything to discuss that we need privacy for."

"It has to do with the mine." She didn't move. "The reclamation process." She still didn't move to perplex him. "I did notice there is one in operation."

"And?" Kari prompted.

Edward stepped in and shut the door. "Caroleigh doesn't seem to know what it means-the possible benefits. As her friend—"

"Are you a good enough friend to know what she would do with those benefits if she became aware of them?"

"Squander them most likely," Edward admitted reluctantly, "but she still has the right to be aware of them if she's receiving them."

"Did that hurt?" she asked tonelessly.

"Yes, terribly," he admitted with a weak smile.

"If she isn't aware of them it's typical of why I haven't brought special attention to it. If she so much as bothered to read her year-end statements, she would be aware of the increase in the principal of her trust. As a friend you would do more for her by not mentioning it. Feel better now?"

Edward smiled shyly. "So much so, you will never know."

"You would be surprised by what I know," she said cryptically.

He studied her before he asked, "May I assume we have a pact of silence?"

"I can't see that you're doing anything to hurt her, but—"

"That I do consider private. No offense. You either, Steven."

"Since I don't know what you're talking about, none taken," Steven answered.

"Terribly rude of us." Edward tipped his head to listen. "Whatever is that racket?"

Kari stood as she answered. "Air ambulance, I'm taking him into the hospital."

"Rather a good idea if you ask me. It looks dreadful."

"Would you show them in?"

"Certainly," he answered and hurried away to do so.

Steven started up only to have Kari plant a hand on his chest. "I can walk," he protested.

"But you aren't."

Minutes later, Steven listened in astonishment while Kari explained his condition from the time she found him and through the early part of the night to the paramedics. She may have 'thrown away' becoming a doctor, but she hadn't forgotten the knowledge.

"All that would scare me to death if I weren't already over it," he said of the technical terms she used.

"Partially," she told him and moved on to describing his condition that morning to the medics.

That was when Caroleigh came in and listened in obvious anger. Just as obvious was who she was angry with. Her features became more and more set as the paramedics not only listened intently but with respect to what Kari had to say. One of the things they did while taking his vital signs was to press their fingers to his ankle to read the pulse into his foot as she had done without Steven realizing what she was doing. An IV was stuck into the back of his hand, and he was lifted onto a gurney.

While Evelyn had fled at the sight of his leg, Caroleigh stood fast and waited. She stepped in front of Kari as she followed the gurney out.

"You should have told us how seriously he's injured, or do you just enjoy making me look like a fool?"

Edward touched her on the arm. "Caroleigh," he implored.

"Are you going to pretend you don't see what she's doing?"

"Quite likely saving his life or limb, which none of us is capable of doing. Now don't be so ugly even I can't love you."

"Go to hell," she retorted and stormed away.

"Most likely," he said with a sigh.

Chapter Four

"I've been prodded, stabbed, and pinched more times than I can count," Steven complained. He shifted his weight; unable to get comfortable, but then lying flat on his back with his leg hung in a sling was not the most natural of positions. He still had the IV in the back of his hand, and a clamp on the end of his finger had been added to monitor his pulse and contribute to his discomfort. "And I'm hungry."

"You've only been stabbed three times, and they'll bring you something to eat soon so stop whining," Kari teased from the chair beside him while she pulled the stick from her hair. The chestnut locks cascaded down her back.

"Your hair is beautiful down like that."

"Now you're reverting to flattery. You must really be hungry."

Steven chuckled and shifted his weight again. The second resulted in pain and an abrupt end of his laugh. He covered it with a cough or rather he tried. He knew he hadn't succeeded when she came up out of the chair reaching for the call button for the nurse. He caught and held her hand.

"There is no reason for you to hurt," she told him, twisting her hand to free it.

"I don't like being drugged." He pulled her hand to his chest. "I wouldn't mind being babied a little though."

"Here?" she asked in mock shock and leaned down closer. "Just how much better are you feeling?"

"Not that well," a voice said from the door. A hearty chuckle followed when Kari jumped back guiltily. Dr. Penmate was a slightly overweight man, slightly bent who carried a solid head of gray hair. He was the one who had done most of the probing and stabbing. "He needed stimulation last night, not today." The way her face reddened made him chuckle more as he shuffled into the room, hand out to Steven.

"Doctor, I hope you're going to tell her I'm fine and let me out of here," Steven said while he received a hearty hand shake.

"Nope," he said cheerfully. He looked at the chart in his hand. "We'll keep you until that fever is normal." He looked up at Kari. "You nailed it on the head, hairline fracture. We'll keep him until the fever is down and the swelling, and then put a cast on it."

"Cast?" Steven asked in dread.

"Perfect excuse for a vacation," Kari told him.

"It'll get in the way," Steven complained, thinking how awkward it would be.

Doctor Penmate chuckled again. "It won't be a full leg," he said merrily. "It shouldn't get in the way too much."

Steven thought about what he had said and the way the doctor laughed. Then he remembered the doctor's comment about stimulation. He looked at Kari and received one of her very blank expressions in return.

"You're a lucky man," Penmate went on. "That was a nasty fall. If she hadn't found you when she did and warmed you up…" He choked up with another chuckle.

"Did you—" Steven started to ask Kari, thinking she surely hadn't told the doctor certain details of their night together.

"She was afraid…" Penmate could barely talk for laughing. "…she…"

"Jeopardized my welfare?" Steven asked with his face flushing like a schoolboy's.

Penmate nodded and took a deep breath. "I told her the stimulation was probably ben-ben…"

"Beneficial," Kari finished for him in a dead-pan voice.

With a vigorous nod and deeper chuckle he walked out of the room. Just outside he had to stifle his laughter to speak. "Hello, Dell. How are you?"

"Fine."

Steven recognized the voice even with only one word and was grateful for the distraction, but confused. "Why is the groomer here?" he asked.

"Vet, but he's probably being the sheriff today."

"Sheriff?"

"Sheriff," said the same voice Steven had argued with on the phone, the same man who had given him such a hostile look after the fire.

Steven began to understand the scowl he'd gotten. He most likely would have really gotten one if the man had walked in on the conversation a few minutes earlier.

Up close, Dell was pretty impressive. His posture suggested military training, ramrod spine, shoulders back, chest out, and chin up type. His medium build screamed weight-lifter, muscles bulging beneath the tan, tailored uniform. He had even, well-shaped features, framed with short, military cut, blond hair. And he wasn't any friendlier.

"Hear you had some more trouble out there," he said to Kari, but his look drilled Steven.

"The bluff steps collapsed, and Steven was hurt." she told him.

"The bluff steps, huh?" He moved closer to the bed. "I've been up and down those, over and over. They've always been solid as a rock. What happened?"

"They fell. I fell," Steven told him shortly.

"You were on them when they fell?"

"That's kind of a dumb question," Kari told him.

"Maybe," he told her to the side and asked Steven curtly, "What's your business here?"

"Vacation," Kari answered.

Dell's gaze never left Steven. "Sure you aren't looking for financial opportunities?"

Kari voice cut. "You really need to work on your communication skills, Dell. You're much too vague."

"Did you see him or those stairs fall?"

"No, but I dug him out of the wreckage and kept him from dying."

"From a banged up leg?"

"From shock, concussion, and hypothermia, or are you going to suggest I mistook an acting job for the real thing?"

"I think his timing could have been off, and it took you longer to find him than he planned. You're too trusting, Kari, even when you know the kind of people Caroleigh drags up here."

"Oh, my," Edward said from the doorway. "Should I knock or just leave?"

"Do come in," Steven said tightly, "and join in on the character assassination."

"I do hope it isn't too severe." He strolled in casually. "You know how sensitive I am."

"What are you doing here?" Kari asked.

"Well, love, the girls were concerned about Steven, and since the phone is still out, we decided a nice little drive was in order."

"Did you leave Emily by herself?" she asked as Caroleigh and Evelyn walked in.

"Do you think us monsters?" Edward queried. "Of course not. She is a brave little girl, but that house is so big."

Evelyn explained more. "She nearly went into hysterics when we told her we were leaving. The spirits are just too much for her."

"Spirits?" Del asked with a derisive snort. He asked Kari, "Are you seeing ghosts now?"

"No," Evelyn answered. "Emily did. A horrid, bloody, one-armed thing."

"Daddy came to visit?" Dell asked Kari in the same tone.

"Sounds like, doesn't it?" she returned tartly.

"That's garbage," he retorted.

"Really?" Evelyn challenged. "Then explain what happened at the séance."

"Séance? What kind of crazy games are you playing up there?"

"Oh," Edward cried and crossed over to touch Kari's hair. "A new do?"

"What?" she asked as her gaze swung to his face.

"A new do, quite becoming."

"It is," Evelyn exclaimed in surprise. "And you've done something else. I know. You've taken off your glasses. You're actually quite pretty."

"Thank you," Kari said dryly.

"You're all loony tunes." Dell retorted. "I'm going to keep my eye on you."

The last was a threat directed at Steven, but Caroleigh took the sting out of it by stepping in front of him as he started out. "Hello, Dell," she said sweetly. "It's nice to see you again."

Dell grunted and pushed by her.

"Was he one of yours?" Evelyn asked in a whisper.

Caroleigh answered with a raised eyebrow and a smug smile, but when her gaze settled on Kari, there was no humor in her eyes.

* * * *

"I thought visiting hours didn't start until seven," Steven said with a strained smile.

"I bribed the nurse." Kari leaned down to kiss him and drew back to question the lack of warm return. "What's wrong?"

"Nothing."

"You are a terrible liar. Are you brooding about what Dell said?"

"No," he said and then amended it. "Not brooding, but it did start me thinking about a few things."

She sat on the edge of the bed, twisted to face him. "Such as?"

"I did tell you I work for a living."

"Then you could take me away from all this?" she teased.

"My business is in Denver, Kari. I couldn't run it from here, and I couldn't—wouldn't quit to live off you."

"You'd be disappointed if you did. I'm not that rich."

"No? What's reclamation?"

"Pretty much what it sounds like. Do you know what a tailing pile is?" At his nod, she continued. "Back then they went after the easy to see and reach stuff, throwing out a lot of low grade ore. I sold the mining rights to what they threw out. I don't have to come up with any of the production costs, and I get a small percentage that helps pay the taxes in exchange for a few arguments over environmental issues and keeping the haul road in good condition."

"Small profit?"

"Yeah, but it beats a kick in the butt," she said, but her voice had lost the teasing tone.

"And the ranch?"

"Non-working, I lease grazing rights to other ranchers with only occasional disputes over herd size and fence repair."

"None of those buildings were deteriorating, Kari."

"Which is where most of the grazing money goes. I supplement that by renting it out to various organizations for summer camps. They carry their own insurance and are liable for damages." She went ahead of him. "The mansion is partially supported by Bed and Breakfast, June through August. What can I say? Appearances are deceiving."

"You could sell that house."

"Not an option."

"Are you saying Caroleigh would fight you on it?"

"I've already told you, Caroleigh has nothing to say about it."

"Is she beneficiary or trustee of any kind in the trust?"

Kari's eyes narrowed. "Which trust would that be?"

"The Morning Meadow Trust."

Kari's back went stiff as she asked coolly, "And how is it you know about that?"

Not seeing the warning signs, Steven answer truthfully. "I had my associate do a title search."

She shot to her feet. "Before or after you fell in love at first sight?"

"What? Hey, wait a minute," he called as she stormed towards the door.

Kari didn't so much as slow at his words. Steven jerked his leg free of the sling to go after her. A split second after his feet hit the floor, he did too. He fell into the bed table and sent it into the wall with a reverberating crash. He went down, twisted and gripped his leg with both hands. The excruciating pain squeezed air from his lungs, and he gasped to catch a breath. He could only answer with a shake of his head when an elderly nurse knelt beside him to ask what had happened.

Penmate ran in and knelt beside both. “What happened, Martha?”

"I found him like this," the nurse said.

"Stupid," Steven ground out.

"Did you try to get up?” Penmate asked.

Martha leaned close to the doctor and whispered. "Just before the crash, Kari ran out of here like her tail was on fire."

Penmate twisted to look over his shoulder. Kari stood just outside the door. He mouthed, “What happened?” She answered with indifferent shrug, but her expression wasn't without concern.

"Screwed up," Steven gasped out. "She thinks…”

"Tell me later."

"Now!" He forced himself up straighter and transferred one clenched hand to Penmate's arm. "Someone’s trying to kill her."

Unconciouness took him under. Hours later, with his brain working before he could control his body, he fought to wake up. As soon as he could open his eyes long enough to focus, he asked, "Kari?"

Penmate, sober and serious, tipped his head toward the other side of the bed. With arms crossed defensively, Kari stood in front of the window, and she looked furious.

"Sorry," he slurred out.

"You should be," she stated curtly. "You snapped that leg, and you've got him so worked up, he won't let me out of his sight."

Steven shook his head in an effort to keep his eyes open. "Commute or something…own the whole state…don't care…work it out."

He shook his head again, fought the drugs to stay awake and reached for the side rail of the bed to pull up. Penmate pressed him back down.

"If you try to get up again, you young fool, I'll put you in restraints."

Unable to keep his eyes open, Steven whispered, "Don't let her be alone."

As much as he wanted to, Steven couldn’t keep his eyes open. He didn’t go to sleep either, but hovered in a middle land, hearing, but unable to respond.

"Well?" Penmate asked.

"Well what?" Kari demanded.

"Are you going to let what happened with Dell spoil—?"

"Oh, for Christ's sake! That happened over ten years ago."

"But that and what Dell said today was in your head. That's why you reacted the way you did. Have Max run a check on him," Penmate urged.

"No. If I doubt him enough for that, I doubt him too much."

"That's not rational thinking, Kari. You have the right not to doubt him or yourself at all."

Steven missed the rest of the terse conversation.

* * * *

When he could finally open his eyes and keep them open, Steven didn't know the person with him.

"Good morning," the perky young nurse told him cheerfully while she pumped up the blood pressure cuff around his arm. "I'm Adie, your day nurse."

His eyes swept the room sluggishly. "Morning?"

"They went home about two." Her head gave a knowing bob. "They wouldn't leave until they knew the medications were taking effect."

"What medications?" he asked, his eyes riveted on the new collection of pulleys and cables holding his leg in traction.

"I am to tell you, specifically, they went home together, and they will be back around seven."

"What time is it now?"

"Six." She stuck a digital thermometer in his ear. "Do you want anything for pain?"

"No," he said quickly.

Adie chuckled with her dimples showing. "Not everything for pain knocks you out. They just wanted you out for the worst of it, new x-rays and that." The last was said with a tip of her head towards his suspended leg.

"What medications?" he repeated, grateful he hadn't been awake during the hanging procedure.

"Layman or tech?"

"Layman, please."

"Okay, anti-inflammatory, antibiotics, fever-reducing, anti-congratulants, pain, and some supplements thrown in for good measure." She pointed to the IV bag hung over his head. "That is to keep you from getting dehydrated. Hungry?"

"No."

"Breakfast will be here soon. Try to eat anyway. You need the nourishment. Is it safe to leave you alone?"

"I won't be trying to get up if that's what you mean."

"It is. Smart man."

He grunted in response and then asked, "Is Dell the only law in this town?"

"Our one and only sheriff, though some will debate with you as to whether or not he's law. Did he give you a speeding ticket?"

"Yeah," he lied.

"See the judge. He throws out nearly everything Dell sends in. Is there anything you want or need before I leave?"

"Water."

"Coming right up."

"What's the judge's name?"

"His Honorable Judge Zachary Powell."

"Is it possible to call him?"

Penmate came in at a rapid clip. "Adie, Mrs. Angelo needs help changing."

"On my way, just as soon as I get him some water."

"I'll take care of it. I don't think he's as impatient as Mrs. Angelo."

"No one is," she quipped and waved to Steven as she hurried out.

Her second wave as she went out the door was the only reason Steven didn't ask where Kari was. He didn't watch Penmate pull her in and couldn't look at her once he had.

"Zack is eighty-nine years old," Penmate told him. "He throws Dell's tickets out because he doesn't like him, not out of judicial fairness or a keen mind. He wouldn't do us much good."

"You believe me," Steven said in relief.

"I believe you believe it. The question is, are you right?"

Kari shoved the door shut. "Can you think of anyone who would want to kill me?"

"No, but—"

"Neither can I."

Steven blurted out, "That was all I was trying to find out, Kari, if someone could benefit."

"Caroleigh isn't doing it."

"Caroleigh?" Penmate asked in shock.

"Then who is?" Steven countered.

"No one."

"There's too much to be coincidence."

"Stop it, both of you," Penmate ordered.

Kari retreated, arms crossed over her chest. Steven went silent and looked to Penmate for help. After Penmate achieved silence, he didn't seem to know where to go next.

"Okay, ah, let's try to put things in some kind of order," Penmate began uncertainly. "You think too many things have happened too close together for coincidence, thereby suggesting there's some sort of conspiracy to cause Kari harm." He scratched his head. "What does Dell think?"

Kari rolled her eyes, and Steven grunted before saying, "The carriage house was lightning, and I sabotaged the stairs, faked my injury, and miscalculated the time it would take her to find me."

"For what reason?"

"To get her money," Steven said in resentment.

"Oh, well, Dell's an ass."

"And territorial," Steven pointed out as much in question as a statement.

"Without cause, which makes him a fool, too." Penmate looked at Kari. "For the sake of argument only, would it have been possible for him to have faked the accident?"

She didn't take anytime to consider, shaking her head. "He couldn't have wedged that timber like that. There were several hundred pounds of pressure on the other end."

"An accomplice?"

"Godzilla maybe," she countered tartly.

"I'm just playing devil's advocate here. Don't get mad at me. I'm trying to cover all the possibilities, including, couldn't it have been just an accident?"

"Yes," she said.

"No," Steven said at the same time. He went on. "By itself, maybe, but not with everything else."

"What everything else?" Penmate asked. "She was a little vague."

"Her dogs disappeared, leaving her with nothing to warn her if someone was prowling around. The carriage house burns down which would have left her without transportation, isolated if her pickup had been in there instead of our cars. The phone goes dead that morning, leaving her with no way to call for help the same day stairs she uses every day suddenly collapse, and all that ghost business, plus the lies Caroleigh tells about her to make it sound like she's crazy."

Penmate looked at Kari in perplexity. "Ghost business?"

"That isn't anything. I'm sure it's Edward's attempts to entertain the girls."

"Emily was terrified," Steven argued.

"Emily gets drawn into conspiracies rather easily in case you haven't noticed."

"You think she was acting?" he asked incredulously.

"She did a lot of screaming, panting, and crying, but she didn't lose her color and her eyes weren't dilated."

"Umm," Penmate said thoughtfully.

"I suppose that means something to a doctor," Steven grumbled.

"Signs of shock," Penmate supplied.

"Okay," Steven snapped, "but what about the blood?"

"Blood?" Penmate asked with start.

"Colored gelatin mixture, fake." Kari retorted, and then asked, "Who came into dinner last?"

"I don't remember."

"Really doesn't matter. Either Edward left it to be found later, or Emily walked around the back hall and left it."

"Why didn't you tell me that before?" Steven asked in a controlled growl.

"I did tell you I thought it was a joke."

"Pretty sick one," Penmate put in.

Kari pointed at Steven. "He said the same thing."

Steven argued. "You don't know if it was just for entertainment. Add that to the things Caroleigh says."

"Yes," Penmate interrupted with. "Let's move on to that. What does she say?"

"She lies about owning the Meadow."

"I told you what that was for." Kari turned to Penmate. "You know how she is. Once she got him to bed, she'd have dropped the whole thing."

"Damn it, Kari," Steven exclaimed in frustration. "She tells people you're mentally incompetent, a brain-damaged drugger."

"Drugs?" she inquired mildly. "That's new."

"How can you just tolerate it like that?"

She half-shrugged. "Keeps the guys she brings up here from hitting on me, usually."

"I didn't—"

Penmate interceded quickly. "Let's not get side-tracked. What about the dogs?"

"They disappeared," she retorted defensively.

"And you're satisfied that they just disappeared?"

Kari shifted and hesitated before she admitted, "Not entirely, but I still don't think it's connected to anything else."

"Okay," Penmate nodded thoughtfully. "What I think is we need someone with more experience in this type of thing. I'm calling Max."

"No," Kari cried.

"Who's that?" Steven asked.

"The best sheriff this area ever had until those fools got dazzled with Dell's flash," Penmate told him. "He'll figure out soon enough what's coincidence or accident."

"Breakfast," Adie announced gaily as she pushed the door open. "And I brought his water. I figured you would forget."

"Just haven't done it yet, you impertinent little brat," Penmate teased. "Set it down and go on with you before I spank you."

"You've never spanked me in my life," she teased back. She sat the tray on the table and draped her arm over his shoulders. "Doesn't look like they've made up yet."

Penmate turned from under her arm and pushed her towards the door. "Out of here you little snoop."

"Grandpa," she complained.

He pushed again and gave orders to Kari. "Get him to eat and then let him rest." He gave Adie one last, little push, winning a giggle from her as they disappeared.

Kari busied herself with filling a glass with water.

"If you'd give me a chance I can explain," he said softly. She cranked up the bed table without a look in his direction. "I don't blame you for being upset."

She still ignored him, but when she turned back to push the table over the bed, her gaze touched his.

He asked quickly, "Will you listen to me?" He didn't wait for her to answer that time. "I was just trying to find out if she—if anyone—could benefit."

"She wouldn't, and neither would anyone else. It became an irrevocable trust when Grandpa died."

"What about the mine?"

Kari threw her hands in the air. "It's nearly worthless the way it is now. If it weren't for the reclamation, we'd have trouble even paying the taxes."

"Your grandfather didn't believe it was worthless. Maybe she doesn't. Remember what you said about dreams of gold that drive to insanity,"

"She wouldn't want to kill me," she insisted stubbornly.

"Would she benefit in anyway if you were found to have diminished capacities?" He added quickly, "If anyone believes even a portion of what she tells people, it's possible that's what she's setting up. Even if she believes it—"

She cut him off. "I don't know what she believes, but I don't believe she's still that mad at me."

"Mad? About what?"

Kari blew a breath out in exasperation. "A silly argument we had years ago."

"Over a man?"

"Hardly," she said in scorn. "She wanted me to go to Europe with her at the last minute during my summer break. I had already made plans and wouldn't change them. We fought over that, not some guy. Why would you think that anyway?"

"I just-ah-just…"

As the words trailed off, she said, "You're embarrassed."

"Yeah," he admitted. "That's what I get for listening to someone repeat what someone else told them. Another of Caroleigh's lies."

"What lie?"

"About the two of you always competing for guys."

Kari gave a short, derisive laugh. "Oh, that." She dismissed it with a wave of her hand. "We never fought over guys, never even liked the same ones. I just stay out of her way since…" She broke off with a sad sigh. "I really miss her."

He found that hard to believe. "Miss her?"

She took the covers off the dishes on his tray. "Not the way she is now. The way she used to be."

"I'm not hungry."

"You haven't eaten much of anything for two days. You need it." She put a piece of toast in his hand. "Try a few bites to see if it stimulates your appetite."

"I'll try to eat if you talk. Tell me the way she used to be."

After a moment of consideration, she agreed. She walked around the bed to the chair on the far side and settled down, but she did not speak a word until he took a bite. “Her father, Jonathan, and my father, Adam, were friends. Jonathan’s father and my grandpa were business partners before that so we saw a lot of them. By that time there weren't many who were considered social peers left up here. My mother left when I was four. My father married Gladys, a real gold-digging vampire, and she didn't really care who knew it. My grandpa hated her so when my father died Grandpa wouldn't let her take me, not that she would have if she couldn’t have made some profit off it. Anyway, she married Caroleigh’s father next to sort of make us related. They liked to travel and didn't want to drag a child along. They didn’t even come home for a year after they were married, and they didn’t ever want Caroleigh around really when they did. Staying with us was free baby-sitting for them, company for me, and Grandpa never minded. She stayed with us most of the time she wasn’t away at school. We grew up together, like sisters.”

She shrugged slightly. “The Meadow was the only real home she ever had, and I won't take that away from her as long as she needs it. She was also the only family I had, except for Grandpa, and she was my best friend."

"That's hard to visualize," he told her candidly of the last. “You aren’t anything alike.”

She pointed to the toast in his hand and waited until he took another bite. "We were a real odd couple, even as kids. She was a prissy, little snob by the time she was six. She played with dolls, wore fancy little dresses, and held mock tea parties, training from her mother and nannies. I couldn't wait to get outside and get dirty. She learned to get dirty, and I learned to pretend to drink tea." She smiled wistfully. "The nannies really preferred the teas. At least then they knew where we were and what we were doing. We had each other, and if there was anything we couldn't handle, we had Grandpa."

When she lapsed into silence, he prompte. "Then she wanted to go to Europe and you wanted to…?"

"Go to Mexico. We had a huge argument, each calling the other selfish, other stupid things. I can't believe she's still angry over that. I think something happened over there, and because I was sick at the time and Grandpa was busy with me, she didn't have anyone to depend on or support her. When she did come back, she was different."

She looked up as Penmate walked in. He finished for her. "She was hateful. And it's time to do something about it."

"If it's gotten bad enough someone actually thinks her capable of murder, I guess so."

"Not only that, Kari. This game she plays is dangerous. You aren't kids anymore, testing your boyfriends. She could get hurt."

"Do I want to know what he's talking about?" Steven asked.

"Dell," she answered in one word with a shrug. "That's where the competition story comes from. It was as much my doing as it was hers because I didn't really trust him, but she's the one that ended up with the bad reputation over it."

"Because of Dell's mouth," Penmate said in disgust.

"He wasn't about to tell people what really happened," Kari pointed out.

"No or admit that his stupid story of you never getting over him is just that, and everyone knows it."

Steven began to understand Dell's possessive attitude better. "What happened?"

"I was a freshman in high school, and without realizing it, a real catch, future guaranteed, or so he thought, me being the only heir and all," she told him matter-of-factly. "I was also inexperienced in the ways of the world. Caroleigh came home for the holidays, took one look at him and told me he was a jerk. I challenged her to prove it. She did, all too easily. After we both told him to go to hell, he told people she had lied to me to break us up because she wanted him, but he didn't want her or me any longer because I hadn't believed in him. That's putting his stories in the mildest form. It really got ugly for her. Most people knew better, but the story still persists. It isn't fair to her."

"Then you did the same thing for her that time when you were in college," Penmate said briskly. "What was his name, Peter?"

"I made a pass at him, but…" she told Steven quickly, "….it wasn't a competition. It was sincerity testing."

With a grimace Steven asked, "You put each other's boyfriends on trial by trying to seduce them?"

"It never went that far. That was never necessary," she retorted.

"I take it no one ever passed."

"No," she said and pushed up out of her chair.

"I guess I failed too." Steven said to Penmate after she disappeared in the bathroom,

Penmate shook his head. "Not for that reason from what I hear."

"Same reason," Steven murmured. "Just a different test."

"I think the jury is still out on that one."

They reached a truce of sorts. Kari agreed to stay either with him or with Penmate even though she didn't believe there was any danger. He no longer stated his suspicions about Caroleigh aloud, but he wouldn't agree there wasn't a threat. They settled into an uncomfortable togetherness. Both fell asleep soon after his disinterested attempt to eat. They were both abruptly awakened.

"That looks awful," Evelyn exclaimed.

Steven jerked awake and reached for his leg. Kari started up, saw who the three visitors were and settled back down in the chair to rub the back of her neck.

"Very good," Edward said dryly. "Being jarred awake does wonders for a sick man's nerves."

"He isn't sick," Evelyn protested while Caroleigh eyed Kari. "He's hurt."

"Somewhat more than before, it would appear."

"I fell," Steven said in answer to the unspoken question.

"In here?" Evelyn asked excitedly.

Edward rolled his eyes. "Something tells me Evelyn sees dollar signs."

"Hospitals are responsible," she answered. "They always pay."

"Pay?" Steven asked sleepily.

"Their insurance, hers too," Evelyn told him with a point at Kari. "You could come out of this very well off."

"Suing," Edward said because of Steven's puzzled look. "Great American past time."

"I'm not suing anyone," he told him.

He reached for a glass of water. Edward saved him the effort. "Tepid, old boy," he said of the glass he took from the table.

Kari stood up. "I'll get some fresh."

"Why not?" Evelyn asked, stuck on the same subject.

Caroleigh spoke for the first time. "What are you doing here?" she demanded of Kari.

"Making sure I don't get sued," she answered indifferently and took the glass and pitcher.

"He was hurt on your property," Evelyn pointed out.

"For how long?" Caroleigh asked, but Kari walked out.

Edward answered. "Visiting hours started half an hour ago." He pulled Caroleigh closer. "Now since we've disturbed his sleep, give him our gift."

With an overly sweet smile, she slinked to the bedside. "We were so shocked to see you like this. Does it hurt terribly?"

"Yes, and I'm not very good company," Steven told her bluntly.

Edward raised Caroleigh's arm to display the gift bag she held. "We'll just give you our gift and…"

At that moment, Martha, the same nurse who helped pick Steven up off the floor the night before, appeared in the doorway. "Two visitors at a time," she said sternly.

"…leave," Edward finished with a grimace. Martha was a formidable looking lady, slim and sharp featured.

"Hello, Martha," Caroleigh said.

"Miss Caroleigh, you know the hospital rules."

"Did Kari send you in here?"

"She did not. I never got in the middle of your squabbles when you were youngsters. I'm not likely to now. One of you has to leave." She half-turned to leave before she added, "You could come to visit occasionally."

"Visit?" Edward whispered after she had gone and shuddered at the thought.

"She took care of us before she became a nurse, and she's really quite fond of me," Caroleigh said brightly. "You go ahead. I'll catch up to you."

"He doesn't feel like visiting."

"Later, Edward," she told him tersely.

"Ah, yes, later." He backed up a step and turned as Kari walked back in. "We were just going for lunch, love. Will you join us?"

"You're asking me?" she asked in surprise.

"She's probably busy," Evelyn said quickly.

Kari's eyes shifted to her. "That's more like it. No."

"Another time then," Edward told her with a wane smile.

"Oh, sure, when I'm not busy."

"Touché, love," he said. He touched her lightly on the arm as he passed, easing Evelyn out ahead of him.

Evelyn complained. "You were being polite. It was no reason for her to be rude."

Caroleigh's cold stare never left Kari. "Where have you been all this time?" she asked while Kari poured fresh water.

Kari held the glass out to Steven without answering.

Caroleigh's voice raised in irritation. "Are you going to play dumb again and not answer me?"

"Deaf," Kari corrected indifferently.

Caroleigh took her arm roughly and pulled her towards the door. "Do you think I don't know what you're up to?" she whispered hoarsely. "Joining us for meals, actually joining in conversations, and..." She flipped Kari's hair.

Kari batted her hand away. "Why not join you?" she asked. "Edward's—"

Caroleigh jerked as if she had been slapped. "Edward?" she exclaimed.

Kari's expression went blank. "...is amusing and..."

"You're not interested in Edward," she snapped. "It's not him you're playing games for."

"I don't play games," Kari stated.

Caroleigh straightened abruptly with a hard glare at Kari before she walked back to Steven's bedside, all smiles again. "We didn't know what to get you really." She handed him the gift bag, then reached inside it while he held it and stared at her. "We just thought this would help you pass the time."

He didn't even look at the electronic game she held up. "Thank you," he said automatically. He watched Kari drift to the foot of his bed as she watched Caroleigh intently.

"You just hurry and get better." She laid one hand on his arm and brushed his side to lay the game beside him. "We'll come back this evening. Maybe you'll feel more like company by then."

She squeezed his arm, giving him a suggestive smile before she left. Two sets of eyes moved to follow her out of sight.

"Was that a declaration of war?" Steven asked.

Kari's eyes swung from the empty doorway to him. "What?"

"Declaration of war?" he repeated.

"Not the reaction I expected from her," she said thoughtfully and then sighed. "I'm not sure what it means." Kari leaned down, arms braced on the footboard. "Have you ever heard the poor, little rich kid story, never sure if you were liked or loved for yourself or your money and what you could do for them?" She didn't wait for an answer. "Caroleigh and I have lived with that all our lives. It's not much of a confidence builder. What she and I did with Dell may have sounded childish to you. It wasn't. It was self-preservation because there are people like Dell who are greedy without conscience or morals. Everyone around warns you to be careful, not to trust blindly, so much so that after awhile you're afraid to trust your own feelings and instincts. I thought maybe that was the real reason why I didn't trust Dell, not anything I sensed about him, and I asked for her help. Getting older doesn't make any of it go away. That's why Caroleigh plays the games she plays, never letting anyone close, never letting anyone matter anymore. The Peter Doctor Penmate mentioned hurt her pretty badly."

"What about you?" he asked softly.

She shook her head slightly. "I haven't been hurt like that, but suspicion and fear are a hidden second nature to us. I didn't look for a reason to doubt you, but I didn't look away when one popped up, either."

"Have you gotten a good report back on me?"

"Excuse me?"

"I couldn't make myself wake up enough to say anything, but I heard you and the doctor talking. Did you get back a favorable report?"

"I didn't order one."

"Because you don't doubt me enough or don't want to doubt me?"

"Both, I think," she told him truthfully. "More than that, I'm afraid of your reaction to even the suggestion of it."

"My pride?" he said somewhere between question and statement.

"And mine."

"Order it."

"You said once you didn't want to take a chance on spoiling something you thought could be important. I'm afraid it's already been done."

"It hasn't, not for me. You're still important to me. Order it, Kari. Get it out of our way."

For a man of his age, Penmate could move briskly. He came into the room and joined the conversation uninvited. "Order what?"

Steven told him. "My investigation or rather the investigation of me."

"Waste of time, but if it will shut up the doomsayers, it'll be worth it."

"What doomsayers?"

"Other than Dell?" Kari grumbled.

"The usual pack," Penmate answered lightly. "Ready?"

"For what?" she asked since the question was directed at her.

"Home, lunch, and rest." Before she could object he added, "For both of you. He needs to know you're safe so he can relax. Don't argue."

Solitude did not provide Steven with rest. He couldn't settle down. He turned on the TV and stared at captions flashing off and on the bottom of the screen, not caring what was on.

"Me again," Adie announced as she bustled in. She glanced at the small screen as she reached for the blood pressure cuff on the wall. "Those things drive me crazy. I can't watch for reading."

"Kind of hypnotizing."

"I suppose you get used to it if you have to. Would you like me to turn them off for now?"

"Doesn't matter. I'm not really watching it anyway."

She lapsed into silence to take his vital signs, but only briefly. "She's great, isn't she?"

He didn't have to ask who she meant. "I think so."

"I'm not prying," she told him. "Not that I don't shamelessly at times. I just think she's one of those genuinely nice people. When her grandfather died, she could have sat back and lived off the trusts, but she didn't. Like her great grandmother before her, she put what she had to work, to help other people. She set up youth camps at the ranch, started a bed and breakfast, and had that horrible road worked on. Because of those things, the kids around here have a work source for summer, and the kids in the cities get to come to the country. Then she opened up that tailings pile. Everyone knows she doesn't make enough off it to justify the headaches, but it's the first time a lot of the men around here have been able to make a decent living in years."

"That's a little different version than the one she gave me."

"Figures, just like seeing to it that we had an air ambulance here. She never advertises the nice things she does. That's why I told you. I've heard some of the garbage Caroleigh comes up with. I don't know why Kari doesn't kick that one out on her butt every time she comes up here for a handout."

"Handout?"

"Yeah, every time she runs through her check before the month is up, she comes up here and lives off of Kari, and Kari lets her. I just don't understand why."

"Maybe for the same reasons she started a summer camp."

"Probably," she agreed cheerfully.

"Ask me…" a voice said from the door, "…there should be a limit."

"Max," Adie exclaimed. "What are you doing here?"

He lounged against the door frame, an indication of how long he'd been eavesdropping and showing he meant for them to know he had. He pushed up lazily. Seventy years old if he was a day, his back was ramrod straight, and he carried his lean body with an impression of packaged energy despite his lazy movements. "Looking for Kari," he answered but walked straight to the bed.

"Missed her. Grandpa took her home to rest. Something I can help with?"

"Nope, could be he can. Nathan Maxwell. We met the other night."

"I remember you," Steven offered his hand.

Max gripped it firmly. "Frightful fire that." With a hold of Steven's hand, his bright, clear eyes flickered under his bushy, gray brows, taking Steven in from head to airborne toes. "Messed you up some."

"Some."

"Gives you a reason to hang around."

Steven pulled his hand free while Adie said, "Hanging being the operative word. Did Grandpa send you?"

"You got other things to be doing?" Max asked pointedly.

"He did send you."

"Go."

"Max, he…"

He turned her by the shoulders and pointed her towards the door. "I'm just going to ask a few questions, not torture him. Go."

She did, but not before she told Steven, "If he gets too insulting, hit the button. Martha came in today, and I'll sic her on him."

Steven told Max with resignation, "I'm glad Kari has so many people looking out for her."

"None of us saw it," Max said to throw him.

"You think I'm right?" he asked in surprise.

Max pulled a chair closer. "In so far as something is going on, yes. Just what, I don't know yet. Those shepherds of hers were getting on, but they could still whip a pack of coyotes without losing their breath. I tracked down the break in the phone line. It was pulled loose from the pole. I couldn't find anything natural or accidental that could have done it, and the wire looked cut, not broken. The 'lightning does strange things' won't fly now. I called in an arson investigator. As for those stairs, it's going to be hard to tell if they were tampered with after the high water that night, but I took samples of those anchor blocks and places where the timbers looked to have broken. Sent those to a lab. They may be able to find something. You got anything to add?"

"Not that I can think of right now," Steven answered numbly.

Max gave a brief nod. "I agree there are too many coincidences to be comfortable, but there is the possibility that's all it is. We're still real short on motive. Any chance someone was after you?"

"Kari already asked me that," Steven said with a shake of his head. "No one, including me, even knew I'd be on those stairs until just before I walked out there."

"Well," Max drew the word out and scratched his head. "I got to tell you, from one angle it sounds like a well thought out plan. From another it looks like just a bunch of screw-ups. Who would plan ahead in getting rid of the dogs so they could prowl around freely to set a trap to burn up her pickup, then not make sure it was in there before setting it off?"

"Does she usually park it in there?"

"Nearly always, but she said she did a lot that day to free up the next, and it was late by the time she got back. She drove around straight to the apartment to get ready in time for dinner."

Steven smiled to himself knowing why she'd freed up the next day. He said, "Maybe they just assumed it would be in there."

"Which would have been sloppy on their part, not making sure. Either we got someone too sure of themselves, or we're making a mountain out of a molehill."

"She's sure it isn't Caroleigh."

Max gazed at him thoughtfully for a moment. "Caroleigh didn't call to let her know she was coming until the day before, which is normal and usually means she had just decided to do it. She could still either be a part of it, or her unexpected arrival is the reason things got screwed up. It threw Kari off her normal routine, put the pickup in the wrong place, which saved it for her to use that morning because she was tired from the night before. She drove over to feed the stock instead of walking the way she usually does. That kept her off the stairs. Damned glad of the last. Been her instead of you under normal circumstances, it could have been days before she was found."

"That's what I thought they were hoping for."

"Which is why we're going to keep a close eye on her. Penmate is going to let you out of here in a few days. Anyone asks she's too busy taking care of you to take care of the ranch and grounds. That's where I come in. You'll see me hanging around, but for now, might be better if we seem on less than friendly terms."

"My being good enough for her being the only issue?"

"Sounds good."

"Am I?" Steven asked bluntly.

Max didn’t miss a beat to answer. "You look good on paper. Some puzzled as to how you ended up here though."

"I seized the opportunity to see the mansion by accepting an invitation from a total stranger, Caroleigh."

"How did you come to meet her?"

"At a party, I heard her say Morning Meadow and barged into the conversation."

"Couldn't be you were interested in meeting who the invitation came from?"

Steven was blunt again. "As in attracted to or hunting?"

"Both," Max answered just as frankly.

"No to both. I didn't know who she was, and I was not—am not—attracted to her."

"I hear she comes on pretty strong."

"She didn't at the party; just flirted like some women do with any man they're around."

"But?"

Steven shifted uncomfortably. "Just in case, I brought my own transportation and before you even bother asking, I didn't leave because of Kari, as in attracted to, not hunting."

"Uh-huh," he said with a nod. "And how did you find out about the trust?"

"I already explained why to her."

"Didn't ask why. I asked how."

"I had my associate do a title search," Steven answered, confused by what difference that made.

"When did you do that?"

"I had just asked him to when the phone went out. I called him back this morning."

"So," Max drawled out thoughtfully, “something like that doesn't take much time and is pretty easy to do?"

"Yes, it's public record."

"So anyone can do it?"

Steven nodded. "Yes, if you know how."

"Give you all the details of the trust, does it?"

"All I asked for was a deed of record. Since a trust has to be recorded, I suppose you could get the details. That wasn’t what I asked for.”

Max gave him details. "It all goes to the state if she dies without issue to inherit it. She’s got full use of it and can use it anyway she wants, but she can't sell it. Something for her heirs, if she has any."

"You think that makes a difference to me?"

Max stood slowly. "Pull your horns in, son. Just telling you. No one benefits from that trust if she dies."

"That doesn't make sense then."

"That's what I said; we're a mite short on motive.

Chapter Five

Since he wasn't sleeping well, it only took a slight sound to wake him. Steven opened his eyes to see Caroleigh moving a chair closer to the bed.

"Sorry. I was trying to be so careful." She smiled sweetly and dragged the chair so close to the bed she barely had room to get in it. "I brought you a milkshake. Kari always brought me milkshakes when I didn't feel well." She looked at the milkshake sadly. "Believe it or not Kari and I used to be very close. It's my fault we aren't anymore. I'd give anything to change that." She sighed heavily. "She can't forgive me. Every time I come up to see how she is all we do is snap and bite at each other."

She had a tear in the corner of her eye. She wiped it away before she stripped the paper off a straw and pushed it through the lid on the cup. "I miss her so badly sometimes…" She broke off with a quiver to her voice.

Steven didn't trust her one bit but asked, "What happened?"

"Something stupid and selfish. I wanted to go on a European tour to mend a broken heart. She wanted to go to Mexico to save sick, starving children. She invited me to go with her. I refused, of course. I told her idiotic things like they wouldn't be starving if their parents weren't so lazy, and she would only save them from starving that summer so they could freeze in winter. I didn't understand about real poverty then, didn't want to. I couldn't be bothered, and I was furious at her for choosing them over me. I really said some hateful things." Another tear formed in her eye. "She got sick down there. Did she tell you about it?"

"No."

"She nearly died. She would have if Grandpa hadn't chartered a helicopter with a doctor and nurses and brought her home from that awful hospital. I got back as soon as I could, but I had already done too much. She ignored me, wouldn't even talk to me. I wanted to take care of her, and she wouldn't even look at me. She looked so terrible. Her hair was all gone in clumps." She ended abruptly with a break in her voice.

"I think you misunderstood," he offered, knowing how Kari felt.

She took a deep breath, blew it out slowly, and shook her head. "You're sweet, but you've seen how she treats me, and she has a hard streak you haven't seen yet." She held the cup out to him. When he took it, her other hand moved to cover his on the cup. "Got it?"

Steven pulled his hand away without the cup.

"Too cold? I'll hold it for you."

He blocked the cup with his hand as she moved it towards his mouth. As she leaned closer he said, "Don't do this."

She tipped her head to look at him quizzically. "Just not interested?" she asked sweetly.

"No."

"Why?"

"You know why."

Caroleigh's smile twisted in something far from sweet. "You are good. You assessed the situation quickly and moved in on her, but you might want to reconsider. Appearances are deceiving. She only has use of the mansion, not ownership. She can't sell it and has to scrap just to support it. Seeing the house and assuming what it meant, you lost your head. I can understand that. What you don't know is I have much more than is apparent, and I share generously. As long as you keep me happy, I'll keep you happy."

Steven didn't even bother with an answer. He pushed the nurse call button.

"Last chance before she catches on to you."

"Good-bye."

Caroleigh chuckled merrily. She half-bowed to him and saluted him with the cup. She had the straw in her mouth as she strolled out.

* * * *

Having a cast put on, a full leg from his thigh to his toes because of the additional damage he caused, took the better part of the morning and left Steven exhausted. He drifted in and out of a drug induced sleep for the remainder of the afternoon, still groggy from the drugs when dinner came. He picked at the food without much interest. He started to actually feel awake just in time for visiting hours and another round with Caroleigh. They could be heard long before they reached the door. Edward talked urgently but softly, and Caroleigh talked loudly. She came in with a package of colored felt pens in one hand and another milkshake in the other. Once they reached the door, Edward fell back with an apologetic and helpless look on his face.

"I brought you a milkshake," she announced loudly. To Kari she said, "You used to bring me milkshakes, remember?" She swung the cup at Steven with a speed that forced him catch it in self-defense while she staggered a few steps and told Steven, "I used to sneak her chocolate. She loves chocolate. Keep that in mind, Steven; Kari loves chocolate."

She weaved while she fumbled to extract one pen from a plastic package. "We brought pens to decorate your cast. They told us we couldn't see you this afternoon because you were getting it, so we brought you pens to decorate it." Her voice trailed off as she concentrated on extracting one pen. One came free, sending the remainder flying. She held the one pen up in triumph. "Let me be the first."

Steven braced himself as she staggered towards the bed. Kari rose up protectively from the chair where she sat quietly. Even Edward moved forward to stop Caroleigh, but all fell back when she slowed and moved with exaggerated caution. She concentrated furiously while she sprawled one long word down the full length of the cast from thigh to ankle. The word was "congratulations."

With a giggle, she said, "I hope I'm not premature." She twisted, swayed again, and looked at Kari. "Did he tell you about our visit last night? Bet not. Bet he didn't want to upset you."

"Don't now," Steven told her sharply.

"You don't know everything," she told him. "She's my sister. I know a few things. She's my sister." She swung back to Kari. "For old time's sake. Yep, for old time's sake." She nodded. "Turned me down flat. I know a few things." She spun and staggered out. "You're welcome."

"Sorry," Edward said before he hurried after her.

"Kari, I…" Steven began anxiously.

Kari moved to the end of the bed and asked, "What did she say when she walked out?"

"'You're welcome.' She's pretty unbelievable."

"I'll be damned."

Steven looked at her, back the way Caroleigh had gone, and back to her. "Are you smiling?"

"Old time's sake," she told him sadly, but with a nod.

Steven groaned. He also pressed at his eyes with the heels of his hand. "She tested me, and I fell for it. Even after you told me what you two did to test your boyfriends, I fell for it. What an act." He mimicked Caroleigh. "She looked so terrible, her hair was gone, I was selfish—"

Kari jerked his left hand down, making him jump in surprise and grimaced over the unexpected pain the sudden movement caused.

"What did you say?" she demanded.

He had to think about what he had said. "She talked about how bad you looked." Kari stared at him in incomprehension. "When she came back to take care of you."

"She didn't come back."

"She said she did."

Kari gripped his hand hard. "What else did she say?"

"She started out saying nearly the same things you had, how close you used to be, how much she missed you, you'd had a silly fight, that you were so mad you wouldn't talk to her when she came back to take care of you."

"You said something about my hair."

"She said it was gone in clumps," Steven told her in confusion. "That was when she acted like she was about to cry and switched to a vamp."

She let go of his hand and backed away. "She was here," she whispered.

"If you mean when you were sick, that's what she said and that you were still so mad, you ignored her and refused to talk to her, to even look at her. Kari, what's wrong?"

"I'm going to find out."

* * * *

Kari was furious. Penmate followed her, making it obvious who she was angry with. She didn't stop until she reached the window where she stood, arms crossed to hug herself and both hands closed in tight fists. Penmate didn't stop until he was behind her. He pulled her around to face him.

"After she ran we couldn't find her," he told her.

"You let me believe she never came."

"We didn't tell you that. We told you we couldn't find her. For God's sake, Kari, you were so sick. Were we supposed to tell you she took one look at you and ran? It was better for you to believe we couldn't find her rather than to know she wouldn't stay."

"She ran because she thought I didn't want anything to with her. Do you know what that did to her?"

Penmate tried reason. "If she had asked anything about your condition it wouldn't have happened."

"You should have told her first. You shouldn't have let her in without telling her."

"No one saw her come in. Martha only saw her run out. I know you're upset, but you need to calm down."

Kari spun her back to him. He tried to pull her back around. She jerked free of his hand. "I'm not listening to you. Go away," she told him. He tried to step in front of her. She turned her head away.

Penmate gave up and backed away. "Tell her," he said softly to Steven, "I'll do anything I can to make it right."

Steven nodded but damned if he knew what to do or say.

She twisted to look at him. "Don't talk to me for awhile, okay?"

"Can I hold you?"

She half-shook her head. It took that long for her to change her mind and go to him. She was draped over the siderail for him to hold awkwardly when Martha came in. Her expression was just as stern as it had always been, but without a word, she went to the side of the bed and lowered the rail to let Kari settle down in Steven's arms. For one brief moment she laid her hand on Kari's back in consolation before she left without a word.

* * * *

"I can't get up, or I would go there," Steven said into the phone.

Edward's droll tone answered. "She's in no condition to go visiting."

"Is she any drunker?"

"Sobering up actually. We've been through several pots of coffee."

"I've got to talk to her before she sees Kari again."

"You can talk to her in Denver. We're leaving in the morning."

"She can't leave until I talk to her," Steven retorted in exasperation. "Damn it, Edward, this is important."

"I take it a message won't suffice."

"No."

"Any hint as to what it pertains to?" Edward asked.

"You can tell her Kari's happiness depends on it."

"Thinking rather highly of yourself?"

Steven was so shocked at how far off Edward was he couldn't think for a moment. "It doesn't have anything to do with me," he finally got out.

"Then it seems you are being a bit dramatic."

"Yes."

"Listen, old boy, she really is feeling rather miserable," Edward told him seriously.

"This will make her feel better, I swear."

"Visiting hours are over."

"I've already talked to Martha. She'll let you in. Just get here." Steven hung up before Edward could think of another argument. After a blown out a breath, he told Martha, "If I convinced him she needs to be here, he's the only one I know of that can get her to come."

Martha's features were just as stern, but her voice was soft. "Gavin loved both those little girls, but he didn't know how to show much affection. They really had no one other than each other. It's time they understood they still do. I'll go watch for them."

No more than fifteen minutes later she was back, leading them in. "Just keep your voices down," she warned and closed the door behind them.

"Real charmer," Edward commented with a shudder.

Pasty colored and drawn, Caroleigh asked curtly, "What's so important? If it involves some kind of pay off to make you move on, you're—"

"She never knew you were here," Steven blurted out.

"Not to seem too much like her, but I have no idea what you're talking about," she said wearily.

"You said you came to see her when she was sick, and she ignored you. I'm telling you she never knew you were here."

Caroleigh's voice rose in agitation. "She was wide awake, staring out the window."

"Did you touch her? Did she look at you?"

"Is this what you dragged me down here for?"

"Keep your voice down," Edward warned.

Steven rolled up on his elbow. "Listen to me, Caroleigh, she was so sick then, Martha said—"

"Stoneface, I'll wager," Edward commented.

"Would you like to stay out of this for now?" Steven asked him in exasperation.

"This is ridiculous," Caroleigh said. "I know she was sick, but not so much that she didn't pretend she didn't hear me."

"That's the point. She didn't pretend."

Edward sat down and said, "She isn't deaf. I thought maybe—"

"Edward, please," Steven implored. "I'm not good at this kind of thing, and you aren't helping."

Caroleigh asked Edward, "Why would you even think she is?"

"Because she isn't stupid." He held his hands up at Steven. "Sorry."

"Hearing impaired," Steven said. "Not deaf, but handicapped. She stares at you when you talk to her because she's lip-reading to supplement what she isn't hearing. She hesitates in answering because she's putting together what she read with what she heard to make sense of it. She parrots back words to be sure she did hear correctly. If you don't get her attention before you start talking to her, she doesn't know it's her you're talking to. She doesn't know which direction a sound is coming from until she sees the source. A lot of the time she doesn't hear you talking at all, depending on how far away you are, how much background noise there is, what side you're on."

Caroleigh cut him off. "She's told you all of this and not me?"

"No. I didn't realize it until tonight when I saw Penmate try to make her face him while he talked to her. She didn't quit her medical training for whatever reason you think. She quit because she would not take the responsibility of making a bad diagnosis because she didn't hear or heard incorrectly. You told me yourself she withdraws when there's a group of people, how she gets lost and confused. You recognized the symptoms, but not the cause." He leaned forward more. "She did not know you were here. They thought it would upset her less to think they couldn't find you than to know you didn't stay. You've both been hurt for all the wrong reasons. You thought she was mad at you, and she thought—"

She stood up abruptly. "I'm ready to leave." She left without waiting for Edward.

Edward told Steven quickly, "She might pull false tears on you to get what she wants, but she hides the real ones."

* * * *

"What would I say, 'Gee sorry, but in Grandpa's efforts to protect me he nearly destroyed you?'"

Kari stood with her back to the window, arms crossed. She was ready to fight anyone or everyone without a real direction for her anger to go. Penmate caught some of it, but she no longer yelled at him, a fact he looked grateful for. He didn't speak, no doubt to avoid bringing her focused attention back to him. He busied himself with an examination of Steven's foot or rather Steven's toes protruding from the cast.

Steven was braver. "How about there's been a mistake?"

"Mistake seems a little inadequate."

"It would be a start. She'd ask what, and you could go into detail."

"Detail?" She tipped her head back to look at the ceiling. "I can't stand what she's thought all this time."

"Then set it right." He raised his voice. "Kari." When she looked back at him he went on. "Set it right. All these years she didn't know you have a hearing loss. Every time you didn't hear her, she thought you were deliberately ignoring her."

"How could she have not known?"

"I didn't until last night."

Kari turned to Penmate. "No one ever told her?"

"I never discussed it with her, and I doubt your grandfather did. He always acted like if he ignored it, it didn't exist."

"I just never…I didn't…" She turned to Steven. "You always look at me when you talk to me, and you speak so clearly I just assumed you knew. It's not something I try to hide."

"I've heard you say you didn't hear or that you didn't know someone was talking to you enough times to know that. I just didn't realize you meant it literally. Neither has she. You need to talk to her."

Going to her wasn't necessary. Caroleigh came through the door at a determined pace and announced to Penmate, "You are not going to keep me out."

Edward, as close behind her as he could stay, braced, it appeared, for just about anything. Adie was behind him, a worried look on her face. Penmate motioned Adie out the door as he went over and stood by it.

"I want to talk to you privately if that is possible," Caroleigh told Kari stiffly.

"There's always the bathroom," Edward said, "if the surroundings wouldn't put you off." When four sets of eyes turned on him, two quite hostile, he added, "Just a suggestion, of course."

"Maybe we could simply shut the door," Penmate said.

"I don't believe that is what she has in mind," Edward told him and asked, "Isn't there an empty room somewhere?"

"I didn't—" Kari began.

"I was—" Caroleigh began at the same time.

Each broke off to wait for the other.

"I wasn't—"

"I thought—"

Kari twisted to ask Steven. "Have you already talked to her?" He nodded. She turned back to Caroleigh "Then you know. I didn't ignore you, and I wasn't mad at you. They never told me you had been here because they thought you'd panicked and ran when I needed you."

"I did," she exclaimed miserably. "I thought you were going to die and leave me alone, and I was so angry at you for going to that awful place, for getting sick, for throwing everything away. You were so brilliant."

"Slower, love," Edward whispered.

Caroleigh looked at him and back. She saw the intense way Kari stared at her and stammered. "I-I…"

Kari rushed at her. "Don't you run." She caught Caroleigh as she turned to do just that. With an arm around her waist, Kari pulled her into the bathroom and shut the door.

"That went well," Edward commented. As Caroleigh's voice rose from behind the door, he added, "I think."

"At least everyone is already up for the morning," Penmate said as he headed out the door.

"Coward," Steven called after him.

"I say, do you think I should run?" Edward drawled.

"From what? You didn't do anything?"

"Fall out." He tipped his head to listen. "They seem to be just talking now." He listened a moment longer. "With a bit of weeping, I believe."

"And you're listening."

"No." He moved closer to the bed. "So-ah-well, how's the leg?"

"I'll live."

"No nasty complications, permanent limp or anything like that?"

"No." Steven shifted weight. "Just the inconvenience of the cast for six weeks."

"Never had the misfortune myself, so I can't emphasize. I hear they itch abominably though."

"I've heard that too."

"Ummm, well, have we exhausted our quota of small talk?" Edward quizzed lightly.

"Probably."

"Shall I just buzz off then, look for a coffee or something?"

"You can tell me if that ghost business is your creation?"

"What a curious subject you've chosen to discuss."

"Is it?" Steven insisted.

"Partially, I thought it would create a little diversion for the girls." Edward pulled up a chair and sprawled comfortably. "I had no idea Emily was such a little performer. She nearly had me believing it, and Gaylord added such spice to the séance. It turned out to be quite entertaining."

"You went to a lot of trouble to entertain them."

"Not much at all really." Edward pointed to the word Caroleigh had scribbled on the cast. "Mine as well, old boy. You realized an opportunity and seized the moment marvelously. Quite an accomplishment, especially with Kari, a very tough nut to crack. What's your main objective, immediate benefits or a long term situation?"

"What is with you people?" Steven groaned.

"Birds of a feather, dear boy. I prefer a little more ready cash myself, but it is a nice house and the connections can be of great benefit."

"Bullshit."

Edward chuckled dryly. "Ah, yes, but one does get addicted to the life style, very easily once you get a taste of it." He leaned forward slightly and lowered his voice. "Tell me, is she—"

"Careful," Steven warned.

Edward leaned back with his lips pursed. "Okay," he said finally. "Just checking."

"How much 'just checking' have you already done?"

With a smile, he asked, "Would you like a break down of your portfolio? I could recommend a few investments of the low risk variety you seem to favor."

With a scowl, Steven told him, "Part of me would like to get up from here and deck you."

"Yes and the other part knows why I did it. You actually had me worried somewhat. Not the usual type Caro chooses for a fling. Had you become interested, it might have gone somewhere."

"You care?" he asked in amazement.

"Now you be careful," Edward warned without a trace of humor in hazel eyes that could go very cold.

"Have you told her?"

Edward laughed bitterly. "I much prefer the steadfast, nearly broke friend treatment, thank you. It's caustic enough at times without her getting it into her head I'm after her money."

"I never realized having money was so demoralizing."

"It does tend to undercut one's feeling of self-worth." He leaned forward again. "Is this going to hurt you financially? I could help out if it is."

"No, but thanks," Steven answered sincerely.

"Well, keep it in mind, discreetly, of course. We wouldn't want to rock the broke steadfast friend boat." He shrugged in response to Steven's perplexed look. "She says she would never marry except for money. I couldn't take that."

"Guess not," he murmured, beginning to understand more of the strange conversation between Edward and Kari that day in the library. Edward, it seemed, was better off financially than he pretended.

Edward changed the subject. "This hearing thing, there's nothing to be done for it?"

Steven shook his head. "The way I understand it, a hearing aid amplifies everything. What she does hear is so loud she can't stand it, and it doesn't really help much with speech. There is an implant, very expensive, a long surgery, no guarantee of success, and the possibility it will cost her what hearing she does have in whatever ear they do it in."

"Pity, though it certainly explains a lot. She's always been a bit of a puzzle to me. I understand now why I get very intelligent answers from her sometimes and answers that make no sense at others."

"You need to stop using that English-accent-slur when you talk to her."

"My dear boy," he protested.

"Her words not mine," Steven told him. "It wears her out trying to understand you. That's why she drifts off. You also need to face her when you talk to her, not look away, up or down, and get her attention so she knows she's the one you're talking to."

"Would raising my voice help?"

"With some it does, some it doesn't. Martha says it depends on the decibel level and pronoucation more than volume. She also said what Kari does hear at a normal level she's hypersensitive to because she lives in a world of so much silence and muffled sounds. That's why she startles so badly when Caroleigh does things like slam her hand down on the table or yells unexpectedly at her."

"You have no idea how much self-recrimination she's suffering right now," Edward confided. "I can't understand why the old man never told her."

"Denial, according to Martha, he never wanted to believe anything was wrong."

Edward smiled sadly. "Her little problem was the way he described it to Caroleigh. It left a very broad field of interpretation. I've known her for three years, and I didn't learn that until last night. Very closed mouthed is our little Caroleigh unless she's a bit into her cups. That's one reason she seldom ever drinks." As if he realized he was much too serious, he quipped, "The aftermath as well, it makes her deathly ill."

"You've obviously seen a side of her most people haven't."

He gazed at Steven so long it seemed he was not going to answer before he said, "There's a sweetness and generosity to her she works very hard to hide. She takes in the strays like Emily, whom she hired when she found her crying in the hall after being dismissed from another position, and Evelyn, who was being completely snubbed at a party. And I adore her sense of humor. Perhaps you will see more of that now."

Chapter Six

Kari's pickup sat in the hospital drive behind the shuttle, a van conversion with four captain chairs and a back cargo area. The van's cargo space was filled with luggage and a pet carrier sat on the far back seat where Rascal scratched and whined to get out. A handsome young man, dressed casually in jeans and flannel shirt over a T-shirt, waited with it. He gave a friendly wave in answer to Kari's

Kari saw Rascal as they approached. "You did find him," she said happily. "I was afraid he had gotten out."

She turned as she spoke and saw first Caroleigh's guilty expression. Second she saw Edward's of well-schooled blandness. Emily quite deliberately looked away while Evelyn watched in anticipation. Steven, confused, wondered what was going on, and Adie, pushing his wheel chair, watched everything.

Kari told Steven tersely, "She had him the whole time."

"It was amusing when you put out food and water," Caroleigh admitted meekly.

"Oh, really?" she asked with a cut, but she leaned forward, gave Caroleigh's hand a squeeze, and grinned. "Good one."

Edward blew out a breath in relief. "Now that's done with, where shall everyone ride?"

"Don't put me in that awful truck thing again," Evelyn exclaimed. "It is dreadful. It bounces, it's noisy, and it was so uncomfortable with four in it."

"One for the van," Edward said dryly. "Two counting Steven, of course. All that dreadful noise wouldn't do his leg much good."

While Evelyn gave him a suspicious look, Kari said, "I could always ride in the back of the pickup."

"Oh, no," Evelyn said seriously. "Let Emily. I'm sure she's used to that kind of thing."

Kari asked Caroleigh out of the side of her mouth, "Where did you find that one?"

Caroleigh took charge. "No one is going to ride in the back. Kari will ride with Steven, Evelyn in the front. Emily, Edward, and I will ride in the truck thing. I'll hold Sir Gaylord, and his carrier can go in the back."

"You're going to hold him again after he threw up all over?" Evelyn asked in horror.

A conspirator's look passed between Caroleigh and Kari. "The pickup is awfully rough," Kari said. "I'll take him in the van."

"Ah, excuse me," the driver said.

"Don't worry, Vern." Kari gave him a wink and a roll of her eyes towards Evelyn to draw him to the 'let's tease Evelyn' game. "I'll take a towel, just in case."

Vern caught on quickly. His pleasant features twitched in a restrained grin as he nodded and leaned casually against the van.

Edward held a hand out to stop Kari from going after Rascal. "I'll get the little creature. You help Steven get settled."

The considerate gesture went all haywire as soon as Edward opened the carrier door. Rascal had other ideas and was quick enough to carry them out. He stayed still until Edward had him half out, and then twisted free and leaped. Edward proved to have quick reflexes, but not fast enough for a determined dog who evaded Edward's hands, body, and legs as he threw himself forward to block the exit. Rascal hit the ground and disappeared under the van, avoiding Edward's efforts to catch him.

"Don't let him in the street," Caroleigh cried.

She ran around the back of the van to the far side. Edward ran around the front. Both disappeared when they dropped to their hands and knees to see where the dog was, and Rascal shot out the opposite side with a leap sideways to avoid Vern's hands.

Caroleigh popped back into view on the far side and shouted, "Why did you let him go?" as she ran around the van.

Edward popped up and ran around the van in the opposite direction and shouted back. "I didn't."

In that time, Rascal skidded to a stop when he saw Emily coming for him, reversed and dashed back under the van. Caroleigh and Edward reversed, ran back around the van and disappeared as they dropped to their hands and knees.

Kari sat on the narrow arm of Steven's wheelchair to watch. "I wish I had a camera."

"Video wouldn't do this justice," Steven chuckled.

"I don't know why she keeps the dirty little thing," Evelyn said with a distasteful sniff.

"You wouldn't," Steven mumbled.

Kari leaned down to hear him which put her in an awkward twist on a precarious perch just as Rascal made a break for it on their side of the van. She startled off balance at Caroleigh's shout to catch him and was left with a split second decision to either keep from falling or catch Rascal as he leaped towards her. She landed on her butt on the concrete with a thud, but she had Rascal in her arms.

"You little—" She broke off in concern and cuddled the trembling little body to her. "It's okay, baby. It's okay. No one's going to hurt you."

Caroleigh, Edward, Emily, Adie, and Vern stood over Kari, frozen in positions of reaching out to help her. Steven leaned sideways over the wheelchair arm, one hand out, also frozen.

Kari looked at all the extended hands and serious faces. "Well," she asked, "isn't anyone going to laugh?"

"Actually, love," Edward said stiffly, "we were wait…" His voice broke. "…ting to see…" He made a choking sound. "…if you're hurt."

His face twisted, and he turned his back to her. Caroleigh turned, shoulder to shoulder with Edward with her shoulders shaking. Steven finished his reach for Kari's arm, not laughing so badly he couldn't help. He just couldn't offer much support from his sitting position as she pulled her legs up under her. With a sniff, Edward turned back, only to stiffen and sober. Two hands slipped under Kari's armpits and lifted her straight up to her feet.

"Oh, I'm impressed," Edward cooed. "Can I feel your muscles?"

Dell's counter was hateful. "It's obvious that isn't why she lets you hang around."

"Walked into that one," Caroleigh mock whispered to Edward as she stepped close to him and slipped her arm around his waist. "But no, Dell, it doesn't take muscles of your variety to satisfy a woman."

Edward gave Dell a smug look, slipped his arm around Caroleigh, and pulled her closer. After Dell stalked away, he asked, "Is he teeny weenie, love?"

"I wouldn't know." She pushed him away. "I have better taste than that."

The pleasant drive home was interrupted abruptly when the pickup ahead of them slammed into the bank and stayed there, sending up a shower of stones and dust as it continued to hurl down the road. Kari dropped to her knees, leaning between the two front seats. "What the hell is he doing?" she asked in alarm.

"Brakes, I think," Vern answered. “He’s using the bank to slow them.”

Steven twisted and leaned over Kari's back to see better. They watched in horror as the pickup ahead of them careened down the mountainside. It veered close to the sheer drop off on one side on a curve before it swung back and slammed against the bank again in a prolonged, grinding sideswipe.

"Can you get in front of him and stop him?" Kari asked.

Dust and debris flew into the air, forcing Vern to back off so he could see. "No, the road’s too narrow. He’ll be okay if he can keep it under control until the next upgrade starts."

The pickup came off the bank, back into the center of the narrow road. They sped by a culvert in a ditch, and the pickup slammed up against the bank again.

With his hand on her back, Steven told her, "I think he's slowing."

Kari gripped the back of the seat with one hand and clutched Rascal to her with the other until he squirmed. Small rocks bounced off the van, pieces of chrome flew over the top of it, and the pickup still scraped down the bank. It bucked wildly, throwing the carrier from the back, sending it flying across the road in front of the van. Vern swerved to avoid it. Evelyn flinched and gasped, the first sound she’d made since the drama began while ahead of them the pickup pulled back into the road. They sped by a second drainage structure. The pickup slammed again into the bank.

"They are slowing," Steven said.

"Yeah, we’re starting up. He’s got it now," Vern confirmed in relief.

Kari shoved Rascal at Steven before either vehicle stopped. The van had barely stopped before she pushed the door open and jumped out. Dust was still settling around both vehicles when she jerked open the pickup door.

"Are you all right?" she cried as Edward crawled out, "Are you hurt?" as Caroleigh slid off the seat to the ground, "Any pain?" as Emily struggled under the wheel to follow. "Did you hit your head? Did you snap your neck?"

Shakes and nods of their heads were the only answers she received during the first rush. There was a chorus of no's to the second.

Edward found his voice to actually speak first. "What a rush," he stated unsteadily.

"I did bite my tongue," Emily said weakly.

"I didn't know you could drive like that," Caroleigh said to Edward in a stunned tone.

"Hell of a job," Vern stated from behind Kari. "Oh, sorry," he added when she turned to look at him. Kari waved away his apology over the profanity. He grinned at her, but told her, "We should move away from it, in case there's a broken gas line."

Kari held to Caroleigh's arm and asked Edward, "Are you sure you're okay?"

"Well, I must admit to being a bit strung at the moment and..." He broke off when Kari gave him a quick, furious hug. As she backed off he finished, "...I could use a drink."

"You're sure you're all right?" She turned to Caroleigh. "You weren't hurt?"

"No, we're fine. Quit worrying."

"Did mess..." Edward touched Kari on the arm and waited until she looked at him. "Did mess your paint job up, I'm afraid."

She waved that away as carelessly as she had Vern's cuss word. "I'm just so glad you weren't hurt."

"We should move," Vern reminded her.

Kari nodded with an arm through one each of Caroleigh and Edward's arms. "Would you help Emily?"

Vern smiled and held his arm out to her. When she took a step and wobbled, he put his arm around her waist to walk with her.

Steven still held Rascal and had gotten as far as pointing his cast in the right direction. He gave the battle up when he saw them coming his way. He also relaxed enough for Rascal to wiggle free.

"Oh, here, baby," Caroleigh called as Rascal raced towards them.

She leaned down, hands out to him, and he dodged to go to Kari. He jumped against Kari's legs to get her to pick him up. Kari did and held him out to Caroleigh. The fight then was for Kari to keep a hold of him as he twisted in an attempt to crawl up her shoulder to keep Caroleigh from taking him.

"Something else you've taken from me," Caroleigh said coolly as she gave up the effort and stepped back.

Everyone held their breath. No one had any idea how strong their new relationship was.

Kari returned just as coolly, "Who do you think you're kidding? You brought him up here to dump on me."

"You're right," she answered flippantly. "He's yours."

"I don't want him," Kari exclaimed.

"Too late."

Caroleigh tried to walk off. Kari pulled her back. "He's the wrong kind of dog for up here. He gets his hair full of burrs and—"

"And he wakes you up at an ungodly hour every morning, but now that's your problem."

"Caroleigh, I am not keeping this dog," Kari stated firmly.

"He absolutely refuses to bond with me," she said in a near whine. "The vet said that often happens with an adult dog. The chemistry isn't right or something."

"Why didn't you find that out before you took him?"

"I took him to settle a debt. She said he was a papered champion. I thought I could breed him and make some money."

Kari's face went blank. "Caroleigh," she stated tonelessly, "this dog is neutered."

"What?" Edward asked with a start.

"How was I to know he didn't have any…?" Caroleigh waved her hand while she searched for a word. "…things with all that hair?"

"He's neutered?" Edward asked with a lilt to his voice.

"I couldn't tell until—"

"You got stung by a lack of things?" Edward crowed.

Straight-faced, Kari asked, "Who would have believed it?"

That was too much for Edward. He made a funny, choked sound. Kari burst out laughing. Edward burst out laughing. An instant later Caroleigh was laughing. In moments they were all laughing, except Evelyn who watched them in perplexity and Emily, who smiled shyly.

Catching his breath and wiping tears from his eyes, Edward said, "Nothing like having the life scared out of you to make you giddy."

"Yeah," Vern agreed. He went by them with a fire extinguisher. "I'm just going to make sure nothing is smoldering."

"I'm going to use your radio." Kari slipped in under the wheel, but she looked at Steven first. "Okay?"

"Fine."

"You need to scoot back and get that leg up. This may take a while." She also answered his look of worry he made no effort to hide. "Later."

Caroleigh sat on Edward's lap in one back seat. Kari sat on the floor between the two back seats, turned sideways to leave room for Steven's cast stretched across the middle. Evelyn's only concession to the crowded conditions necessary to get them all back to the mansion in one trip was to lean against the door to avoid contact with Emily. Emily perched on the console between the two front seats. Fortunately it was a relatively short trip. The tow truck had been called, but they didn't wait for it to come. Steven didn't complain, but Kari insisted he needed to get where he could stretch out and elevate his leg properly. No on argued with her. No one, however, wanted to wait for Vern to make two trips.

The good laugh had relieved much of the tension, but they had all been badly shaken by the incident. It seemed to have affected Emily the worst. She huddled and swayed as the van swung around curves and whispered apologies to Vern every time she bumped into his shoulder.

Kari touched her on the back. "Are you sure you weren't hurt?"

Emily brushed against Vern when she twisted to face Kari. "I'm fine, ma'am, really I am."

"How's your tongue?" Caroleigh asked.

"It's fine." She turned back, swayed badly and briefly put her hand on Vern's arm to steady herself. "I'm so sorry."

"No problem, Miss. You just lean against me if it will help any."

"It is very difficult to keep my balance if you're sure you wouldn't mind."

"Not at all."

Kari turned her head to face Caroleigh and tipped it towards Emily. Caroleigh raised her eyebrows speculatively and then tipped her head towards Vern. Kari gave a nod.

"That was remarkable," Edward commented to Steven. "Make you feel a little left out?"

"I think I got the drift of it."

"Drift, yes, but I suspect something much more concrete will come of it than a drift." He asked Caroleigh in a whisper, "Matchmaking, love?"

"Mind your own business," Caroleigh told him sweetly. "Here we are."

"Thank goodness," Edward gave her a light pat on the bottom. "Ah, there's our welcoming committee. We missed them before."

Two large shepherds came from the porch as the van entered the drive. They ran along side the last few feet and stood back as the van came to a stop.

"Don't," Kari said quickly as Edward reached for the door handle. "Vern, wait."

"I'm waiting. I recognize those brutes of Max's." He told Edward, "If you open that door, they'll tear your arm off."

Edward's hand sprang back from the handle at shoulder height. "Not a welcoming committee?"

"What are they doing here?" Caroleigh asked. "Especially if they're dangerous?"

"Max has been looking after the place for me." Kari told Edward. “The next door neighbor."

"There is no next door," Edward said, watching the dogs through the window.

"His ranch is five miles north," Kari told him. "That's next door up here. Honk the horn a couple of times, Vern."

Vern did. The immediate reaction from the largest of the dogs was to drop its head, curl back his lip, and growl deeply. Rascal came up from Kari's lap like he'd been shot from a catapult. He wedged himself between Edward and Caroleigh, jumped furiously at the window and barked ferociously.

"A debarking might be in order," Edward remarked with a grimace.

"That's inhuman," Kari returned.

"Depends on your point of view," Edward told her with a pained expression as Rascal jumped up and down in his lap. "Claws next, perhaps."

"Oh." She grinned and went to his rescue. She swung Rascal around and dropped him on top of the luggage where he devoted himself to barking out the rear window even after the dogs had trotted off.

"We can get out now," she told Edward.

"You're sure?"

Vern opened his door. "They never would have left unless Max called them off." As he walked around the rear of the van, he waved and called out, "Hey, Max, how's it going?"

Max trotted to them. "It's going."

“Thought maybe we were going to have to drive in the front door to get out.” He opened the passenger door and took the hand Evelyn extended. With Evelyn out, he leaned down to carefully help Emily. When he realized Max was watching him, Vern explained. "Poor little thing had a bad scare."

Caroleigh worked her way off of Edward's lap and explained further. "Brakes went out on Kari’s truck. Hello, Max."

"Caro," he said with a nod. "Haven't seen you in so long, figured you wouldn't remember me."

"I always remember men who threaten to arrest me."

"Arrest?" Edward asked in interest, but he moved slowly off the seat to lean back casually against the van beside her.

"It was Kari's fault," she told him with a flutter of her eyelids.

Max grunted and asked Kari, "The brakes went out on your pickup?"

"Yes." She slid into the seat vacated by Edward. "Coming down the grade." She climbed out to stand beside Edward and laid her hand on his shoulder. "He drove through it and got them stopped." For just a moment her hold tightened, then she leaned close and whispered, "Can you walk yet?"

Edward was surprised by her perception and smiled slightly. "I expect a nearly immediate return of feeling in my lower extremities." He looked apologetically at Caroleigh. "Sorry, love. As lovely a bottom as it is, it—"

"No!" Kari cried. With an open door and freedom beyond, Rascal evaded her hands and hit the ground at a full run. "Go get him."

The last was directed at Caroleigh. "He won't come to me, Kari. You go on. We'll take care of Steven."

"Go," Steven told her. He had both crutches out and himself moved over, cast stuck out the door.

Kari shouted back as she ran off, "Stay beside him in case he loses his balance."

"What about those dogs?" Edward asked in alarm.

"She helped train them," Max stated.

Vern answered with a chuckle. "It was your arm they would have torn off."

"Or yours," Edward joked back.

"That's why I didn't open the door."

He started for the rear doors, and Caroleigh stopped him. "Vern, Emily is still badly shaken. Would you mind helping her in?"

"Sure," he agreed readily.

"What about my things?" Evelyn asked stiffly.

They all stared blankly at her. Edward was the first to recover with a sardonic, "Soon, dear. In times of crisis, we all have to make allowances and sacrifices."

"There is a limit. I endured that dreadful motel room, staying alone while the two of you ran off together."

Caroleigh exclaimed, "You said you didn't want to go."

"That hospital was even worse. I simply cannot tolerate these crude and primitive conditions any longer."

"You don't need to," Edward assured her. "We're back here now. The ordeal is over."

"*Here* is an ordeal." She turned to Caroleigh. "Haven't we had enough? Let's go back to town."

"I can't leave now."

"I thought we were friends."

"Friendship has nothing to do with it."

"I see."

Evelyn walked away, leaving Caroleigh with her mouth open. "What was that about?" she asked no one in particular.

"Feeling left out, perhaps," Edward suggested.

"It's her own fault if she is. She doesn't have to be such a snob."

He reminded Caroleigh what a snob she could be at times with a bland expression and neutral tone. "Her upbringing, I'm afraid, terribly difficult to overcome."

"Ass."

"My upbringing."

From the door, totally vexed, Evelyn shouted, "The door is locked."

"Try turning the knob," Max shouted back.

"It's locked, you Neanderthal."

Max stalked towards her while Edward whispered under his breath. "She does seem more than a little…"

"Pissed," Caroleigh finished for him.

They all chuckled lightly, or in Emily's case smiled shyly, while they moved to the house. Edward drew up in a jerk when Max turned the knob and pushed open the door, letting Evelyn flounce in the house.

"What is going on with that door?"

With Rascal draped over her arm, Kari rejoined them as they reached the hall. "Vern, it's so late now, why don't you stay for dinner? You too, Max?

"I'd like that," Vern answered.

"Got things to do," Max told her. "Some other time." He pointed to Rascal. "That thing needs some obedience training."

"Would you train him?" she asked eagerly.

"For bait."

"Max."

Max chuckled and started for the door. "You know how. Just don't think because he's little you can't discipline him."

From the drawing room doorway Evelyn said, "You probably beat yours."

"Only the spoiled bitches."

"Max," Kari said in warning.

His look told her he didn't care one whit about offending Evelyn. "See you tomorrow."

Evelyn did not thank Kari for speaking in her behalf. She stalked by them. "I will have dinner in my room," she stated and walked up the stairs.

"This is not a hotel," Kari retorted.

"You take care of Steven," Caroleigh told her. "I'll take care of her. Emily, do you feel well enough to help me fix something for this bunch to eat?"

"You're going to cook?" Edward asked in disbelief.

Emily smiled shyly. "Her hot ham and cheese sandwiches are very good."

"This I have to see."

Caroleigh walked off with the others behind her, leaving Steven and Kari alone.

Steven watched them walk away. "I can't believe the change in her."

"I will never be able to thank you for what you've done. We would have gone to our graves, still thinking the other was angry."

"Something would have happened to get you talking again."

"I don't think so. It was getting worse every time she came up. She was coming up less, and I was staying away more while she was here." She touched him lightly on the face. "You look tired."

He nodded slightly and put a kiss in the palm of her hand. "But we need to talk."

"I know."

"How often does someone else drive your truck?"

"Never, but at least now you can't believe it's Caroleigh."

"At least now you're taking it seriously."

"I don't—" She broke off as Steven and Rascal both jerked and looked up the stairs. "What?"

"Evelyn is screaming her head off."

"Hurt or mad?" she asked, braced to run if need be.

"You'll be able to tell soon enough. She's coming this way."

So was the group from the kitchen. They all met at the foot of the stairs as Evelyn ran down the steps. She waved clothes in each hand, still screaming. "Look at this! Look at what that miserable old man did! Look at my beautiful clothes!"

It was difficult to see what she raved about the way she flailed them. Edward caught one, a frilly blouse, and pulled it from her hand. He held it up, and light shone through the slashes in it.

"You see?" she shrieked. "See what he did!"

"Who did?" Edward asked as the others stared in astonishment.

"That miserable old man."

"Max?" Caroleigh asked. "Why would he do that?"

"He's mean and hateful."

"That's personality, dear," Edward told her, "not a reason."

"She put him up to it." She pointed an accusing finger at Kari. "She doesn't want me here."

"Maybe the ghost did it," Emily suggested quietly.

"There is no ghost, you moron."

"Yes there is. I saw him."

"Not now, dear," Edward told her.

"I did see him. He was right there." She looked as she pointed, gave one of her ear piercing screams and nearly crawled up Vern's chest.

"Jesus," Caroleigh breathed. She back-handed Edward in the chest, showing she had known all along that he had been responsible for the tricks. "Turn that off."

Edward could only stammer. "I-I-I…"

The man, though obviously not a real man since he was transparent, stood just inside the front door. He was bloody from gashes on his forehead, and more blood dripped from a severed arm.

"This isn't funny," Caroleigh yelled at Edward. "Turn it off."

"That isn't mine," he croaked.

"Kari, no," Steven shouted.

He grabbed for her and missed her arm as she stepped towards it, but she heard him and twisted to look at him in puzzlement. When she looked back, the man was gone.

"Jesus," Caroleigh gasped again.

"I don't think so, love," Edward quipped weakly. "The clothes were all wrong."

"That wasn't funny," she shouted at him.

"I didn't do it," he shouted back.

"You're the one," Evelyn shouted at Kari.

"What?" Kari asked in distraction and jerked her eyes away from the landing behind Evelyn.

"What were you looking at?" Steven's question was lost in Evelyn's screeching.

“You’re the one who blocks him. You’re probably the one who calls him just to-to…just to-to…”

As she stammered to a stop, Kari half-shook her head and murmured in perplexity, “Why would I call him only to block him? You’re not making any sense.”

Evelyn threw what was left of her clothes to the floor. “That’s it. Take me back to Denver, right now.”

The last was directed at Vern. He had not made a sound or moved except in reflex to protect himself from Emily's strangle hold around his neck. When Evelyn yelled at him, he gulped but still didn't move.

"Take me now," Evelyn ordered with an edge of hysteria to her voice.

Edward shook himself. "Evelyn, dear, it's—"

"I won't stay here one more minute, not one minute. You aren’t making me stay."

"Okay, okay," he said quickly. He turned to Vern. "You better take her before she does something rash."

Vern looked at him helplessly.

"Yes, right, well, ah, Emily, would you like to go back to town as well?"

Emily dissolved into tears and nodded vigorously.

"If you could just give me a hand," Vern said weakly, "I'll be glad to take them."

They had to work Emily’s arms loose first. Edward had to help Vern support her once they did. Evelyn needed no help, not even with the van door. She was outside and in the van before the other three could reach the porch. Edward slipped a credit card into Vern's hand with orders to charge his fee and get whatever the women might need before he hurried back. He was met with two sets of accusing eyes and one curious.

He answered the accusers with, "I didn't do that. I didn't."

"How would it be done?” Steven asked, not in the least sure he believed him.

"I don't know. Some kind of projector, but…" He shuddered. "It looked so…so…give me a minute." They waited the second or two it took him to collect himself. "Okay, a projector of some kind. Did anyone notice a shaft of light going into him…it?"

"All I saw was blood," Caroleigh said quietly.

"He bled to death," Kari said.

"What?" all three asked.

"My father, he bled to death on the front veranda. He couldn't get in. Grandpa had locked the door. He couldn't get in, not until now."

Edward asked nervously, "Are you saying you've seen that before?"

"He's never made it in the house before. The door always stopped him until now. He must have gained strength through Evelyn's anger."

"This is cruel," Caroleigh told Edward angrily.

"I didn't do it," Edward exclaimed again.

Kari's gaze turned inward as she stoked Rascal. Steven was the first to notice she was drifting away from them. He touched her on the arm lightly.

"Doesn't seem to have bothered him any," he said gently.

"They don't frighten him anymore. He's gotten used to them."

"Them?" Edward croaked.

Caroleigh groaned and sat down on the stairs, her face in her hands.

"That's why I sleep in the back," Kari explained. "They don't go there."

While all of them stared at her, she batted her eyes.

"Damn it, Kari!" Steven shouted. "That wasn't funny!"

"It was a joke?" Edward asked dumbly.

"Got ya," Kari told him.

"Oh, thank God." He dropped to sit beside Caroleigh.

Kari remarked matter-of-factly, "Steven thinks someone is trying to kill me."

Caroleigh stared at her.

"Another joke?" Edward asked hopefully.

"No," Steven answered once he recovered from the shock of her blurting it out without any warning.

"Why for God's sake?" Caroleigh asked.

"The accidents," Kari answered.

"Who?"

"You."

"That's ridiculous," Edward retorted.

"I'm a bitch, Steven," Caroleigh said emphatically, "but not lethal."

"That's what I told him," Kari told her.

"You called me a bitch?"

"Stop it," Steven exclaimed. "No more damned joking around."

"Let's go to my apartment," Kari said quickly. "You can lie down, and I can fix something to eat."

* * * *

They were a pretty sober group. Caroleigh and Edward sat in overstuffed chairs perpendicular to the couch. Steven stretched the length of the couch with his leg propped up on pillows, and Kari sat on the floor, her back against the couch. Rascal was asleep in Kari's lap.

"I thought it was all settled," Kari said. "Just Steven misinterpreting things because of the tension between us and that Max would prove it wasn't anything."

"Why that gamey old man?" Edward asked.

"He was the sheriff here forever," Caroleigh answered. "He retired last year."

"After trying to arrest you?" Edward asked Caroleigh.

"That was years ago, and it was Kari's fault."

"I didn't ask you to join in," Kari told her, letting them know Caroleigh wasn't joking.

"Like I was going to let you tackle those sick, little bastards alone." She added for Edward's benefit, "There were four of them, tormenting some injured dog."

"They were torturing it," Kari interjected.

"The worst bullies in the school, and she tears into them."

"Really?" Edward asked in amusement. "And who won?"

"We did," Caroleigh said proudly. "That was why Max thought about arresting us. Grandpa set him straight in a hurry."

"Then he let us have it," Kari added.

"Did he ever, my ears rang for a week. Was I ever glad Martha had already left. If she'd put her two cents in, we'd have been grounded for the rest of our lives."

Edward teased. "At least he didn't lose his sheriff's job over so silly a mistake."

"They had it coming," Kari said seriously. "The dog had to be put down. He was too mangled to live. But Max didn't retire, he got voted out. People thought they needed someone younger and stronger."

"Too bad they didn't include intelligent," Edward muttered.

"What?"

"Smart," Caroleigh answered. "Dell is not the brightest bulb around."

"No and he's lazy. He isn't even a good vet."

"You know," Edward said thoughtfully. "We are alone here, without transportation. Should we make sure the phone works?"

"Not tonight," Kari answered. "I don't want to deal with anymore tonight."

Caroleigh got up, going to the computer center. “Why didn’t you ever tell me this was here?”

“You never asked.”

Caroleigh made a face at her, snatched up the phone, and told her, "You may be taking this lightly, I'm not."

"I didn't catch that."

"She isn't taking it lightly," Edward supplied and then added, "Neither am I."

Caroleigh listened to the phone’s dial tone and sighed in relief, at least over that. "If that had been you on those stairs instead of Steven with no one here to even miss you…” She ended with a shudder and dropped back in her chair. "I hate you being up here all alone."

"But we were here," Edward said thoughtfully. "Doesn't that make the timing rather off?"

"Not if they needed a fall guy," Kari said pointedly.

Steven shrugged that off. He’d already apologized to Caroleigh for what he thought at first. "Or had everything set up before they knew you were coming," he suggested. "That wouldn't have worked with the storm though."

"What wouldn't?” Edward asked.

"A timing mechanism.” He yawned deeply. "Sorry. I'm getting so tired I can hardly think, but I thought it was synchronized with the storm to pass the fire off as a lightning strike."

"Unless the storm set it off in some way," Edward said thoughtfully. "I shouldn't think it would be difficult to rig a trigger the storm would activate."

"Like what?” Caroleigh asked.

"A lot of chemicals are water activated."

"I've never heard of any that water ignites," Caroleigh said.

"You're not following. I'm thinking more of a trigger held in place by something rain would dissolve and release. Makes sense, rainy season is coming, get rid of the dogs so they can sneak about without them alerting Kari, set it up, and wait, miles away."

"And Daddy comes to warn me that something's amiss?” Kari questioned dubiously.

"I'm going to have a bit of a look around for a projector." As Edward stood, he asked Caroleigh. "Care to give a hand, love?"

"As if I would know one if I saw it," she grumbled as she stood. "I'm only going so you two can be alone."

"Thank you," Steven told her.

Kari told them. "You don't need to stay away for long. He's going to sleep."

Once they were alone, Steven asked, "How are you doing?"

With one arm hooked under Rascal, she rose to her knees to face him. "Are you angry about me telling them?"

"No." He smiled wryly. "I did nearly have a heart attack when you blurted it out like that though." His hand went to her shoulder to stroke her hair. "You didn't answer me."

"What with watching them careen down the mountain on Daddy's grade, then Daddy showing up, pretty drained," she confessed. "You?"

"Tired."

"Pain?"

"A little," he admitted. As her hand went to his cheek, he added quickly, "I don't have a fever."

She started up. "It's time for your medications."

He pulled her down. "In a few minutes."

* * * *

None of them moved back into the mansion bedrooms. Steven was asleep on the couch, Caroleigh and Kari were in the bedroom, and Edward sat at the computer. Without discussion, he and Steven had come to an agreement that one of them would stay awake. Steven had simply fought sleep until Edward announced he was going online to do some research and would probably be up all night.

Steven roused at four and asked, "Did you find anything?"

"Some." Edward spun around in the chair. "By comparison to the last home projector I remember seeing you can get some really fascinating digital stuff now. Some of them are even designed for this type of thing. My guess is it's hidden in that massive chandelier."

"It would take a pretty big ladder to even reach it."

"With her hearing and no dogs, an army could have gone through there without her noticing."

Steven nodded in agreement. "Is something like that hard to operate?"

"Not according to the ads, though I suspect it would be a little more involved than they make it sound. Basically you need a recording, video or computer generated for the small equipment, then the projector. Those things are really small, some with remote control and wireless transmission. Can I ask you something?"

Steven lowered his cast to the floor with both hands. "Not another test, is it?"

"No. I just wondered why you yelled at her when she started towards it."

"Because it scared the hell out of me," he stated tersely. "I don't care how many times you say you don't believe in ghosts when something like that pops up in front of you, primeval fear comes out of nowhere."

"She wasn't afraid of it."

"Obviously or she wouldn't have started towards it."

"It was like a ghost didn't surprise or shock her, just who it was, and it didn’t seem to frighten her at all."

"Don't tell me you think the place is really haunted."

"I'm just curious as to how long it's been going on.” Edward pointed to the computer screen. "These things can be put on timers. Things like we saw may be going on and off all the time all over the place."

"To drive her crazy," he murmured.

"Saying she was seeing ghosts would be a sure way to kill her credibility if she had gotten suspicious and tried to enlist help."

"We all saw it."

"Yeah," Edward said, his brow furrowed in puzzlement. "And that thing wasn't designed for fun, not for her. Appearing right after the brakes go out on the same grade that killed her father? That's not fun. That's malicious and cruel. Honest to God, if all of this actually goes together in some way, we're dealing with a total psycho. I know we're guessing about a lot, but if we're right about half of it, you've got ingenious devices all left to chance. It just doesn't make sense."

"Kari and I made more sense out of it when we eliminated the ghost thing. What made you think of that to entertain the girls anyway?"

Edward shrugged. "The subject of haunted houses came up when we were talking about coming up so I threw together a couple of gags." He laughed derisively. "Really inept by comparison and all but two of them burnt up in the carriage house. I didn't even get a chance to use them. The blood came from a joke store, and the noise in Evelyn's closet was a tape recorder in mine. We were next door to each other. Other than asking Emily to start setting things up by saying she saw something, that's all I did. Imagination did the rest, like seeing a good and evil spirit coming out of the heater vents."

Steven smiled wryly in appreciation of Edward's understanding of what Kari said that night. "I've got to admit, I wasn't sorry to see Evelyn go. Caroleigh didn't seem upset either."

"No, she was getting tired of her. She felt sorry for her to start, and she, ah, goes through friends rather quickly, ones from that mold anyway. I didn't know her from before she and Kari had problems, but I knew something was eating her up. I hope her constant self-assassination stops now." He sighed deeply and wearily. "I think you'd better get that leg back up."

"I will, but it's your turn to sleep."

"I think you're the one who should be the most rested, old boy. I don't have the slightest idea how to handle all this."

"What makes you think I do?"

* * * *

Max stood on the veranda in front of the French doors. "I want you to pack a few things and come over to my place until we find out what's going on around here."

"The brakes were sabotaged," Kari stated wearily.

"There wasn't any obvious evidence of tampering, but there was no brake fluid. You take better care of that truck than to allow that to happen. Come out here and talk to me."

That was his second request to talk to her privately. She refused again. "What we…" She emphasized the pronoun. "…want to know is if the fire and stairs were an accident."

“I got some more reports back, one of them on your new friend."

"Did you find out anything about the fire and stairs?"

Max was as dogmatic as she was. "He knows all about bombs. They taught him in the army," he stated bluntly. "He was also married, conveniently to a woman whose father died, leaving her his business. Then the wife died, leaving it to him."

"The fire? The stairs?" she asked single-mindedly.

"Caroleigh brought him up here. You two haven't talked to each other in nearly five years." He jumped forward to block the door with his arm as she tried to close it. "You may be able to forgive and forget, but I'm not so sure she is, and Gavin did cut her completely out of his will."

"I won't let you do this, Max. I won't let you destroy my trust in the people I care about."

"She's never caused you anything but grief. When you needed her, she…"

"Shut up, Max," Kari warned.

"...was no where to be found."

"Shut up."

"Once you got back on your feet, she…"

Kari let go of the door and hit him with both hands in the chest, pushing him back.

"That other one is a professional driver," Max told her in determination.

She slammed the door in his face.

He shouted. "The whole thing could have been staged."

"No one I know would agree with him," Edward said drolly as Max gave up and stomped off.

"What?" Kari asked.

He sobered and answered. "In my young and wild days I followed the stock car circuit for a time. I wasn't very good."

"Does that have to do with what he yelled?"

"He said I was a professional driver, and the brake thing was staged. I was just saying I wasn't considered professional by anyone who was."

"You were good enough for me," she said vaguely. "I'm going to take a shower."

As she disappeared through the bedroom, Edward sighed. "I'm afraid we've lost her."

"How could he put so many things together so wrong?" Caroleigh asked miserably. "Hundreds of thousands of men have been in the army, and he's thirty-five years old. It would have been unusual if he hadn't been married, not that he had."

"And that company wouldn't have ever been more than mediocre if he hadn't taken it over." Edward added.

"And it's not like he could have predicted his wife would die of cancer." She looked at Edward suddenly. "How do you know about his company?"

"The same way you know his age most likely."

"Is there anyone who hasn't checked me out?" Steven asked wearily.

"It wasn't personal," Edward said quickly.

"No," Caroleigh agreed. "It was just a precaution, and she doesn't believe any of that, not the way he said it."

He shook his head and fumbled with the crutches. "It isn't her. She accepted me and what happened between us for what it was, which was pretty damned beautiful. It's the people around her that have turned it into some damned, devious plot. It's no wonder she hides on top of a mountain to stay away from everyone."

* * * *

Long walks and inexperience with crutches did not go well together. Steven decided to go only as far as the library. As he reached the door he thought he saw movement out of the corner of his eye, a figure disappearing into the drawing room. He backstepped and turned to follow.

"Kari?" he called just as his head exploded.

The searing pain was still there when Steven woke up. It radiated from the bloodied back of his head in pounding waves. Dazed, confused, and disorientated, Steven tried several times to reach for his head before he could understand why he couldn't. He was face down on the library floor, wrists taped behind his back and tape over his mouth.

"Not such a big man now, are you?"

Steven rolled up on his shoulder to see who spoke to him. When he could see the speaker, he blinked repeatedly, unable to make any sense of it.

Dell squatted at Steven's head, amused to the point of laughing. "You come up here, flashing your money around, strutting like you're better than everyone else. Think I don't know your kind? You're too good to marry our women, but they're good enough for you to take your pleasure with. They're good enough to give you a bastard you won't claim while you chase the ones with money." He took Steven by two handfuls of his shirt and pulled him up to his feet while he hissed in his face. "Does it make you feel like a man? Huh? Making a baby then abandoning it? Huh?"

He let go with a shove. Steven would have gone down if the door frame hadn't caught him in the back. He hopped on one foot, the cast out stiff in front of him, and barely caught his balance only to have Dell shove again. Landing hard on his right shoulder with a grunt followed by a groan, Steven laid there, fighting for breath.

Squatting at his head again, Dell told him, "This is one bastard that's going to teach you a lesson, one bastard that's going to make you pay."

Straightening, he held a handful of Steven's collar, flipping him to his back. He dragged him down the back hall to the kitchen, from the kitchen down the hall to the laundry room, through to the basement stairs. He laughed at the torture Steven suffered from being dragged down those stairs head first, unable to keep the cast from dropping heavily with each step.

"Dell," Caroleigh cried, "What are you doing?"

"One more bag of rich trash," he answered and dropped Steven.

A dull thud sounded as Steven's head hit the natural rock floor. Other than a grunt and the sounds of his struggle to breathe with his mouth still covered, he didn't make any sound or move, but his furious glare remained on Dell.

Caroleigh sat on the floor, wrists and ankles taped together, not far from where Steven landed. She huddled against Edward, who was bound in the same way.

"At least take that tape off his mouth so he can breath," Edward implored.

"Dell, what do you want?" Caroleigh shouted. "Just tell us what you want!"

"Want? Want?" he asked and laughed. "I don't want anything from you, not anymore. You had your chance."

"Muffed it up, did you, love?" Edward asked with an elbow pushed at her ribs.

"Yes," she answered. She caught on quickly to Edward's urging and both tried very hard not to watch Steven inch his body around behind Dell. "Yes, I did. I always regretted it, always."

"I knew you would," Dell told her smugly. "So did Kari. She was always sorry she listened to you. She never stopped loving me."

Steven rolled and kicked. His foot caught Dell in the side of the knee to stagger him. Edward, anticapting Steven's move, double kicked with his taped ankles and caught Dell on the hip instead of in the gut where he wanted to. Caroleigh's attempt hit only air as Dell hopped away.

Dell laughed at their efforts and moved around Steven's feet to his right side. Steven was between him and the other two, putting Dell a safe distance from their feet, and Steven couldn't move fast enough to avoid Dell's retaliation. Dell easily dodged Steven's attempts to kick him while he kicked Steven's cast.

"Stop it!" Caroleigh screamed. "Stop it, Dell, stop!"

Steven's entire body heaved in his efforts to draw air into his lungs, and Dell turned his attention to her. "You're nothing but a slut. He's…" He pointed to Edward. "…no more than a male whore, sniffing after your money. And you." He turned back to Steven. "You're a gold-digging piece of scum."

Still in a struggle to breathe, Steven managed an understandable, "You son-of-a-bitch," behind the tape.

"Bastard," he corrected cheerfully. "And we're going to get it all. Not you." He looked at Caroleigh. "And not you. You just get the blame." He looked at Edward. "You get nothing but dead. You prostituted yourself all this time for nothing but dead."

"You're crazy," Edward stated calmly.

Dell shook his head. "We've planned everything perfectly, a couple of accidents, the mansion gone with all of you inside to break the trust."

"What do you mean the mansion?" Caroleigh asked. "What are you going to do?"

"We will get everything, everything that always should have been ours."

"We who?" Caroleigh asked. "Who are you talking about?"

He smirked and started off. "Got things to do," he told them cheerfully and laughed to himself. They could still hear his laugh after he disappeared around the turn in the stairs. He still laughed, the sound muffled, as he shut and locked the door.

Edward and Caroleigh moved immediately. They inched their way to Steven on their knees. Edward reached him first and clumsily peeled the tape off his mouth.

Through the first gasp for a lungful of air, Steven asked, "Where's Kari?"

"She's not a part of this," Caroleigh exclaimed. "He doesn't mean her."

"I don't think that's why he asked, love." Edward told her.

"Where is she?" Steven demanded.

"We don't know," Caroleigh answered miserably. "We thought she was still in the bathroom, but the hall door was open when he brought us down here."

"He didn't look for her," Edward said reluctantly.

"She is not a part of this," Caroleigh insisted.

"I just said—"

"She either got out or she's hiding," Steven said firmly.

"Just what I said," Caroleigh told him. "Or another possibility, as upset as she was, she may have gone off somewhere and doesn't even know anything is happening."

"How long has it been?"

"Have you been unconscious?" Edward asked.

"Yes," Steven answered angrily. "He blindsided me."

"An hour," Caroleigh told him, "Maybe a little longer."

"I've been out for an hour?"

Edward answered. "Assuming he got you right after you left us, yes."

Steven squeezed his eyes closed with a groan. "What the hell would she be doing for an hour? Did she even take a shower?"

"No." Kari made all three of them jump. She stood at the base of the stairs. Rascal was draped over her left arm, and she held a large kitchen knife in her right hand, with the twelve inch blade parallel to her arm. "I went out to talk to Max."

"Kari," Caroleigh exclaimed in shock.

"Quiet," Steven warned.

"Have you come to finish us off, love?" Edward asked with his perplexed gaze on the knife.

"You keep asking questions like that and I might," she answered absently with her eyes on Rascal.

"Quit screwing around and cut us loose," Steven ordered angrily.

"That's better," she commented, but she still didn't move, watching the dog draped over her arm instead.

"What are you doing?" Caroleigh asked.

"Shh," Edward warned with a nod at Rascal.

Rascal looked at the ceiling. His eyes moved across it rapidly. When his ears perked up and his head turned towards the stairs, Kari backed quickly to a dark space under them.

"Clever," Edward murmured in appreciation as the door rattled several times and opened. "Back for more?" he called out.

Dell tossed Steven's crutches down as he ascended, laughing as Edward and Caroleigh twisted in a useless effort to dodge them. He laughed more each time they flinched from the impact of being hit. Then he laughed some more and held up a bundle in his other hand for them to see. "Your demise."

"Rather crude," Edward said of the sticks of dynamite duct taped together with an old fashioned wind-up kitchen timer. "Mail order?"

"Just a simple little bomb," Dell told him. He tucked it under his arm to pick up the roll of tape he had last used to bind them. "It's going to be real unfortunate for you when it goes off prematurely, blowing yourselves up along with this…this…"

"Abomination?" Edward queried.

"I've forgotten, Dell, why is it I'm doing this?" Caroleigh asked.

"To break the trust, love," Edward helpfully reminded her.

"It's not breakable."

"That's what you think," Dell told her. He stood on the bottom step to reach the dangling light wire and taped the bundle above the bare bulb. "Because you don't know about the changes Gavin made, just before he died."

"He didn't…" With a quick nudge of Edward's elbow, she changed what she was going to say. "…leave me enough? Is that the idea?"

"He didn't leave you anything. Everyone knows that."

"Why would he?" she asked in confusion. "I wasn't his."

"You thought you had wheedled your way in. You thought you would benefit."

"Right, so I want the Meadow so badly, I'm going to blow it up to get it?"

"Caro," Edward warned quietly.

"That is what he said," she retorted.

"You think I'm stupid, don't you?" He started up the stairs and tossed the tape to the floor. "Well I'm not. We will have everything that should have always been ours." At the turn of the stairs he looked down at them. "Like they say in the movies, I'll be back."

"The man is positively nuts," Edward exclaimed.

"Kari?" Steven called hoarsely

As soon as she appeared, Edward pleaded, "Cut us loose, love, please."

She stared at the bomb. "Is it turned on?"

"Not yet," Steven retorted. "Cut us loose."

Instead she moved close enough to look down into his eyes. "Were you unconscious?"

"Don't start that," he retorted furiously. "Cut us loose."

"Not yet," she murmured, turned, and ran up the stairs.

"Kari!"

"Come back here!"

"Bloody hell!"

"Keep him awake," Kari shouted down to them, already out of sight.

"What the hell is she doing?" Caroleigh cried.

"Maybe she…" Edward began.

"She is not with him."

“Who could he mean?” he asked reluctantly.

“I don’t know, but it isn’t Kari.”

Edward hesitated for a second before he asked, "Wasn't that door locked?"

"He just forgot to lock it this time," Caroleigh said in dismissal.

"Before," he said regretfully. "When she came in."

"Grandpa probably unlocked it for her," Steven grumbled. "Right now that makes as much sense as anything."

"Dell left the key in it," Caroleigh argued, "and he was just too stupid to realize it was unlocked."

"Not to argue for his intelligence, but—"

"She is not a part of this. She's…she's…"

"She's trying to keep us safe…" Steven told her tightly, "…while she takes him on alone."

"Oh, God," Caroleigh groaned with a catch in her voice.

"By locking us in with a bomb?" Edward asked.

"An unarmed bomb," Steven pointed out, and he moaned in pain. "I've got to get off my arms.” He raised his head a few inches before he let it back down carefully.

"He's right," Caroleigh told Edward in dread.

"Let us help," Edward told Steven. He knee-walked his way close again. Of Caroleigh he asked, "He’s right about what?"

"Did you see—no, Edward, I'll take his leg. You're stronger than me."

They changed sides. Edward went to Steven's shoulders, and Caroleigh went to his cast.

"About what?" Edward asked again. He worked both hands under Steven to help him roll.

"The way she was carrying that knife?" She lifted the cast and guided Steven’s leg. "Max taught us years ago how to slash anyone who might attack us. He said girls should be able to defend themselves." Her voice caught in a gasp. "My God, Steven."

Once he was able to roll to his side, they were able to see the back of his head.

"Looks worse than it is,” he told them in a strained voice while he wiggled to be able to go all the way over to his stomach.

"How do you know?” Edward asked grimly. "You can't see it."

Steven turned his head so they couldn't see it either. "I'm fine.”

"Anything we can do?"

"Get my hands loose."

Caroleigh snorted. "We've been trying to get ours loose since he brought us down here."

"Poor Caroleigh has broken two nails, and I'm quite sure I've chipped a tooth. Damnably tough stuff, despite how easily you see them work it off in movies. He does a rather pitiful Arnold, don't you think?"

"Oh, Eddie, not now," Caroleigh said with a sigh.

He crawled to her. "Providing a little levity is all I seem able to do. Give a lean, love, while we think of something. I've been totally useless."

Caroleigh did lean on him, but she asked him sternly, "Just what were you suppose to do? He had a gun to my head."

"And such a pretty head. I was, I will admit, sick with dread that he would damage it."

"You're so sweet," she said dryly.

"Do you see that, Steven? I give her a compliment and she—Steven, are you awake?"

"Yes," he grumbled distantly. "What are the terms of that trust?"

"The one I'm basing all this on or the one I don't know about?" Caroleigh asked tersely.

"You know about a second?" Edward asked in surprise.

"Of course I do. Grandpa talked to me before he revised it, and he sent me a copy afterwards. If Kari had wanted to keep any of this for herself, all she had to do was say so. He wouldn't have given it away, the rights to it anyway."

"Who would he give it to, and why wouldn't she want it?"

Caroleigh answered one of the questions. "She and her heirs have full use of it for as long as she wishes, but if she dies without heirs it goes to the state as a museum and park."

"What happens if it burns down?" Steven asked.

"I don't know."

Edward answered. "Theoretically no mansion, no more trust. It may be possible to break it that way, but there wouldn't be anything left but the land it's on."

"Twenty acres has been set aside with it," Caroleigh supplied. "It's crazy."

"Does any of this seem sane to you?" Steven asked.

"Point well made," Edwards said.

"I don't think either of them ever really wanted to live here," Caroleigh said sadly. "Grandpa said it was his responsibility to stay in his father's and the children's home. She stayed because of him."

"What children?" Edward asked.

"His and his father's," she said with a sigh. "Ten died all together, a wagon accident on that horrid road took great Grandpa's and an epidemic took Grandpa's."

"Not a very cheerful heritage," Edward said with a grimace.

"No, it isn't." She straightened with determination. "I am not going to just sit here and let Kari do this alone or die with everyone thinking I'm an insane bitch."

"Which part bothers you, love?"

She made a face at him and rose up to her knees. "We haven't had any success with our wrists. Let's see what we can do with Steven's."

Caroleigh reminisced to fill the time while they diligently worked on the tape around Steve's wrists and waited for Dell or Kari's return. Together they had worked loose four inches, not enough to even loosen the bond around Steven's wrists.

"Too bad some of Kari's childhood friends aren't around to help us, although she was the only one who saw them. She called one Albert. We had to set a place for him and pour him tea just like we did for ourselves. Winnie and Penny played in the yard with her."

"Sounds as if she had a very vivid imagination," Edward commented in preoccupation. "And a lonely life."

"Both I guess. I'll never forget the day Martha told her—"

"Martha? Not old stoneface?"

"Be nice, Edward. She stayed longer than most, and she wasn't always such a stone face, although she never had much imagination or tolerance. She told Kari to stop talking about people no one else could see, or she would be branded simple in the head and taken away where we'd never see her again."

"That seemed a bit harsh. There's no harm in imaginary friends. Don't you agree, Steven?"

Everytime he grew quiet for more than a couple of minutes one of them either asked him a question or deliberately prodded him. Steven had given up telling them it was unnecessary. He said enough for them to know he had followed the conversation. "No harm."

"She really spooked me when she started talking about 'them' after that thing showed up," Caroleigh continued. "I remembered the ones she used to talk about when we were kids and instantly started thinking ghosts instead of imaginary friends. When she batted her eyes at us, I—what?"

Edward suddenly lifted his head to listen. "Dell, I'm sure. Kari certainly doesn't walk that heavy."

He motioned for her to move back and quickly tucked the tape they had worked loose out of sight under Steven's wrists before he followed her. They were back to where they had been when Dell left them, huddled together, when Dell came down the steps, humming in satisfaction. They watched silently as he reached above his head and turned the timer to a full hour. Once finished, he turned it carefully so they could see the face clearly.

"You can count the seconds off together," he told them

"Aren't you just the most thoughtful thing ever?" Edward taunted.

Smile gone, Dell told him, "I'd love to stick around to hear you start screaming."

"Bet you tore wings off of flies as a boy," Edward countered ruefully.

"He tortured helpless dogs," Caroleigh retorted and then thought of something else. "I thought I taught you better than to trust bitches, Dell. Whoever she is, she'll cross you the first chance she gets."

Dell ignored the inferred question. "She loves me."

Caroleigh snorted. "I remember when you said that to me. Maybe she's the one who should be careful."

"And I love her. When things are right, we're going to get married." He started up the stairs. "We will have everything, everything that always should have been ours."

Edward picked up on the subject Caroleigh started. "As soon as she gets what she wants, she'll dump you."

"I really would like to teach you a lesson," Dell answered nastily and looked at the timer, "but I don't have the time."

"Teach me," Steven challenged. "Or are you too much of a coward?"

"Darling," Caroleigh simpered, "even tied and with a cast, you're too much competition for him. Besides, he doesn't have 'her' here telling him what to do."

"You better shut up," Dell warned. His hand dropped to his holstered gun.

"Your substitute manhood?"

When Dell took the gun out Edward interceded quickly. "A bullet hole would spoil your little scenario."

"No," Dell said coldly. "It wouldn't." He swung the gun, not to point at Caroleigh, but to point at Edward. He grinned, pulled the trigger, and waited for Caroleigh's scream to end in a whimper.

The impact threw Edward to his back, and Caroleigh struggled to her knees to hover over him. "What do I do? What do I do?" she cried as Dell laughed and walked out.

"Pressure," Steven ground out. He fought to get the knee he could bend under him and braced his shoulder on the ground. He gave the struggle up when Kari bounded down the stairs the knife still in her hand and rolled up on his side to watch her.

"Press on it, now," she ordered. She changed directions and went back up the stairs.

"I can't," Caroleigh wailed and stared in horror at the blood spreading over Edward's chest.

"Do it now," Kari shouted over the sound of metal grinding on wood.

"Go ahead, love," Edward coaxed. "You can do it."

She set her jaw, took a deep breathe, and leaned on her hands on his chest. He set his jaw and stifled a groan.

Kari came back down the stairs two at a time and jumped the last three. "Keep the pressure on while I check for an exit wound."

"Did you…" Edward caught his breath in a groan when she pushed him to his side towards Caroleigh. He let it out in a whoosh when she let him back down flat.

"The bullet is still in there," she told him.

His nod meant nothing more than that he had heard her. It was several gasps later, while she kept her fingertips to his throat and her eyes on her watch, before he could ask weakly, "Did you lock us in or him out, love?"

"Him out, dear, though it won't hold him for long," she answered absently.

"Did you forget…?"

"Keep the pressure on," she told Caroleigh. "Don't let any air in."

Kari was already up. She went one direction long enough to snatch up the roll of tape Dell had left behind, then another to drop on one knee in front of Steven.

"Look at me," she told him at the same time she pulled a length of tape loose.

"Forget about me for now. Take care of him."

She evidently had seen what she wanted to see. "Lay back down," she ordered, pushed back and twisted in one motion to put herself next to Caroleigh.

Fear was in Caroleigh's voice and eyes "Kari?" she asked helplessly.

Edward returned to the question he had attempted to ask before. "Have you forgotten about the bomb?" Kari didn't answer. She concentrated on cutting strips of tape to form a solid square by overlapping the edges. He told Caroleigh, "Ask her."

"She hasn't forgotten. There's nearly an hour."

"With Jamie," Kari murmured. “He fine.”

"What, love?” Edward asked, his voice losing strength.

When she didn’t answer, Caroleigh asked slowly, as much to keep her voice steady as for Kari to hear. "How are we going to get out?"

"The root cellar." She continued to prepare a make-shift bandage. A patch of tape six inches square lay ready on Edward’s chest. She slipped out of her over-shirt next and hacked off the sleeve.

"No, Kari," Caroleigh said. "How are we going to get out?"

"Not now. I can't stop to concentrate on what you're saying. I'm going to guess what you want to know." She cut Edward's shirt away from around Caroleigh's hands. "There’s a door under the stairs that goes to the root cellar. Dell's bound to be out there somewhere watching so we can’t cross the lawn. We can't hide in the house either.” She twisted to look up at the bomb.

"Don't even think about it," Steven told her. "It’s homemade and unstable as hell now that it's armed."

"He said—” Caroleigh started.

"I can hear him," she cut her off with. "When I tell you, move your hands as quickly as you can. Steven, can you walk?"

"Yes."

"We have to move you, Edward, and we can't take the time to be gentle. We have to be clear before that thing goes off. We should have plenty of time."

He gave her a game smile and said, "Nice day for a walk in the park after all."

She rubbed the blood from his chest with the remains of her shirt sleeve as close to Caroleigh’s hands as she could get. "The percussion may be enough to bring down some of the unstable areas. It's pretty steep too."

She concentrated so intently she didn't see the confused looks on their faces. Caroleigh questioned what she said. "Are you talking about the mine?"

"As soon as I get this in place. We're going to have to sit him up so I can bind it in place."

"Free your hands, I think," Edward said as a guess to what question Kari thought she was answering.

"That wasn't what you asked?" Kari paused to ask.

"No. I asked if you were talking about the mine."

"Yes."

"Why?"

"That's how we're going out."

"It's miles away," Caroleigh exclaimed.

"The tunnel isn't. Get ready to move your hands."

* * * *

None of the three had any concept of how extensive the mine shafts were or how close they came to the mansion. Kari had only learned of the tunnel from the house to the mine a few weeks before her grandfather's death. In rambling reminiscences Gavin had talked about how his father had liked to observe his workers without them being aware of it. To accomplish that he had simply dug a tunnel from the root cellar into one of the extended tunnels and concealed the entrances with a wall in the cellar and a door in the mine. Kari only knew where it was and how to get into it because out of curiosity on a boring day she had hunted it down. She admitted that after one look inside she had resealed it, prepared to forget it ever existed. One look inside and they understood why. With only a string of bulbs draped from the roof down the center of the tunnel, it was so utterly dark it seemed to absorb the light. Only the top center wasn't hidden in shadows.

"That isn't so bad," Caroleigh said bravely. "At least there are lights."

"All the comforts of home," Edward said. He joked even though he couldn't stand alone and only managed to stand at all by leaning against the root cellar shelves with an arm draped over Caroleigh's shoulders.

Steven leaned on his crutches. His head hung, and he stared at the tunnel floor in puzzlement but made no comment.

Concerned, Kari moved in front of him. "Do you…" she began.

Without moving his head, he turned his eyes to look at her. "Yes," he told her with a crooked smile.

The smile she gave back was faint and forced. She touched him lightly on the cheek and asked, "Which one?"

"I've got a headache."

She leaned towards him as if she wanted to put her arms around him only to pull back suddenly. "I can't do anything about it now," she told him crisply.

"I know," he answered, his brow furrowed in puzzlement again. "I'm doing okay. Let's get going."

"I'm sorry," she whispered softly before her manner returned to all business.

With one hand she took a flashlight from a shelf behind Edward. The other hand pulled his free arm over her shoulder. One quick on/off of the switch told her the light worked, and she pulled Edward up.

"Why do you need that?" Caroleigh asked.

"The lights only reach to the end of the tunnel. The mine doesn't have any power."

"How far is it?"

"The house."

"No, I asked…" The struggle with Edward's weight required too much effort for her to talk. "Nevermind."

"What?"

"She asked how far," Steven told her, short of breath himself.

"Not far. If whatever you want to ask can wait," she told Caroleigh, "Do."

She nodded in agreement. As soon as they started again, she whispered to Edward, "I still don't understand what she does and doesn't hear."

Edward only nodded in agreement, his breathing labored. Heavy breathing with only the thud and shuffle of feet, the clicks of rocks kicked and flipped, and the thud and scrape of Steven's crutches echoed eerily while each struggled for different reasons. All four staggered before they reached the heavy door at the bottom of the steep incline, two from the exertion of supporting a man's weight, and two from weakness and pain.

Steven leaned heavily on the crutches to use both hands to try to pull the door open. It barely moved.

"I'll get it," Kari told him. "Rest for a minute."

She helped Caroleigh brace Edward against the wall before she went to the door. To pull the door open on hinges that shrieked from rust and disuse took both of her hands and all of her body weight. Once she had it open, she blocked it with her body and used both hands to slide a heavy rock in front of it. She was panting with exertion by the time she finished but she didn't stop.

"I don't think that flashlight is going to do much good," Caroleigh said of the pitch black void beyond.

Kari said, "It isn't much further to the pickup now."

"What pickup?" Caroleigh asked in confusion.

"That's why," Steven murmured.

"What pickup, Kari?" Caroleigh persisted when Kari looked at Steven.

"Footprints," Steven explained to no one in particular. He had seen fresh footprints in the tunnel floor.

"It's only twenty or so feet," Kari told Edward. "Not far now before you can lie down."

Edward shook his head. He pulled his arm back when she took his wrist. "Can't, love."

"Yes, you can," Caroleigh said sharply. "We'll carry you if…" She broke off when the lights flickered. "Kari?" She whimpered when the rumble started.

The sound began low and ominous and gained in volume as it cannonballed down the tunnel at them. The ground beneath their feet vibrated, gained in velocity as the sound amplified. The vibration accelerated to a tremble and then to a quake. Portions of the ceiling fell, and the walls began to crumble. Dust first, then small rocks, then large stones thudded to the ground to strike anything between.

Kari and Caroleigh moved together to shield Edward. As the shock wave increased, and he went down, they went down, huddled over him. Each flinched, jumped, and jerked as the rocks hit near them. Each grunted in pain when they were struck. Dust still hung in a thick cloud in the air and rocks still plunked and tumbled. The flickering lights went out completely, leaving them in total darkness, but the shock wave had passed.

"Steven?" Kari asked with the sound of her hand patting the rock floor.

"Okay," was his muffled reply.

"He says okay," Caroleigh said loudly.

"I heard."

"I don't know how you could at all," she told her in a shaking voice. "I barely can for the ringing in my ears."

The flashlight beam cut through the dark, and Kari's fingertips moved to Edward's throat. She swung the light wildly to locate Steven. He sat leaning sideways against the wall, the crutches still in his hands. His cast stretched out in front of him, rocks and debris surrounded him, and a trickle of blood worked its way down through the dirt on his face from his forehead. He flinched from the light in his eyes and turned his head away.

"Can you get up?" she asked.

"Yeah, just get the light out of my face." He positioned the crutches to get up. The light was still on him. "I'm okay."

Kari laid the light on the floor, a faint beacon in an engulfing dark. She showed Caroleigh what she wanted her to do rather than take the time to explain. She pulled Caroleigh's arm around Edwards's back and squeezed her hand to take a handful of his waistband at his side. Her arm crossed over Caroleigh's, and her hand did the same on the opposite side.

"When I say go, pull him up." She waited until Steven was up. "Go."

"Isn't that Max's pickup?" Caroleigh cried as they approached the crew cab pickup with the cages built in the bed. "Where is he? Why isn't he helping us?"

"He's dead," Kari answered tonelessly.

"Oh, God," Caroleigh gasped. "Dell?"

Kari gave no indication she would answer even before Edward went down. The question was forgotten, but then they already knew the answer.

"Leave me," Edward gasped.

"Don't be an ass," Caroleigh hissed. "We won't…" She paused briefly to listen to a stone tumble some distance away. "…leave you."

"Pull him by his waist band. Try to put as little pressure on his chest as possible." Kari guided Caroleigh's hands to accompany the words. When she said "go," they each had one handful of waistband and one handful of his shirt at his shoulders. They dragged him the last of the distance to the pickup, but it took all three of them to get him into the back seat of the crew cab. Caroleigh squeezed in the floor beside him. Steven, twisted to be able to wedge his cast in the short floor space, and sat in the passenger seat. Kari, tense and silent, drove. She hunched over the wheel to guide the pickup through the rock littered tunnel by headlights.

"What is he saying?" she asked of the murmurings she could hear from the back.

"He's telling her he loves her," Steven told her.

"He is not going to die," Caroleigh retorted angrily.

"All the more reason to listen to him," Kari told her.

Kari visibly relaxed as they pulled into the light and through a smashed gate in front of the entrance. She eased the pickup to a gentle stop and then became a flurry of movement. After a quick check on Edward's breathing—signs of the physician in her—she searched the pickup. She flung open every door to see under the seats, into the door pockets, and empted the glove box in her haste. She poured old Kentucky bourbon over her hands, a hunting knife, and a straw, hurrying the last when Caroleigh cried out in panic.

"He isn't breathing. Kari. He isn't breathing."

"Get out of the way."

She crawled in on her knees on one side, hands held high while Caroleigh crawled out the other. Caroleigh hovered, and Kari took the time for a quick glance at Steven. He sat with his head braced against the door post.

"What are you going to do?" Caroleigh asked with her eyes riveted on the knife.

"Shut the doors and get in behind the wheel."

"Kari, what…?"

"Move, now!"

The sharpness of her tone made Caroleigh cringe, but she ran to do what she was told. Fortunately for her she did not climb back in until after Kari had punctured Edward's chest with the knife. She didn't see the spray of blood from inside his chest or the straw Kari inserted into the new wound. Kari leaned over him, doing chest compressions as much to hide the blood dripping from the straw to the floor from Caroleigh as to pump air into him.

"Hit the horn, three short, one long," Kari ordered.

"What?" Caroleigh asked in a near panic. "Why?"

"Just do it," Steven said quietly.

"I thought you were asleep."

"He's in and out," Kari told her. "Hit the horn, just the way I told you. We have to get them back into the cages before the helicopter gets here."

Chapter Seven

Kari cupped her hand to Steven's cheek and pressed her cheek to the other. She whispered softly, "I'm sorry. I'm so very sorry." He wanted to tell her she didn't need to be sorry for anything. He wanted to tell her he loved her when she whispered she loved him and kissed him tenderly on the lips. He couldn't make himself move or speak. He knew she was telling him good-bye. He knew it and fought to keep her. He fought to break free of the paralysis that held him to catch her hand as it slipped away from his face. He fought while he heard voices he didn't recognize speaking around him, not to answer them, but to tell them to leave him alone. He had to catch her. He battled darkness and silence without knowing time had passed or where he was until finally he could force his eyes open. He saw and reached for Kari. Kari caught his hands, though not to hold them. Hers were caught in his grasp as she lowering them to his chest and started to pull away.

Content in his drugged state to hold on to her, his eyes closed again. "Edward?" he asked faintly.

"He came through surgery without complications. He's in I.C.U. for at least twenty-four hours."

"Okay?" He opened one eye briefly to look at her. "He'll be okay?"

"Yes, and you. I'm sorry, Steven. I knew you were in trouble, but I couldn't…"

"Breathing is more important than a headache."

"Concussion," she corrected, "but no fracture or inter-cranial bleeding, and they didn't have to re-set your leg. You do have some nasty looking bruises and twelve staples in the back of your head."

"Taking advantage again?" When she didn't answer his tease, he forced one eye open again. "Are you okay?"

"Some nasty looking bruises, no staples," she said with phoney sounding lightness. "Caro's a borderline basket case. She didn't get enough bruises to keep her down, but Doctor Penmate is threatening to sedate her. She's driving them crazy in I.C.U."

"I'm sorry about Max."

She shied away from the subject. "Dell blew himself up," she stated bluntly. “That’s why the bomb went off too early.”

"What? How?" he asked with both eyes popping open.

"That's all they're saying so far, accident probably. They think he tried to disarm it for some reason, but we aren't supposed to discuss it.” She tipped her head towards the door and the uniformed guard in a chair just outside. "They want to question us separately first."

"You make it sound like they think we'd lie about what happened."

"They just want to be sure. I'm sorry you got dragged into all this. You don’t deserve any of what's happened to you."

"Neither do you. It's not your fault some psycho targeted you and Caroleigh."

"Caroleigh was just catching flak from being close to me, you and Edward too. It was all because of me." She shook her head and blew a breath out. "Maybe Grandpa was right. I thought he was just getting senile, but I'm beginning to wonder if the meadow isn't cursed.”

"If you feel like that, leave it."

The chair in the hall creaked as the officer stood. "Ma’am," the man said softly.

"He's talking to you," Steven told her.

She made a face, pulled her hand from his and said, "Go back to sleep."

"Wha—where are you going?” His effort to sit up to reach her ended with an intense throbbing in his head that stopped movement quickly. She didn’t look back as she walked out of the room. "What's going on?" he asked the officer with both hands to his head once Kari wasn’t there to see how much he hurt.

With an apologetic expression, he said, "Nothing that won't be settled soon, sir.” He glanced down the hall in the direction she’d gone. "Beside, the doctor wants her to get some rest."

* * * *

Penmate stood beside Caroleigh who stood beside Edward in the second bed. She held Edward’s hand. Three state policemen, two in suits and one in uniform arrived just moments before Kari. The suits moved to the wall, lining up with the aisle between the beds. The uniform stayed at the door. That left him a few feet from Kari when she came in as far as the foot of Edward's bed. She barely glanced in Steven's direction, and she didn't look well with circles under her eyes so dark they looked like bruises. She was also tense to the point of brittleness.

"I'm Inspector Eden," the oldest of the suits informed them. He was a non-descript man, early forties, medium height, medium build, and medium brown hair with touches of gray at the temples. He hooked a thumb over his shoulder towards the second man. "He's Canterbury."

Slightly taller, darker hair, and younger, he also had nothing to distinguish him in appearance. A slight nod was his response to the introduction before he stepped to the side.

Eden opened a thick folder and scanned through several pages. He deliberately made them wait, but if his intention was to make them nervous, he failed. Caroleigh and Edward turned their attention to each other. Penmate took a chair from against the wall and moved it to the foot of the bed for Kari. Steven gave Eden no attention at all. He watched Kari who deliberately didn't look at him.

"There are a few things we're not clear on," Eden stated to start. He still looked at the pages while he asked abruptly, "When did you resume your affair with…" His eyes flew up dramatically to Kari's face. "…Mr. Webber?"

"Excuse me?"

"She," Caroleigh told him tartly, "never had an affair with Dell."

"You let her answer for herself. I'll get to you later."

"I never had an affair with him either," she shot back.

"Nor I," Edward drawled out slowly. "You, Steven?"

"You think this is some kind of a joke?" Eden demanded.

"Certainly not, it hurts too much," Edward answered.

Immediately concerned, Caroleigh leaned over Edward. "Do you need something?"

"No, my love, I'm…"

"Hey!" Eden snapped.

"Keep your voice down," Penmate warned. He leaned around Caroleigh to take Edward's pulse.

Disgusted, Eden turned back to Kari. "How long have you been having an affair with Webber?"

Kari eyes went from one to the other of them in an attempt to keep up. "I never had an affair with him either," she stated calmly.

"Why is his number on your speed dial?"

"He's…was…the sheriff and…"

"His home phone?"

"…and the vet," she finished.

"So you saw a lot of him?"

"As little as possible. I didn't like him."

"Because he jilted you for her?" He pointed at Caroleigh.

Caroleigh responded. "Because he was a jerk."

"I told you to keep quiet."

"I don't think I have to, and I sure as hell don't like your attitude."

Behind Kari the uniform man moved forward and leaned down. Inches from her ear, he shouted, "Are you…"

Kari didn't just startle. She jerked convulsively with each word, staggered to her feet, and spun to face him.

"I thought you were deaf," Eden said smugly.

"We thought you were an ass," Caroleigh shouted. "Looks like only one of us is right."

"I don't have to put up with your mouth, lady. All that crap about her not being able to hear on the radio was just that, crap."

"She isn't deaf, you imbecile."

"Caroleigh," Steven said urgently. He raised his voice to make her hear him. "Caroleigh."

She looked where Steven looked. Penmate looked where Steven looked. They both moved at once to a trembling, ashen-faced Kari. Caroleigh pushed Penmate aside to reach her first. Kari didn't see either until Caroleigh's outstretched hand touched her shoulder. She startled violently.

"Don't," she cried as she backed away.

Both froze. "Deep breaths," Penmate told her. "Deep breaths."

"I know what to do," she told him with her chest heaving. She backed further from them with a wild look in her eyes until the wall stopped her. She jerked violently again.

"Let me get you a tran—" Penmate began.

"No!"

She slid down the wall to the bathroom door and clawed at the knob. Her hands didn't work right.

"I'm not through with you," Eden told Caroleigh. Then he made a mistake. He started after Kari.

Penmate stepped in front of him as Kari disappeared through the door. "Yes, you are," he promised.

Eden turned on him, ugly and threatening. "I'm conducting a criminal investigation."

"What you just did was criminal." Penmate was not in the least intimidated. "She's hyper-sensitive to sound, her nerves are already to a breaking point, and…" His finger jabbed at Eden's chest. "…you did that deliberately."

"If you continue to interfere," Eden went on smugly, "I will arrest you for obstruction."

Penmate didn't argue anymore. He pushed by Eden and stormed up between the beds to the phone.

Up on his elbows, Steven asked, "Is she okay?"

"She will be," Penmate promised. He punched in a number, shoving the phone with each jab. Into the phone, he said. "Get me the Judge, right now."

"You think some hick judge is going to scare me?" Eden asked derisively.

"You are going to be so sorry," Caroleigh told him.

"Maybe—" Canterbury began.

"Shut up, Mayberry," Eden told him with a derisive misuse of his name, displaying his opinion of his companion.

Canterbury's face closed up. He leaned back against the wall, arms and ankles crossed, withdrawing from the situation. The stunned uniformed officer wisely left the room.

Eden was sorry.

* * * *

Canterbury entered the room literally with a flag of truce. A white handkerchief waved from his fingertips, held at arm's length.

"Second string," Edward muttered without amusement. "Good cop-bad cop."

"Too much television," Canterbury said. "Remorseful cop. I'll tell you the truth, after what happened, I don't want to be here anymore than you want me."

"Then leave," Caroleigh told him.

"Sorry, I can't." He looked at Kari in the far corner, her back against the wall, and spoke slowly. "I apologize for what happen. Nothing like that will happen again, I swear."

Penmate came in quietly behind him. "It had better not."

Canterbury looked from Penmate to Martha beside him. She looked more formidable than usual, and the look she gave him was not friendly.

"Watch out for the Colombo act," Edward warned.

"More Sheriff Taylor," Canterbury said good-naturedly.

"Mayberry, we know. We heard," Caroleigh retorted. "Can we get this over with?"

Canterbury nodded and pointed to the chair against the wall opposite the beds, neatly centered. The gesture was unnecessary. It had obviously been placed there for him. He sat down with Eden's folder across his legs and took a small notebook from an inside pocket.

"There are just a few things we're confused about," he began easily. "Motive for Mr. Webber's actions for one."

"He was crazy," Caroleigh retorted.

"Certainly seems so, ma'am, but we usually find the crazies have a reason, even if it makes no sense to anyone other than themselves. If we're able to understand them, no matter how distorted they are, it sometimes helps with the next case."

He cleared his throat to continue. "Often in the case of stalkers obsessed with their victims they imagine and come to believe in certain outcomes. When they fail to materialize they end up killing in frustration. That would explain Miss O'Keefe's belief that Webber delayed killing the three of you while he searched for her, theorizing a jealousy of her relationship with Mr. Chase and the belief that you, Miss Fitzhugh, came between them in that high school incident. He may have wanted her to see your demise."

"He didn't say anything like that."

"If you'll excuse me, you were all three a little vague on just what he did say."

"Because none of it made any sense. He said he was going to own the mansion by blowing it up to break the trust. What kind of sense does that make?"

"It doesn't," he agreed. "No more than being obsessed with her when he believed he was Adam O'Keefe's son." He threw the last directly at Kari. "Your brother."

"He wasn't," she stated flatly.

"By all accounts his mother agreed. Everyone we've talked to say she claimed it was an older man. Your father would have had to have been fifteen."

"Sounds like you've done your homework," Penmate commented.

With a nod, he said, "He was obsessed with her though. We found an entire wall of photos of her in his basement."

"What else did you find?" Steven asked.

"I can't go into details, but I can tell you enough to know he was responsible for the fire and collapse of those stairs. They're still pulling internet how-to pages off his hard drive."

"Computer?" Kari asked with her stare fixed on Canterbury.

"Yes, ma'am. With him being your vet and the dogs being familiar with him, it would have been easy for him to get close to them as well." Kari still stared at him and didn't answer. "Well, ah, so if you could just clear up a couple of points, you can all put this behind you."

"Here it comes," Edward muttered.

With a game smile, Canterbury asked, "Where were the dogs?"

"What?" Kari asked.

"Mr. Maxwell's dogs, where were they?"

"In their cages in the pickup."

A quick glance passed between Edward and Caroleigh. Steven's expression held to stoic, with an effort. None of them knew why Canterbury was asking or why Kari seemed to be lying about the dogs, but they would not say anything to contradict her.

"They were when the paramedics arrived. Where were they when you found Mr. Maxwell?"

"In their cages."

"When they received your first radio call, you were saying something about the dogs tearing him up. You were pretty upset and not speaking clearly…"

"They would have torn him up if they'd been loose when he shot Max," she stated emptily.

"They weren't loose at that time?"

"What do the dogs have to do with anything?" Penmate asked in confusion while three very deliberately stayed silent.

"We're trying to determine why Mr. Webber couldn't seem to get out of the house. All the exterior doors were locked, and we can't find any of the keys. The missing keys also confuse us as to how he could have locked you in a bedroom."

The last was again directed at Kari. "If you're asking me where they are, I don't know," she told him.

"Which locks?" Caroleigh asked.

"Which keys did you see?" Canterbury countered.

"None lately, but the old keys were on a huge metal ring." She made an eight inch circle with her hands. "Pretty hard to miss."

"And the dead bolts?"

She made a smaller circle with her hands, about four inches. "They hung on pegs in the pantry."

"We haven't found either of them. None of you actually saw him with either of them?"

Three shook their heads. Kari didn't respond at all.

"Wait a minute," Caroleigh said suddenly. "You said he couldn't get out. That's silly. Even if the doors were locked, there are windows."

"It was obvious he tried, but something panicked him. He emptied his gun into the front door and then spilled all the shells out of the spare cylinder trying to reload. From there he ran through the house, knocked over tables and chairs in front of the windows, but he never opened one more than a few inches, as if something was chasing him inside or something was outside, following him from window to window."

"I would say it was Daddy…" Edward began dryly.

"Dell created that ghost. Nothing was chasing him," Caroleigh retorted.

"Which brings us to another point," Canterbury said. "We can't find any projector."

"Then he took it out."

"Reasonable, but where did it go. We didn't find one anywhere in the house or in his car."

Edward answered. "It was probably small enough he had it in his pocket."

"That's a possibility, of course. They're still shifting through the debris. It and the keys may turn up yet." He turned to Kari again. "Why was it you didn't take them out of the basement the first time, Miss O'Keefe?"

"With Steven on crutches with new injuries, I didn't think we could out run Dell. I thought they would be safe there as long as Dell didn't have me. I was obviously wrong," she said tightly.

"What did you do with the meat?" When all he received was a blank look for an answer, he explained. "You said you were taking meat from the freezer in the pantry for dinner when you saw Webber taking Miss Fitzhugh and Mr. Van Philips to the basement. What did you do with it?"

"What the hell difference does that make?" Caroleigh asked.

"It's the little details that trip up criminals," Edward said cynically.

"We aren't the criminals."

"The kitchen, I think," Kari said in answer to Canterbury's question.

He nodded. "How well do you hear on the phone?"

"Depending on the voice, pretty well, I have to have some things repeated, but generally I catch enough to know what they're saying."

"But not on the radio?"

"That was the first time I tried," she said with a slight shrug. "Maybe someone with better diction, not him."

"You had trouble with the paramedics too," he pointed out.

"They were in the air. I couldn't hear them over the chopper."

He made a note on his pad. "Did you go to the apartment before or after trying the phone?"

"I tried the phone in the apartment."

"After you determined Mr. Chase wasn't there?" Kari nodded. "You said when the little dog alerted you that someone was coming you went out the exterior door and hid to watch Webber through the window. Do you know why he destroyed your computer?"

"Internet access probably."

"The phones were dead."

"I have satellite access."

"You do?" Caroleigh asked in surprise. "When did you get that?"

"Last year."

"Excuse me." Canterbury took back the conversation. "How would he have known that?"

"Everyone in town knew it," Penmate answered.

"She didn't," Canterbury pointed out with a tip of his head towards Caroleigh.

"She wasn't in town when the truck pulled through."

Canterbury smiled slightly. "Big news in a town this size," he said in understanding. "I know how anything out of the ordinary is noticed."

"Then you also know how the ordinary can become twisted," Penmate said tersely.

"Yes, sir," he nodded sagely. "That doesn't mean having his plans to marry Miss O'Keefe spoiled in high school didn't twist Webber's mind up. Do any of you know who paid for his education?"

"He won a scholarship," Penmate supplied.

"No. Every year a cashier's check was sent on his behalf. No return address." He shifted his attention to Kari again. "Your grandfather?"

"No," she stated flatly. "After I dated…" She emphasized the word, "…Dell, he came to Grandpa, claiming to be his grandson. Grandpa asked his blood type and sent him on his way. It wasn't possible."

"But he continued to believe it."

"I wouldn't know. He never mentioned it to me." Her temper began to show. "But then he wouldn't, would he if he was obsessed with me and suddenly did all this because he was jealous?"

"Shades of Rome," Edward mumbled wearily.

Canterbury understood the reference. "He wouldn't be the first sicko to have an incestuous obsession," he agreed. "It sounds like he wanted the mansion, which he considered rightfully his, and her."

"So what's the problem?" Caroleigh asked.

"A few things that don't fit quite so neatly."

"Such as?"

He turned his attention to Kari. "You told them you were going to take a shower. Instead you went outside to talk further with Mr. Maxwell." Kari nodded. "After failing to find him you returned inside, going to the pantry to take out meat for dinner." She nodded again. "It seems a little strange that as upset as you were you would be thinking about dinner."

"We had to eat," she said tonelessly.

"What would your normal routine for the morning have been?"

"To go over to the ranch to feed the animals."

"But Mr. Maxwell was doing that for you?" He received another nod. "Is it possible Webber was in the house before Mr. Maxwell arrived that morning?"

"I suppose so. We were in the apartment. You think he saw me go out and thought I was going over to the ranch?"

"That's what I think."

She squeezed at the back of her neck with both hands. "That makes sense. I thought it was just his colossal ego making him so sure of himself. He wasn't in any hurry because he thought I would have had to walk around, and it would take me hours to get back."

"Why are there key locked deadbolts on all the bedroom doors?"

"Say that again?"

"Why are there deadbolts…?"

"Grandpa did that years ago," she answered as soon as she heard what she had missed. "From what I understand it was to keep my father and his new wife from stealing from him."

"His own son?"

"More Gladys, I think."

"A real winner," Caroleigh said with a snort.

"In what way?" Canterbury asked.

"Try cannibal."

“My grandfather didn’t like her,” Kari said. "He blamed my mother’s leaving on my father’s affair with Gladys."

"Where did she go?"

Kari shrugged. "They never heard from her again. Father divorced her, claiming desertion. Grandpa didn't approve of any of it."

Canterbury didn't seem surprised, just curious. "So he cut him off?"

"Put him on a wage and made him work for it. It wasn't enough for Gladys, and she didn't like living there away from all the parties.”

"Are you a gossip at heart?” Penmate asked.

"Just background," he said sheepishly. He looked quickly back down at his notes. "You all agree it was approximately an hour from the time Mr. Maxwell left to when Webber dragged Mr. Chase to the basement so that means he spent approximately half an hour doing what?"

"I don't know what he was doing." Kari was the only one who could answer the question. "I only know he was in the library until he dragged Steven to the basement."

"You watched through the windows on the front veranda,” he said with a nod. “So you don’t know what he was looking for?”

“I didn’t know he did look for something.”

“Tore the library up pretty good,” he stated as if it really wasn’t important. “That was when you assumed he was taking Mr. Chase to the basement also and went around to the root cellar.” He looked up. “That presents a problem for us. There are dog tracks over yours around the perimeter of the house." When she didn't answer immediately he prompted. "They had to have been there after you went back inside the first time at least and after you came back from the ranch, yet you didn't mention seeing the dogs during that time."

"I didn't."

"But they do respond to commands from you?"

"I helped train them."

"What is your thing with the dogs?” Caroleigh asked.

Canterbury answered bluntly. "Eden believes she set those dogs on Webber, that they're why he couldn't get out a window."

"So what?" Caroleigh said with a flip of her hand.

Edward took it more seriously. "Is he thinking of charging her with something?"

"If she deliberately set the dogs on Webber, preventing him from leaving the house where she knew there was a bomb, he could."

"It was his bomb," Caroleigh retorted. "And he meant to deliberately blow us up. Excuse me, but I don't feel sorry for him."

"The dogs were in their cages," Steven stated firmly.

Canterbury asked Kari, "Why would you leave them in the pickup when you took the time to leave the little dog safely in the greenhouse?"

"I put Rascal in the greenhouse to free my hands. I knew Steven might need help."

"You could have left him in the pickup with the other dogs."

"Not in the cages with the big dogs. I would have had to put him in the cab, and he's undisciplined. I couldn't take the time to worry about him if he ran off, and I didn't plan on driving through the mine when I left the ranch. I didn't think of it until I approached it."

"Does she need a lawyer?" Penmate asked in concern.

"Why would Mr. Maxwell leave you everything?" Canterbury asked her.

"What?" Caroleigh exclaimed.

"I don't think I heard that right," Kari stated.

"Why would Mr. Maxwell name you as his beneficiary, leaving everything to you?"

"He wouldn't," she stated. "He has children."

"He left provisions for them, but he left the bulk of his estate, the ranch, to you."

"Why would he do that?"

With a crooked smile he told her, "That's what I'm asking you."

Kari shot up and went to the phone. "Do you know anything about this?" she asked Penmate while she punched in a number. Penmate shook his head while she started talking. "What's this…you're damned right you're hearing from me. What's this nonsense about…?"

She stopped to listen, slammed the phone down, and headed for the door.

"Wait a minute," Canterbury called after her.

She was already gone.

"Just what is it you people think?" Steven asked.

Canterbury's eyes shifted from one to the other of them as if he were making a decision. "There's no doubt Webber was crazy," he finally said. "It's just that some people aren't sure someone wasn't manipulating that insanity with an alternative motive."

"Because of the business with Max?" Penmate asked.

"That's the stupidest thing I ever heard," Caroleigh said explosively.

"They think it could have been a very elaborate plan to hide its real purpose."

"To get Max's ranch?" Caroleigh asked incredulously. "Why, for God's sake? She has a ranch."

"Kind of like a wart compared to the frog," he told her. "Hers is small and non-productive; barely enough income to keep it going, and it's really all she owns. The mansion is not hers. The mine barely provides an income, and neither it nor the mansion is something she can turn into a large sum of money like she could by selling his property."

"She helped Grandpa set up the trust," Caroleigh retorted. "She doesn't own the Meadow because she didn't want it. It's a white elephant and maintenance on it is a money eater."

"She may have wanted money to support it," he said and then asked quickly before she could retort, "She told you she helped set up the trust?"

"Grandpa told me before he revised and recorded it."

"If all that is true, and she didn't want it, why has she hung onto it instead of turning it over to the state?"

Steven answered that one. "For Caroleigh. Kari told me it was the nearest thing Caroleigh had ever had to a real home, and she wouldn't take it away from her as long as she kept coming back."

Canterbury watched but didn't comment on the stunned effect Steven's words had on Caroleigh. "She discussed the terms of the trust with you?" he asked of Steven.

"Not specifically, but I know the basics," Steven answered tightly.

Canterbury's eyes shifted to him. "And you're okay with that?"

"Very."

"After what Maxwell told her, was she reconsidering her relationship with you?"

"You're jumping around worse than water on a hot griddle," Edward complained. "I suppose you think he was part of the plot."

"No," Canterbury answered bluntly. "I think he has his own agenda."

"Don't even start," Caroleigh warned.

"Just stick to one subject, please," Edward pleaded. "Keeping up with that is wearying enough."

"And you better make it quick," Penmate put in and motioned Martha to Edward's side.

"To the point then," Canterbury said stiffly. "To some it looks like she never intended for any of you to get hurt, but she manipulated Webber into killing Maxwell, then made sure Webber didn't live to tell anyone about it after getting the three of you to safety."

"That's as crazy as he was," Caroleigh retorted.

"For the record, I don't believe it. I ran some tests with the canine unit. The dog left at the mansion was able to hear the signal from the ranch to come. It wasn't familiar with the area the way Maxwell's dogs would be, but still made it to the handler at the ranch quickly enough to fit the time frame. Maxwell's dogs could have been at the mansion, circled the house after she went back inside, and still returned to the ranch before Webber reached there for Maxwell to put in their cages. I think Webber went to the ranch expecting to find her following her usual routine. When he found Maxwell instead, he killed him as a potential witness. The time it took her to drive back through that mine after she found Maxwell, climb up to a second story window and—"

"What? Stop a minute. Climb to what second story window?" Caroleigh cried.

He laid his pen down. "You don't know what she did, do you?"

"We weren't supposed to talk about it," she retorted even though without discussion they all had obviously failed to mention the woman Dell had referred to as well as the dogs being loose when they came out of the mine.

"Then you don't know what she went through on your behalf. She has a lot of guts." The last was said in admiration. "I think the reason Eden and some of the others have a problem believing her story is they have trouble believing the route she says she took. I had trouble with the climb up that house, and I passed on the fingernail trip down that cliff face."

"The old Indian ladder?" Caroleigh asked in horror.

"That is what she called it."

"It's hand and toe holds chipped out of the rock," Caroleigh explained, assuming Edward and Steven didn't know.

"To follow Webber to the ranch, she went down that cliff with that little dog in a pack on her back," Canterbury told them. "I had a rock climber do it and added his time to the time it took me to run to the edge from the house and then from the creek to the barn. It fits. She used the radio in Maxwell's pickup to call for help. She was nearly hysterical to start, not making much sense, but she calmed herself down, told them she couldn't hear what they were saying so just listen. Once she calmed down, she was blunt and to the point, 'He killed Max and has my sister and two friends locked in the basement with a bomb. I'm going back to stop him.' and cut off. Next she called for the air ambulance, told them she had a beating victim, head injury, status unknown and needed them there as fast as they could get there. Because they were already on a call and weren't sure how soon they could get there, they ordered the land unit, which turned out to be fortunate since there ended up being two of you who needed medical assistance. She was already in motion when she called them. They heard that gate go down before they lost contact. She drove through the mine, went up that tunnel, into the root cellar, out and up the side of the house to get back in without Webber seeing her. Once inside, she let him see her and chase her into a bedroom. He was obviously familiar with the house and knew the deadbolts locked on both sides with a key. Rather than fight to get her out, he locked her in. She went back down the outside, into the root cellar, and in to get you."

By the time he finished, Caroleigh had found a chair, her color gone. Steven gripped a spindle in the rail of his bed. Martha had both hands to her face in horror. Penmate leaned against the wall for support.

"And you wanted to know why she left the dog behind?" Edward asked in awe.

"Unbelievable," Penmate gasped.

"That poor child," Martha whispered. "She must have been terrified."

"And they're trying to make her the villain?" Steven demanded angrily.

Canterbury nodded. "Along with what I've already mentioned, there's the insurance."

"Insurance?" Penmate and Caroleigh said together.

"On the mansion. It goes to the trust as principal. She controls the trust."

"The principal is only to be used on the mansion," Caroleigh said numbly.

"Our legal department is still examining that. Maybe you could save some time by telling me what happens if there isn't one left? You did say he intended to destroy it with all of you inside."

"Yes, but…" She broke off in an effort to concentrate. "I don't remember if the trust even covered that. I'm too tired to think straight."

"You all are," Penmate said quickly. "Time's up."

Canterbury didn't argue. He folded his notebook and put it inside his jacket. "She seemed angry about that will thing," he commented as he stood.

"Yeah," Caroleigh said glumly. "She works for years to give everything away, and he gives her more. Ironic, isn't it?"

* * * *

Caroleigh gave up on sleep. As soon as she stood, stretched, and rolled her head to ease a stiff neck, Steven's eyes opened.

"Can't sleep either?" she asked softly. She moved closer to him, but watched Edward sleep. Next to Steven's bedside, she said in a rush, "I should never have pulled her off when we were kids. If she'd killed him then, none of this would have happened."

"I don't know what you're talking about."

"The time Max nearly arrested us. She didn't just want to stop them. She wanted them, especially Dell, to remember what would happen to them if they ever tortured an animal again. She did, she hurt him, which was what made Max so mad. He thought we'd abused what he'd taught us. She probably did let those dogs out, hoping they could catch Dell before he got back in the house."

Somehow it didn't surprise Steven to learn Dell was the bully Kari had stopped. It wasn't, however, what concerned him at the moment. "I don't care about the dogs or her administering justice as a kid. I want to know what's going on with her now. Why won't she talk to me?"

"She's…I…upset probably." She gripped the bedrail with both hands. "I don't know what the hell she's thinking. We haven't been able to talk."

"Have you ever heard about a curse on the Meadow?"

"That old thing? It's nothing. I know the O'Keefes have a pretty sad history, but it doesn't have anything to do with some Indian curse."

She turned as Kari walked in and immediately went to Kari, her hand out, careful not to touch. "What's wrong?" she asked.

Dazed, Kari shook her head. She either hadn't heard or couldn't answer. Steven didn't think Caroleigh knew which any better than he did. Caroleigh moved closer, and Steven pushed up on his elbows.

Kari looked at the hand Caroleigh extended towards her and whispered, "He did it. He didn't think it was fair for Grandpa to give the Meadow away."

"You don't have to take it."

"No." She shook herself and gave a short, bitter laugh. "His kids are sure to contest it. I won't fight them."

"Then it isn't a problem."

"No," she said, but she didn't look any better.

Caroleigh reverted to the comfort of a childhood nickname. "It'll be okay, Kay-Kay."

"He's our uncle."

"What?"

"Our uncle, Great Grandpa's son, Grandpa's half-brother, our uncle."

"A bastard?" Caroleigh asked in astonishment. “Great Gramps had a bastard son?”

"Max—our uncle," Kari repeated, closed her eyes and groaned. "God, I can't take this all in. I don't want to take it all in."

"Just forget about it." Caroleigh touched her on the shoulder then. "It doesn't mean anything now."

Kari stepped away and pulled herself up straight. "I have things to do."

"You need to rest."

"No, no, not yet.” She shook the remainder of her daze off and spoke briskly. "As soon as they will let me in the Meadow, I'll have your things brought down. Vern can drive you to Denver."

"Oh, no you don't—Kari, come back here."

Kari was already out the door with Caroleigh right behind her.

"Damn it," Steven muttered helplessly.

"I do believe," Edward said drowsily, "she means it this time."

* * * *

"I don't believe I've ever seen you look quite so guilty," Edward teased.

Caroleigh squirmed. "I had to tell her something."

"In regards to?” When she glanced at Steven, he added, "Come, come, my love, I've never known you to be bashful."

"She was going to go up to the ranch and stay by herself. There isn't even a stick of furniture in that house so…so…so." She went from stammering to rushing the words out in a tumble. "I told her we were getting married, and she had to stay to help with the arrangements. You did say you love me, and she thinks I'm terribly selfish. You do love me, don't you? You were going to propose?"

"Heart and soul, my love, and yes, but—"

"I know. You want your mother and father here."

"I see no reason to spoil the happiest day of my life with their presence."

“Are you ashamed of me?”

“No, my love, them. I really don’t want them here.”

"Of course you do. They can get here in three days, can't…"

"Three days?" he repeated in an astonished start followed by a wince of pain. "That…that is a bit soon." He recovered to joke. "The solicitors couldn't even prepare pre-nuptials in three days."

"I don't care anything about pre-nups, Eddie. I know I've said some stupid things, and I have more than you think. I'll tell you about it, but—"

"I have a bit—"

"I don't care. I just want us to be married. I love you so damned much it hurts and when…" Her voice got unsteady. "…when I thought I was going to lose you, I…I…"

"Don't you do that," he said quickly when she turned slightly to look for a way out. "There's nothing wrong with tears." He held his arms out to her. "Please, Caro, don't run."

She hesitated while years of old habits warred in her. When she did go to him it was to break out in sobs. "You looked so horrible. I couldn't breathe when you stopped. I would have died if you had."

"I didn't. Uh-oh." Martha appeared at the foot of his bed. "She's—"

Martha waved a hand to silence him. "She's doing what she should have done days ago. Good for her. This wedding…" Caroleigh and Edward held their breath. "…good for Kari. You've got her raving. Good to get her mind off this other business."

Caroleigh sniffled and wiped her eyes. "You'll come?"

"Of course, I'll come, child. And so will the boy. Now get off his chest."

She walked out, leaving Caroleigh with a giggle strangled in her throat.

"Dare I ask who is the boy?" Edward asked.

"Vern, her nephew, she raised him."

Edward considered that for a moment. "Fortunately for him there is no family resemblance."

She did giggle then and hugged him until he gasped. When she recoiled, he chuckled. "Just the chest, my love. The shoulder is fine."

She settled down with a sigh, head on one shoulder and hand on the other. "I do love you," she whispered.

"And I love you, but are you sure you don't want a large bash for a wedding?"

"Absolutely." Her head snapped up with a new thought. "Steven, you have to stay. You're the best man." Once said, she asked Edward quickly, "That's okay, isn't it?"

"Perfectly. Be honored, old boy."

"Only if you quit calling me old boy," Steven told him.

They all laughed, but Steven's humor did not reach inside.

* * * *

Simple and lovely was the easiest way to describe the wedding. Kari arranged it all in three days time with taste and efficiency. Adie rolled Steven down the aisle of the small hospital chapel to take his place as best man. Martha pushed Edward behind him. Adie sat on the bride's side next to Penmate's wife, an elegant little lady. Martha sat on the groom's side next to Vern and Judge Powell's wife, a wizardly lady with a mischievous glint to her eyes. The judge stood in front, tall, slim to the point of emaciation, but still straight for his years. Edward's parents were unable to make it, for which he was grateful.

A stand of white roses, baby's breath, and pink carnations stood to each side of the judge. The single carnation with ribbon streamers Kari carried matched those in the stands. Her dress, a deep rose, was full length batiste in Victorian style with lace at the throat, hem, and wrists.

White was saved for the bride. With a radiant smile on lips that trembled and tears in Caroleigh's eyes, she carried a dozen white roses with streaming ribbons on one arm, and baby's breath was weaved in the curls in her hair. Her free hand lay in the crook of Penmate's arm as he walked her down the aisle with the honor of giving her away. Her dress was a true heirloom, Kari's grandmother's, of Victorian lace and satin with a floor length veil. She walked to a taped recording of the wedding march to Edward who grinned like a school boy.

Simple, old fashion vows were exchanged and simple gold bands sealed their promises to each other. When Edward, with the help of Vern, stood long enough to kiss his bride, Adie snapped the first picture. Many more were snapped while congratulations and hugs were given. Tears flowed freely and openly down Martha's cheeks, while Kari and Adie brushed theirs aside furtively. Through it all, Kari stayed well away from Steven. It was obvious she intended to do the same when the others started to leave.

"Kari," he said loudly. "I'd like to talk to you."

Penmate touched her on the arm, and Kari nodded. Though she did not look at Steven, she had heard, and she did stay.

"What's going on?" he asked bluntly as soon as they were alone.

"A return to reality," she stated tonelessly. "It's nothing against you. You're a fine man."

He scoffed angrily. "That's the first time you've ever said anything to me that sounded like an insult."

"It wasn't. You're a good man and attractive. That night in the greenhouse I got carried away by both. It was exciting and romantic, but I've realized it was an emotional reaction. Adrenalin was high and—"

"It took quite a while to get over an adrenalin high," he told her with a curl to his lip.

"You are attractive," she repeated. "Your attention was flattering. I've been alone for a long time, and I was lonely. The idea of falling in love was what I was reacting to, not love."

"Couldn't stand my performance as hero?" he asked bitterly.

"Excuse me?"

"Having to save my ass twice must have spoiled the romance. A real poor showing."

"That's absurd," she cut him off with before he could say more. "You don't have that fragile an ego or misplaced pride. I don't for a minute think you lack in ability or courage. Nor do you. It just isn't there for me. Be glad I realized it before I allowed gratitude to carry it any further. We come from two different worlds. Once you get back to yours, you'll realize it isn't for you either."

Chapter Eight

Steven sat in his new Dodge four by four pickup and stared at the gate. The one time he'd been on that road from the ranch to the Meadow there had been no gate, or any signs forbidding trespassing, or warnings of patrolling guard dogs. There certainly had been no radio call box perched on a post. He knew once he punched that button if Kari answered, he would never get beyond that gate.

The few times he had phoned, she hadn't answered, no matter what the time, and he could tell from Caroleigh's behavior whether or not Kari was nearby. If Kari was there he had gotten short answers to his polite questions on Edward's condition, the weather, or whatever else he could think of until they hung up. If Kari was not there Caroleigh's chatter overflowed with friendliness. During those calls, he learned Kari had seen to the complete refurbishing of the old house before Edward was ever released from the hospital, all in a matter of days once Caroleigh convinced her they had nowhere to go and their funds for the month were exhausted. A house that started as a boarding house in a mining camp had been painted, curtains and drapes hung, and carpet put in. Furniture and appliances had been purchased, lamps and wall decorations either new or favorites like grandpa's hand painted map from the mansion had been hung. The cupboards and refrigerator had been stocked, all entirely for their benefit. Kari had fully intended to return to her apartment in the Meadow. It had taken a nearly hysterical fit from Caroleigh proclaiming her inability to care for Edward alone to change her mind. Kari agreed to stay with them, but she knew Caroleigh had been acting, and Caroleigh knew she knew. It caused tension between them.

"I don't know why, Steven," she confided the night before, "but I'm scared. She says she put in all those security things so we wouldn't worry. I think it's something else, something she's not telling us, and Max's dogs scare the hell out of me. She won't let us out of the house, even to sit in the garden, without one of them being with us."

"Where is she now?"

"That's another thing; she's gone all the time, longer and longer. She won't tell us where, not really, or what she's doing."

"What do you think she's doing?"

"I don't know."

That had been the deciding factor for him. He was packed and on his way the next morning only to be stopped with indecision at a locked gate. He nearly jumped out of his skin when the radio shouted at him.

"Who's out there? What do you want?"

"Caroleigh?" he questioned hopefully.

"Steven? Is that you? Oh, God, it's Steven, Eddie. Come in here. Come in." With a loud click the gate rolled open. "Oh, oh, drive around to the back. I'll meet you on the porch."

Steven wondered if Caroleigh wasn't a little drunk. She sounded giddy, and she acted giddy when he pulled in. She waved her hands excitedly and bore down on him at a run.

"Careful," Edward warned before she reached him.

She skidded to a stop to stare at the cane in Steven's hand. "Oh, God, Steven are you crippled?"

"Caro," Edward abolished.

Steven burst out laughing. "No, I'm not crippled. The leg's just weak, and the cane is for support."

She flung herself at him, nearly knocking him over. "I'm so glad to see you."

Edward held out his hand when he reached them. Steven shook it awkwardly. Caroleigh still hung from his neck.

"Cabin fever," Edward told him in answer to his stunned expression.

"I'm just happy to see him," She stepped back finally. "Can't I be happy to see an old friend?"

"She was nearly as happy to see the satellite man," he teased.

"Eddie." She gave Edward a playful punch and fell against him as his arm went around her. "Tell us what you've been doing. How are you feeling? Does your leg hurt?"

"Cabin fever," Edward repeated.

She pushed away from him. "Just get his bags." She hooked her arm through Steven's. "You look good, a little thinner. Are you eating well?"

Edward followed with Steven's single bag. "It will take her about half an hour to wind down."

"Does she stop for breath before then?" Steven looked back over his shoulder to ask. His smile froze, and he stopped so abruptly it jerked Caroleigh to a stop.

Edward stopped, his shoulders hunched slightly. "She's coming?" he asked with a grimace.

Barely moving his mouth, Steven said, "Like a locomotive."

Kari bore down on them, dressed as she had been that first morning in her apartment. No glasses, hair braided, and no over-sized shirt hiding her slim figure, but a large German Shepherd trotted in front of her, and Rascal hung over her arm.

"Stiff upper lip, old chap," Edward advised quickly and turned to stand beside him.

"Look, Kari, Steven's come to visit," Caroleigh called out. "Isn't it wonderful?" She took a protective step forward. "Don't you let that dog jump him."

"I don't have him on guard," Kari retorted. She stopped several feet from them. The shepherd stopped and sprawled on the ground in front of her. Rascal kept his eyes on Steven and growled softly.

"I guess he still doesn't like me," Steven said of Rascal.

"Why are you here?" she asked bluntly.

Caroleigh answered in a challenge. "To visit,"

"To talk to you," he corrected.

Edward held up both hands defensively. "I am not getting in the middle of this."

"We have nothing further to discuss," Kari told Steven.

"I think we do, and I think there's something you should tell them."

"I have no idea what you're talking about."

"Yes, you do." As her eyes narrowed dangerously, Steven added. "If you don't, I will."

"Fine," she said with a flip of her hand. "Let's see what you think you know."

"Gladys." Kari jerked as if he'd slapped her. "Still think I don't know anything?"

"You're interfering in something that is none of your business," Kari told him coldly.

"Being dropped off a cliff, smashed in the head, and nearly blown to hell makes it my business."

Caroleigh and Edward melted together while Kari and Steven had a stare down.

Kari broke the silence. "Why don't you just stay out of it?"

"You know why, but we'll save that conversation for later."

"Shit," she retorted. With a snap of her fingers the shepherd's huge head turned towards her. With another signal, he lunged to his feet and loped off. "Come in the house."

As she stalked by, Edward blew out a breath and rolled his eyes. "Round one to you," he whispered. "Let's hope she doesn't strangle us before round two."

Their wariness didn't lessen once they went inside. Edward and Caroleigh sat side by side on the overstuffed couch done in pleasant floral upholstery. Steven sat perpendicular to them in a matching overstuffed chair. Kari, deliberately separated, was across from them in a second chair with a low table between. Rascal still growled.

"Kari, make him stop that," Caroleigh, a bundle of nerves, pleaded.

With a touch of her fingers to his throat, Rascal stopped and wiggled free of Kari's arm to lie in her lap.

"Looks like you've been working with him," Steven commented.

"He's really a little marvel," Caroleigh began.

"No small talk," Kari ordered.

"What is wrong with you? A friend comes to visit and you act like—"

"He isn't here for a friendly visit," Kari shouted at her.

"Yeah, well maybe it's time you stopped acting like everything is—"

"Don't tell me how to act."

"Kari," Caroleigh ground out, "something is very wrong. We have to stop ignoring it, face it."

"You don't know what you're talking about anymore than he does. You should not have asked him to come here."

"I didn't. He came because I told him I was afraid."

"Of what?" Kari asked in scorn.

"Whatever you're hiding. You've always been a secretive little bitch, but whatever this is, it's eating you up."

Steven interrupted, asking Kari, "Do you tell them or me?"

"Go ahead, and tell them whatever it is you think you know," she challenged.

"Fine," he shot back with determination. "Canterbury said they thought someone was manipulating Webber."

"Steven, you can't think—" Caroleigh began.

"Hush, my love," Edward whispered. "Now is the time to listen."

Steven picked up where he left off. "Even though none of us told them the things Webber said about some woman he was working with, they thought someone else was involved."

Caroleigh couldn't stay quiet. "It couldn't have been Gladys. She's old enough to be his mother."

"If I'm right, she is his mother."

Caroleigh's mouth dropped open. "And who…who…"

"The father?" he finished for her. "Probably William Fitzhugh."

"My grandfather?" Caroleigh shook her head. "She didn't marry him. She married my father."

"William wouldn't marry her, but he did pay her to go away and get rid of the problem. That's what Webber was raving at me about, rich men who abandon their bastards."

"How did you find out?" Kari asked quietly.

"You knew?" Caroleigh exclaimed. "You did know! Why didn't you tell me?"

"I didn't for sure, but would you ever want to think Dell was your uncle if I did?"

"I never wanted to claim any of them. What was one more? This is great, just great. There wasn't one of them that wasn't a sick, twisted pervert. Now there's a murdering psycho as well. Just great."

"It gets better," she promised solemnly. She asked Steven again, "How did you find out?"

"I hired some damned good detectives."

"What made you think of Gladys?"

"The way both of you talked about her more than anything. Neither of you came right out and said it, but the insinuation was you both believed her capable of murder. That and what seemed like too many convenient coincidences. Kari's mother disappears, Gladys marries her father. Caroleigh's mother dies. Kari's father dies. Gladys marries Caroleigh's father. All of it happening within a year."

"You missed William," Kari told him tonelessly. "William would have blocked any marriage of his heir to a woman like Gladys, and he controlled the money. All of those other coincidences wouldn't have done her any good until he died." Caroleigh stared at her dumbfounded. Kari half-shrugged. "William was notorious for not keeping his hands off the help. You knew that."

"Yeah, but to go from mistress to murderess is quite a jump even for Gladys."

"Grandpa always thought she was responsible for my mother's disappearance, but since no trace of her could be found, he couldn't prove it. He hated locked doors, but he put those locks in, not just to keep her from stealing, but to keep her away from me."

"Jesus, Kari, maybe Evelyn was right and your father does protect you."

"If it had been left up to him, I'd have been drowned in the bathtub."

Shocked, Caroleigh began with, "I know he was never much of a father."

Kari shot to her feet. The movement was so sudden she barely caught Rascal to pace and talk. "Dear Uncle Max felt it his duty to inform me of a few things. He left a letter and some journals, along with his will. The letter put it all in a nutshell. The journals went into detail, all noted as it happened. I told you I couldn't take it all in. Well, I still can't. You called them perverted, and you're right, sick, twisted minds, and not just William and Jonathan. Father…my father—ha! He was just as bad. At least he had the excuse of being a weak-minded drunk and addict. No, no the cruelest thing he did was before he started drinking."

In one turn she saw the looks on their faces and stopped short. As abruptly as she had left the chair, she dropped back. Rascal went to the floor, and she leaned forward, her face in her hands. "You don't know what I'm talking about," she moaned. She straightened back up when Rascal stood on his hind legs, front paws on her arm in concern. She picked him up automatically and leaned back, dog in her arms. "The only good thing about all of it is you," she told Caroleigh. "But I couldn't tell you without telling you all of it."

"All of what?" she asked, frightened and confused.

"Max only went back three generations. For all I know, the world is full of them."

"Full of what?"

"Bastards, O'Keefe and Fitzhugh bastards." She drew a deep breath and began. "It all started because the love of Grandpa Gavin's life was Caroleigh Winchester."

"My Grandmother," Caroleigh asked in astonishment.

"A lady too good for the likes of the son of an Irish tramp got lucky, according to her family," she confirmed. "When Grandpa asked to marry her, her parents dragged her off to England, not knowing it was already too late to save her virtue. Once they realized there was a scandal in the making, they bought her a husband of suitable title, William Fitzhugh, poor and desperate enough to accept a spoiled bride."

"You're saying Jonathan, my father, was grandpa's bastard?"

Kari nodded. "After a reasonable time, meaning they could claim the child was months younger than he actually was, William brought your grandmother back to her family, to their mine, and their share of the Morning Glory, his payment for marrying her. William, however, was full of hatred for the father of the bastard he was forced to claim as his own and immediately began a feud without Grandpa even knowing why."

"If Jonathan was Grandpa's then we're actually cousins," Caroleigh stated to skip over the rest of what she heard.

"Not quite," she answered, confusing them all. "William, though some perverse sense of revenge, taught Jonathan to hate Grandpa and on into the next generation to hate his son, Adam."

"Adam was your father?" Steven asked in a struggle to keep it all straight.

"Yeah," Kari answered derisively and went on with the story. "William tried to swindle Grandpa over and over. Grandpa, being much smarter, always avoided his little traps or turned it around on them so William and Jonathan attempted a con on Adam instead, not realizing, scum that they were, that Adam would ask Grandpa's advice. That's when everything pretty much exploded. They thought they owned a worthless played out mine and lied to Adam to get him to buy it. Grandpa, being so damned much smarter and ahead of them, knew that for the right price it could turn a tidy profit with some new mining techniques. You can imagine how swindled the swindlers felt when Grandpa built it up and sold it for triple what he put up for Adam to buy it. To get even with Grandpa, William told Grandpa Johnathan was his. When Grandpa tried to talk to Jonathan, William denied everything, claiming Grandpa was lying to cause trouble between them. Jonathan, to get even with Grandpa, put on a mask and raped Adam's fiancé a week before their wedding."

"Oh, Christ," Caroleigh murmured.

"She came out to the Meadow to call off the wedding, and Grandpa talked her out of it. He believed Adam really loved her and would only be hurt by the truth. He believed she had been raped, he didn't think Adam would ever know, and if she was with child, it was so close to the marriage date, Adam wouldn't know that either. Adam, being a little worldlier than Grandpa realized, did know his new wife wasn't a virgin and threw her out of his bed on their wedding night without ever completing the consumation. He wouldn't believe she had been raped as she claimed or that she didn't know who, especially after they discovered she was with child—me. He should have sent her home to her family, in disgrace if need be, but no, his pride wouldn't let him do that. He kept her and punished her. He also started drinking, and Jonathan was only too happy to help him down that road of destruction. He or William, Max wasn't sure which, brought Gladys back to assist. Gladys was then much better educated thanks to William's payoff money."

Kari took a deep breath and let it out slowly. "God, this all sucks. Gladys seduced Adam, and they were not discreet in their affair. After my mother disappeared, Gladys married what she thought was going to be the golden calf. She didn't take into consideration how Grandpa would react to it or realize he controlled the money. He hated her and wouldn't give her a thing. The only money he gave Adam was what he made Adam work for."

She sighed again and sank down lower in the chair. "She learned a lesson though. A few months later William died from what was assumed to be a drunken fall down a flight of stairs. A few weeks after that your mother succumbed to a lingering illness. Less than a month after that Adam died tragically, but only after a very dramatic and public display. Gladys told Adam at a party the seduction version of who my biological father was when he was staggering drunk and it was storming furiously. She included the fact that Grandfather had always known just to twist the knife. Adam left the party, screaming he was going to kill that interfering old bastard, that bastard child, and Jonathan. Just in case the road didn't kill him, Gladys called Grandpa and told him Adam was on his way and why. She set him up, either to die in that car or hoping Grandpa would kill him when he got to the house. All Grandpa did was lock the door, take me upstairs, and lock the bedroom door. We never heard him, never knew he was out there until the next morning. They didn't put a gun to his head, but they murdered him just as efficiently."

When she finished it was dead quiet in the room. Three sets of eyes riveted on her face, and no one seemed to want to talk or know what to say.

Edward broke the silence first in a strained voice. "Coffee anyone?"

The sound of his voice ignited Caroleigh. In an instant she was across the room to kneel in front of Kari, her hands on Kari's knees. "We are sisters, we really are sisters. He really was my Grandpa."

"The only good thing out of all of it."

When Kari stood, Caroleigh stood with her. Her arms wrapped tight around Kari as she told the men, "You guys get out of here."

"Kitchen," Edward said and led the way in a hurry.

"He loved you, Caro. It killed him that he couldn't tell you," Kari told her in a strained voice.

"I know he did a lot for me, but he did so much for—oh, God, not all of those kids he helped were his, were they?"

"No," Kari laughed shakily. "Only Vern."

"Vern? Vern! Martha?"

"She didn't go back east to take care of a sick and pregnant sister who left her with a child to raise."

"Does Vern know?"

"He's always known." Kari choked back a sob. "He's the sweetest man."

"Oh, Kay-Kay."

In the kitchen Edward eased the door shut. "Having a good weep now. Whew, did you ever open a can of unsavory worms. How did you ever find all that out?"

"I didn't," Steven told him numbly, moving away from the door, feeling only slightly guilty in listening as long as he had. "All I knew was that several people thought Gladys was in a family way when she left here, and she had been working for the Fitzhughs. William had a reputation for messing with the help and sending them off with a bit of money to get rid of the problem, and she came back a year later with some new polish and a pocketful of money. The rest was matching a few dates and conjecture."

"You were bluffing?"

"Yeah." Steven admitted. "I thought if I could get her talking…" He let the sentence trail off. "I didn't suspect all of that. What a shock." He shook his head in disbelief. "Caroleigh seems to be taking it all pretty well."

"Ha. Right now she's concentrating on the positive, but let me tell you, after she's thought about it for a while, they can all be glad they're already dead. Coffee?"

"Unless you've got something stronger."

"Only in the living room," Edward answered with a grimace.

"Coffee is fine," Steven answered quickly.

Edward went to the coffee maker. Steven stood where he was, lost in thought.

"They were a piece of work, weren't they?" Edward asked to draw Steven back.

"Is that kind of behavior normal for people with that kind of money?"

"That kind of behavior isn't limited to people with money."

"I wasn't including any of you."

"I know," Edward said with a chuckle and pointed to a chair at the table. "Have a seat. They may be a while." He joined him. "To answer your question, that kind of behavior in those days was seen more in the aristocrats than just rich. William's attitude that woman servants were for his pleasure was archaic even then, but still fairly common. I'm happy to say not all abused it to the extent he did. Still English history is full of bastards, legitimate and illegitimate."

"A bastard is a bastard."

"Not if it isn't known. Jonathan, for example, was born with benefit of a wedded mother. Legitimate on paper, but still a bastard in reality. The illegitimate didn't have that protection. That type of thing doesn't mean as much now, but then she'd have been thrown out into the world with the stigma of mother not wed, social disgrace, and all that. Jonathan and his mother were spared that, though I suspect both paid dearly at William's hand."

Steven asked tightly, "And Kari at Adam's?"

"Not physically from what Caro remembers. He ignored her as well as her mother. I can understand why now. Kari had her grandfather though. From everything I've heard of the old duffer, he doted on her."

"But he never told her the truth."

"I'm not so sure dear Uncle Max should have. They're soul sisters. That was enough for them. They didn't need to know all that other garbage. Some skeletons should remain in the closet. Knowing it serves no purpose." Edward paused and asked, "Does it, in the current situation, I mean?"

"Not that I know of except it gives us a pretty scary idea of what Gladys is capable of."

"Your boys happen to tell you where she is?"

"The last they could find on her was over six years ago when Jonathan Fitzhugh died. They haven't been able to find anything more recent."

"Not knowing where a creature like that is can be rather frightening. However, it may well tie into what my fellows were able to find." He shifted uncomfortable under Steven's quizzical scrutiny. "Okay, I haven't been entirely at ease either. Webber was such a buffoon I found it hard to believe he was capable of those clever things. The screw-ups, yes, but the overall plan, no. I gave my boys a blank check and told them to find whatever they could even if it hurt."

"So what did they find?"

"A parking ticket in Denver to start, one of those no parking on this side after such and such a time. It was nearly a year old, but with a little canvassing, they discovered he was a frequent visitor to the area, a rented house to be exact, rented by an agent, cash for a year in advance. His visits were rather spaced out to start, about once a month, but increased steadily until during the last month he went every week. It was common knowledge in the area that the house was not actually lived in, and since a lady's arrival coincided with his, it was believed to be a love nest."

"And the lady?"

"That's the rub. No one could give a very accurate description of her, dark sunglasses, hat or scarf always over her head. She even drove a different car each time. They did do some cross-checking though, dates the neighbors could remember, and it could not..." Edward put special feeling on the last two words, "...have been Kari."

"I never thought it was."

"Nor I, but now if Canterbury comes up with anymore of his garbage, we have something to fight back with."

"Did Caroleigh ever tell you more about that nearly getting arrested business?"

"Enough to know little Kari has the moxy to have set those dogs on the bastard, and I don't have a single qualm about saying they were in their cages the entire time."

Steven grinned ruefully. "She was younger and smaller and beat Dell up in front of his friends."

"Between the two of them, they beat the friends up too."

"He probably started plotting revenge against her then. Can you imagine what it would have been like for her if she and Caroleigh hadn't pulled that test business on him?"

"He probably would have made William look like a piker if he'd ever gotten her to marry him."

Frustrated, Steven asked, "Why didn't the first Caroleigh just tell her parents to go to hell and marry their grandfather? Look at all the misery it would have prevented."

"She was a product of her time and circumstances. Frankly, I'm surprised she was brave enough to have gotten herself in that kind of a predicament. I don't think either of her granddaughters inherited her disposition."

"No," Steven agreed with a scoff. "They would have told them to go to hell."

* * * *

The gathering wasn't particularly comfortable. Kari sat back from the table at one end, arms crossed. Each of the looks she gave Steven, though brief and few, were hostile and belligerent. He pretended not to see them. He sat on one side, up to the table, his hand beside an untouched cup of coffee. Caroleigh and Edward sat across the table from Steven, their chairs close together, and they held hands, braced for a confrontation.

"I don't know that Caro should be grateful for being enlightened with that bundle of trash," Kari began coolly, "but at least she knows now what was bothering me. Now you can all go away and leave me alone."

"It was quite shocking," Edward said. "Bitter-sweet to be sure. However, we need to discuss—calmly…" the last he injected quickly when her expression began to harden, "…the current situation."

"Which one is that?" she asked tartly. "The one where you won't go the hell away and leave me in peace?"

"The one where you've been pushing people away," Steven answered.

The look she gave him could have cut stone. "If you mean you, forget it," she told him. “Maybe I wasn't clear enough, but our little fling is over."

"Our fling aside," He gave the word the same twist she had, "you heard enough of what Dell said to be scared."

"I heard enough to know you all lied to the police because you think I was involved."

"Kari, no,” Caroleigh cried.

"She's trying to distract you again," Steven warned.

"It might be better to get this bit out in the open," Edward advised quietly.

"You didn't lie to the police?” Kari challenged.

"Yes, but not because we believed Dell."

She scoffed on that point and jumped to another. "I did turn those dogs loose hoping they would get back to the Meadow and rip Dell’s throat out before he could get in the house."

"We know that,” Edward told her.

"And it doesn't bother you?"

"Not in the least, nor does it Steven or Caroleigh. The blighter had it coming."

"You've all discussed it?"

"We are all in agreement. There's no need for the police to know."

She smiled coldly and went back to the first point. "Even if it proves I meant to kill him to hide my involvement."

"You weren't involved with that maniac," Caroleigh retorted. "We don't believe that, not then, not now."

Kari's eyes dropped to the floor. She also dropped one hand to Rascal's head where he stood beside her, his front paws on her leg. "I thought you did," she said softly. "I thought you believed his delusional ravings."

"They weren't delusional," Steven stated.

"Steven," Caroleigh implored.

"He was parroting something someone told him, and she knows it."

She took Rascal into her arms to stand. "Now you're having delusions."

"You heard something that scared you to death. You're afraid anyone near you is going to get caught up in it again."

"Dell was the only one."

"Bullshit. He was an imbecile, the stupid brawn for someone's brain. You sit down and talk to us, or I will tie you in that chair," he threatened.

"I don't think you want to try that."

"There's no sense denying it, love," Edward said quickly. "Steven and I have both hired detectives to—"

"Both of you too?" Caroleigh asked with a start.

"And you, my love?" Edward asked with a grin of appreciation. "What did yours find?"

"I had them really dig into the trust to see if it could be broken, who could possibly benefit from it, and who's been interested, that kind of thing. They traced Dell down as a looker, but that's not much help."

Kari dropped back into the chair in defeat. "What a waste of money."

"You too then?" Edward asked. He received a nod for answer. "And what did yours find, love?"

"I had them looking for bastards."

"Why?" Steven asked.

"To possibly find someone who had a twisted idea they had a right to the Meadow," she told him impatiently.

"More history?" Edward asked with his face twisted with distaste.

Caroleigh's face was a mirror of Edward's. "How many?"

"Quite a few, but they didn't find them, not yet anyway." She sighed and let Rascal down to her lap and leaned forward, hands folded together on the table. "Max told me about them in his letter. Great Grandpa only had one, Max. Other than Jonathan, Grandpa only had Vern, and Vern always knew. Grandpa would have given him anything, but the only thing Vern ever accepted was his van just before Grandpa died. Martha let him pay for her nurse’s training, but wouldn't take anything more after that. Adam had one, a boy that died shortly after birth. Jonathan, however, followed Williams’s example with zeal. He had two in England, one in France, and one in the states somewhere. Grandpa gave them all generous trusts to support them, and they could only claim the principal at their maturity if they signed a waiver, surrendering any claim on the estate by them or their descendants."

"Would that be binding on the descendants?” Steven asked.

"More importantly, did any refuse?” Edward asked.

"None refused that Max knew of,” Kari explained. “The waiver for them was legally binding. As for the descendants, that's questionable as to whether they could win in court or not in claims against the estate, but they could not break the trust. There's no way they could get the Meadow so all of this is moot."

Caroleigh shrugged that off. "Who are they?”

"Max didn't know their names or where they are, just the number and countries. The particulars of those trusts and names are sealed and locked away in some lawyer’s office only to be opened if a claim is filed against the estate."

"Does anyone else know all this?”

"Gladys knew about Jonathan and me, obviously. Martha suspected a lot of it, but she never questioned Grandpa. He told her it was a man's responsibility to see to the care of any child or grandchild that was his if the father wouldn’t or couldn’t, no matter what the circumstances of their birth. That was one of the things she respected about him."

Caroleigh asked with a grimace, "Did you tell her everything while you were asking?"

"Hell, no, I didn't. I was too embarrassed. I asked if she knew of any others. That was what she told me."

"Why didn't they ever get married?"

"He was more than thirty years older than her, and she never felt he loved her. She felt he was lonely, and she was lonely and handy."

Before anyone could comment on that—not that any wanted to—Edward said thoughtfully, "You said some lawyer’s office. Not the worthy Judge?”

"No. Grandpa took all of that out of the area so there would be less chance of anyone finding out. He didn't believe the sins of the fathers should be visited on the children."

"Denver, probably. I could put my chaps on it."

Kari shook her head. "Even if they find the right lawyer, they'd have to break in to get the information."

"Do you think it was Gladys?" Steven asked.

Kari shrugged and returned to stroking Rascal. "She's just the only person I've ever known who was cold-blooded enough to do anything like this. The problem is there is no way she could benefit even if the trust could be challenged successfully. Her only possible legal tie was Jonathan. That ended when he died."

Caroleigh said, "My guys say that trust is unbreakable."

"So do mine, but we're assuming that was the objective or that they know that." Steven pointed out. "Dell believed what he was saying. That doesn't mean he wasn't lied to."

"What he said sounded so much like her," she said faintly and crossed her arms again. "You know how sometimes you hear something and it triggers a memory of something you haven't thought of in years. When he said 'we'll get everything that should have been ours' I had a flashback so vivid it gave me the chills."

The memory obviously still did. Her arms wrapped tighter. "God, I hated that woman. She terrified me. I was always afraid she would take me away from Grandpa some way. She threatened to, over and over. He always laughed at her. He did the day of Adam's funeral too, but instead of making some hateful remark and walking off, she started yelling at him. I understand better what she meant now that I know Jonathan's real parentage, but then I was just frightened. When I walked in, she grabbed for me, and Grandpa went for her. I'd never seen him lose his temper before, even when he and Adam fought."

"He never had to," Caroleigh said. "He scared the hell out of you just by raising that bushy eyebrow."

Kari smiled sadly. "He was a man of awesome appearance." The smile faded completely. "That day he was…he was…" She broke off with a deep ragged expulsion of breath. "He wanted to hurt her, really hurt her, and I think he would have if I hadn't screamed. He was holding her by her hair and had his fist drawn back. She was kicking and screaming when he threw her out, literally by the hair of her head. She stopped screaming, got back on her feet, and told him, 'I'll just keep the other one. Blood is blood, and when I'm through, I'll have everything that should have been mine.'"

"Just change the pronouns," Edward observed.

"There isn't any chance she was related, is there?" Caroleigh asked though her expression showed she hoped not.

"No. Her family moved to the area when she was a small child. Her father was a teamster."

"Rather a rough lot, weren't they?" Edward asked.

"Very, but she was ambitious, smart, and pretty. She schooled herself enough to get a position at the manor house."

"There's a manor house in the area?" Steven asked in quicken interest.

Kari tipped her head to look at him. Edward chuckled while Caroleigh stared in disbelief.

Edward said, "I would think with all the difficulties an interest in one house in this area has caused you, you would be reluctant to show interest in another."

"I'm a slow learner," he grumbled in embarrassment.

"Obviously," Kari retorted. "Or you wouldn't have come back here. No matter what you think may be going on, it is no longer any concern of yours."

"Assuming you're working on the premise that I'm safe away from here…"

"There's no reason for you to be involved."

"…you're wrong." he finished. "Someone tried to run me down."

"What?" Caroleigh gasped.

"A couple of days ago," he told her matter-of-factly. "Tried to take me out while I stood at the corner waiting for the light to change."

"You were the main fly in her ointment," Edward commented thoughtfully as Caroleigh gasped again. "You're the one that put everyone on alert."

"You're lying," Kari accused.

"What did the police say?" Caroleigh asked quickly.

Steven ignored Kari's accusation and told Caroleigh, "They'll look into it, but they pretty much chalked it up to either a drunk driver or random violence."

"After what happened here?"

"I didn't mention here. They asked if I had any enemies, I told them none that I knew of and left it at that."

Kari did an erratic shift. "It burnt down," she stated, putting Edward and Caroleigh at a temporary loss. Steven nodded. "The town was three or four times as big while the mines were opened. All the big homes, manor houses and mansions, either burnt down or were torn down after there was no one left who could afford to live in them."

"Except for Sinners Palace," Caroleigh told him, though she looked confused over why Kari had suddenly diverted the subject away from someone trying to kill Steven. "It was turned into a hotel with special accommodations." She accented the last with a suggestive wiggle of her eyebrows.

"It closed years ago. The county took it for back taxes and bulldozed it down as a public hazard," Kari said in preoccupation. She grew quiet and thoughtful while they continued to talk.

"Another fine piece of history lost," Edward quipped.

"It was where Dell and his mother lived," Caroleigh told him.

"Oh? And was she one of those special accommodations?"

"They say so."

"Wait a minute," Edward said in confusion, "if she wasn't his mother and Gladys was, how did she explain a baby?"

"She went away for a while and came back with an infant she claimed she had adopted. No one believed it and was sure he was her illegitimate son."

"Oh, my, what a life, a prostitute mother, what a stigma to put on a child."

"And make him hate," Steven said.

Kari settled something in her mind and rejoined the conversation. "At that time, it was probably more a way to rub it in William's face, with a threat of telling the truth if it was."

"Like he would care," Caroleigh snorted.

Steven told them what he had discovered. "Gladys and the Webber woman were both patients in the county charity ward at the same time. One gave birth to a healthy boy; the other had one that died in a couple of hours. It would have been easy to make a switch. Dell's mother of record never had a visible, stable source of income, but she always had enough to support them. Then there was his tuition appearing every year."

Edward grunted. "Did dear Gladys teach William or did William teach her?"

Kari shook her head. "Neither one needed lessons." She blew out a breath of frustration. "We don't know that Dell was her son or that she was behind it. There just isn't anyway she could benefit."

"Have you considered plain, old revenge?" Edward asked.

"She never did anything if she couldn't profit from it."

"How would she profit from attempting to run over Steven?"

"If anyone did."

Steven ignored her again without going into any details over how close he'd come to being hurled across an intersection and told Caroleigh and Edward, "Now you know why she's been trying to get rid of you."

"We aren't leaving," Caroleigh said firmly. She pointed a finger at Kari. "You're going to stop trying to make us leave and start leveling with us. What else do you know that you aren't telling, like where did that old key ring go?"

"I don't know where the damned keys went," Kari retorted in frustration and shot to her feet. "Grandpa lost the old ones years ago, and Dell never had the others that I saw."

"He didn't lock the doors?" Edward asked.

Steven asked, "There was someone else there?"

"Then who locked them?" came from Caroleigh.

"For all I know Grandpa did." Kari said in answer to all three. "I've got to call the dogs in."

After she disappeared out the back door, Edward's attempt at a laugh died in his throat. "I wish she wouldn't do that," he admitted. "I know she's putting us on or being sarcastic, but that ghost business still gives me the willies. That specter looked to me like he wanted to kill."

"If you had been locked out and left to bleed to death, wouldn't you want to kill someone?" Steven asked.

"They never knew he was there," Caroleigh argued.

"According to her, he was going there to kill," Edward pointed out.

"Who's Jamie?" Steven asked abruptly.

Caroleigh suddenly got busy. "I'd better get something started for dinner." She went to the cabinets and pulled out pans. "All this from scratch stuff takes time."

"You could just answer me. I'll find out eventually."

"Don't sound so mysterious. There isn't anything to find out. We probably just misunderstood what she said, the same way she misunderstood the question."

"Things were a bit muddled." Edward leaned back in his chair to watch them.

"Yes," Caroleigh agreed, "and she was confused."

Steven would not be put off. "She misunderstood what was said, but her answer wasn't confused. Who's Jamie?"

"Oh, all right." She popped the pan in her hand down with a thud. "But it doesn't mean anything. I think she thought the question was where was Gaylord. Jamie was one of her imaginary friends. He always stayed in the greenhouse." When Edward shivered, she added quickly, "I think it was just an association thing with the greenhouse and his name came out. She had so many things on her mind at once. It doesn't mean anything."

"What were the children's names?"

Caroleigh turned back to the cabinet. Puzzled, Edward asked, "What children?"

"Great Grandpa and Grandpa's."

Caroleigh snapped, "I don't know, I don't care, and I am not going to find out."

Chapter Nine

After dinner Steven was treated to a meeting with the dogs. That meant he was introduced to them as one who was supposed to be there, therefore, they shouldn't attack him. The smaller of the two, by no means a small dog, was called Fred. He was the one who had been with Kari when he arrived. He gave Steven a cursory sniff and wandered off to lie down and immediately closed his eyes. The larger, Sam, as big a shepherd as you're ever likely to see, gave Steven a more thorough examination and had to be ordered away. He took up a position at Kari's feet. He didn't lie down, and he did not take his eyes off Steven. Even with the coffee table between them he was only one leap away from Steven's throat, and Steven wasn't convinced that was not exactly what the dog wanted to do. The dog's attitude seemed to mirror Kari's. She had been backed into a corner and did not like it.

She didn't share information willingly and only did so after being badgered. "Dell hated computers," she finally told them. "He couldn't understand them and couldn't operate one. The dispatcher at the sheriff's office had to do anything that required a computer. Dell wrote all his reports by hand. She had to enter them. His receptionist at the clinic had to do it there. He could barely manage the fax machine."

"Common knowledge?" Edward asked.

"Both of them complained publicly over the additional work it made for them. He was no mechanic either. There's more than one story of something he messed up while trying to do something so simple a six year old could have done it. The only thing he was good at was memorizing. It took him through school, but he had no ability to apply what he memorized. No one in this area took their animals to him if they could help it for anything more basic than vaccinations."

"That mechanic bit makes you wonder when the brakes were supposed to have gone out," Edward observed.

Steven's thoughts were on something else and he said thoughtfully, "She probably gave him some excuse for moving the computer from the house in Denver."

"Are you carrying a gun?" Kari asked suddenly.

Steven looked at the dog. "Is that why he keeps watching me like that?"

"You should have told me." She got to her feet. "Don't move."

Steven didn't move. He didn't speak. She sat Rascal on the floor as she took her first step toward him. The large dog was right beside her, head lowered, eyes trained on Steven. The second dog, not as asleep as he seemed, got quickly to his feet.

"Just blink twice for yes. Shoulder holster?" He didn't blink. "Waist?" Steven blinked twice. She leaned down, hand on his stomach. His muscles contracted involuntarily, and Sam inched closer. "Easy," she warned.

She lowered herself slowly to one knee. While Steven held his breath, he watched her face just inches from his. She leaned in closer. Her hand went around his waist, followed the band of his pants to find the gun in the center of his back. She was nearly laying on him, a closeness that caused some vivid memories for Steven. She worked his jacket up to give her access to the pistol. When the safety strap snapped free Sam's hind legs twitched. The longer she was that close to Steven, the more nervous Sam became, and the closer Fred moved. She extracted the heavy automatic and leaned against Steven's chest to hold the weapon out to the dogs.

Edward whistled. "You don't mess around when it comes to weapons."

"Hush, Eddie," Caroleigh breathed in a terrified whisper.

Sam and Fred moved forward. Sam's eyes never left Steven's face while he sniffed the weapon. Fred gave a quick sniff and sat down to wait. Kari gripped Steven's forearm with her free hand, rolled his arm palm up, and put the gun in his hand. Steven suffered split second reluctance when she started his hand towards Sam's mouth, one armed with long canine teeth. Fred pushed Sam aside slightly, took his smell and left, no longer interested. Sam lingered. He smelled the gun, Steven's hand, and up Steven's arm.

Rascal, for whatever reason in his little dog brain, decided to be included. Just as Fred circled to lie back down and Sam was relaxing, he leaped into Steven's lap. Steven's reaction, understandable considering the tension, was to nearly jump out of the chair. Kari was as tense and jerked violently. Sam leaped forward, mouth open, and Fred started back towards them in a lunge.

Kari threw herself in front of Steven and over Rascal. "Stay!" she shouted. "Back."

Fred stopped where he was at the first command and went back to lie down. Sam stopped, a response attributed to his training, not because he did so willingly to judge from the way he looked. He gave every appearance of wanting to take a big hunk out of Steven and restrained himself only because of her command.

Kari modified her tone. "Go lay down, Sam. It's okay." He whined and fidgeted. "It's okay, baby." She patted Sam reassuringly on the shoulder. "Go lay down."

"Can't you put him somewhere?" Caroleigh pleaded. "You know how nervous he makes me."

"No." She stood and pulled Rascal away from his curious and energetic examination of Steven's hand and gun. "Put it away," she told Steven with a signal to Sam to back.

Sam backed two feet and waited for her. He was at her feet again when she sat back down in her chair.

"Rather unnerving, isn't it?" Edward asked with feigned lightness as Steven carefully returned the gun to its holster.

"That one is dangerous." Caroleigh was still frightened. "The other one does what she says when she says it, but that one—one of these days, Kari, you aren't going to be able to control him, and he's going to kill someone. He should be put down."

"No."

"That's a little harsh, Caro," Edward said in the dog's defense. "He's just missing Max. He'll settle in."

"He's dangerous. Everyone knows it."

"Everyone that matters," Kari stated coolly and got back to her feet. "I'm going to bed."

"We haven't finished talking," Caroleigh protested.

"Talk all you want. I'm going to bed," she said as she walked out, one dog in her arms and two following.

"She's still hiding something," Caroleigh said glumly.

"She got rid of all the farm animals?" Steven asked.

"All but a few chickens that run loose. She cancelled all the camps for the summer and all the bed and breakfast reservations."

"Why did you call her secretive?"

"Because she is, always has been. Little things usually that really don't mean much, but she hoards them like treasures. Why? Do you know what she's hiding?"

"I just wondered," he said evasively, then asked, "Is Canterbury still playing Mayberry?"

"Colombo in the sticks," Edward answered, "but you can bet they picked up on that computer business, and he hasn't said a word about it to us."

"He came out one day," Caroleigh said with a giggle. "She didn't have the gates in yet, but she had the warning signs up. He ignored them, drove right to the house and got out of his car."

"Never seen a man dive through a window and roll it up so fast," Edward finished for her. "Quite comical."

"He's not stupid though," Steven said seriously. "Cops like that have radar. They know when someone is lying."

"Which makes him keep looking and maybe actually come up with something useful."

"Or," Caroleigh said glumly, "as twisted as what they already came up with."

* * * *

"What the hell for?" Kari demanded furiously.

Steven, Caroleigh, and Edward continued to eat breakfast. They were deliberately nonchalant in anticipation of Kari's reaction to their plan.

"To draw her out, love," Edward answered. "Can you think of a better way?"

"Aside from making us all leave and taking her on alone?" Caroleigh asked.

"If there really was someone else, do you think they would be crazy enough to attempt to murder me during some trashy party at the Meadow?"

"Afterward while the dogs are still locked up to protect the guests. We'll even take the warning signs down so everyone knows," Caroleigh told her around a mouthful of bacon. "And with all those people coming and going, it would be the opportune time for her to hide, wait until everyone is gone, and then surprise us."

"No."

"Try some jam," Edward told Steven.

As a hint to get him to join in the conversation, it didn't work. Steven was deliberately staying quiet, hoping his silence would keep Kari's anger from turning on him. It didn't work.

"Is this your idea?" she accused.

"No," Steven answered briefly.

Caroleigh told her quickly," It was ours."

"Any excuse for a party, love." Edward threw his hands up protectively when she scowled at him. "Okay, look, love, you haven't been able to get rid of us, and it's made you nervous. The more nervous you've gotten, the more security you've put in. That's going to make her more cautious, plan more, and drag things out longer."

"Not really," she answered indifferently.

"Meaning?" Caroleigh asked tersely.

Steven answered. "One power pole."

"You're quick." Kari's tone bit. "I will give you that."

He ignored the sarcasm. "What are you using for backup?"

Caroleigh exploded at being ignored for so long. "You are just about to really piss me off! You think I'm so stupid and such a coward I couldn't possibly contribute anything. All you want to do is ship me off and get rid of me." She shot to her feet. Her hands slammed down on the table. "I am not going to let you do it, Kari Anne O'Keefe. She nearly got us all killed. We have as much right to go after her as you do, and despite what you think, you are not the only one smart enough, brave enough, or strong enough to do it. Quit the crap. Admit you think it's Gladys and that she's after you."

She finished leaning well over the table and out of breath. The other two held their breath waiting for Kari's reaction. Only Rascal moved. He stood with his front paws on Kari's leg, uncertain and frightened by the angry voice. When he scratched at her leg, Kari pulled him up into her arms.

In exasperation, Caroleigh asked, "Did you even understand what I said?"

"Enough," Kari said quietly and slowly stroked Rascal's head. "I have battery back-ups and a generator in the basement. They're on a trigger. If the power goes off, they come on."

"How will you know if it goes off when you aren't in the house?" Steven asked.

"High frequency alarm. The dogs are trained to find and alert me. I also carry a beeper that goes off the same way. It alerts me if there's anyone at the gate too."

Steven drew in a deep breath to steel himself and asked, "How many of the buildings have tunnels?"

"Tunnels?" Caroleigh and Edward asked together.

Resentment flashed in Kari's eyes before she sighed in defeat. "Nearly all of them." She stood still stroking Rascal's head and moved to the basement door. "I'll show you."

Following her, Caroleigh was the first to react to what they saw. "How the hell did you get all of this in here?" Caroleigh exclaimed.

She referred to a bank of six monitors. Four showed the outside from each corner of the house. One displayed the area between the house and barn. The last was mounted on the greenhouse, aimed back towards the house.

"I brought them in, in food and furniture boxes."

Caroleigh twisted to look at her. "Long before we came out here," she accused.

"This looks to be quality goods, love," Edward observed. "Did your detectives round all this up for you that fast? Must be bloody good. Did they install it too?"

"I installed it after you got here."

Caroleigh retorted, "You went out the front door and back in here through tunnels you've never told me about?"

Edward leaned down to study the monitors. "Can you change the angles?"

"One through four are at fixed angles. You can adjust five and six manually for up to a ninety percent arch."

"What's their range?"

"They aren't wireless."

"Tunnels again?" Caroleigh asked.

"All right," Kari cried in exasperation. "I didn't know about them until a couple of years ago, and you weren't talking to me. Remember?"

"What was wrong with telling me when you were sneaking down here to do all this?"

"I wanted you to go away. Damn it, Caroleigh you were happy for the first time in your life. I didn't want to take that away from you. She's a vicious bitch, and I don't want you hurt or killed."

"We're staying."

"I got that."

"Okay." After a couple of deep breaths, Caroleigh's voice dropped an octave. "Now show us how to work all this crap."

The two men began to relax only to tense back up when Kari turned on Steven.

"Did you take that cast off yourself?"

"No, I didn't. The doctor did."

"A.M.A?"

"I don't know what that means."

"Against medical advice. Did you pressure them into taking it off too soon?"

"Yeah," he returned sarcastically. "I wanted to be in running condition."

"If that bone has not properly—"

"It has." He held his hand up to stop her next question. "They x-rayed it, took the cast off and started me on physical therapy. The cane is just for show to give me an edge if I need it. The leg is fine."

Her eyes shifted to Edward. "And you've been faking weakness as an excuse to stay here?"

"Yes, love," he admitted freely.

"Good. I was beginning to wonder if you were a pussy." She left him with his mouth gaped open and unlatched a section of the wall. A dark tunnel lay behind it. "I still think a party is a stupid idea."

The tunnels, more products of Great Grandpa's advanced age and an example of how eccentric he had gotten, were actually one tunnel dug in a circle with a tail that led to a shaft of the mine. From that circle short spokes went to the barn, bunkhouse, and greenhouse, all accessed by a vertical shaft with a ladder and trapdoor hidden by some inconspicuous feature in the interior of the building. The house and mansion were the only buildings with a basement to have a door hidden in a wall. Not only did Kari give them a tour and instructions on getting in and out of the entrances, she revealed another secret that infuriated Caroleigh again.

Kari tried to calm her down. "They aren't secret passages, per say, they're utility and plumbing access. DeBain knew electricity and phones would spread to even remote areas like this and designed the house to make installation easier," she explained patiently.

"That's how you got in the basement the first time," Edward exclaimed. "You went straight down from the bedroom he locked you in."

She shook her head. "I did climb down from the bedroom because I didn't know where he was, but once was enough for me. I went in that way the second time. I didn't mention them because of the way Eden was acting."

"And you didn't want to share your little secret," Caroleigh retorted.

"So you can get in every room in the house?" Steven asked.

"Pretty much. They go into all the bathrooms, and if you squeeze, there's a space enough between the main walls."

"And out, which was the most important to us," Edward pointed out.

"Who else knows about them?" Steven asked singled-mindedly.

"Probably no one. Great Grandpa put in the original electric and phone. Grandpa did all the up-grading."

"Because they wanted to, or to keep them a secret?" Steven asked.

"Both probably. Neither of them ever wanted to pay money to someone to do something they could do themselves. I don't know about Great Gramps, but Grandpa was bored too. He was always puttering around those passages and the mine." She gave a rueful laugh. "And the tunnels. They're all maintained better than I expected."

"And he kept all of it a secret?" Steven mused thoughtfully.

"Like someone else I know," Caroleigh grumbled.

Edward, in response to the puzzled look on Steven's face, told him, "You've heard the old adage a rich man is eccentric; a poor man is crazy, haven't you?"

"I'm neither," Kari stated.

"No, but you always liked keeping your little secrets," Caroleigh said pettishly.

Temper snapping, Kari countered. "Are you going to talk to me about secrets?"

Suddenly embarrassed, Caroleigh returned defensively, "There are some things other people don't need to know about how much money I actually have."

"Point made," Kari retorted. "They kept it secret for three generations. I felt like I should too."

Caroleigh waved her hand at the tunnel surrounding them. "Are you sure you trust me now?"

"For myself, I feel quite honored," Edward quipped lightly. "You, Steven?"

Steven shook disbelief off to answer. "Very privileged, I think."

"Something bothering you about all this?" he asked.

"Yeah," Steven admitted. "I just don't understand the reasoning behind something so extensive and extreme."

"Ours is not to reason why, but to make use of it. How are we going to do that?"

Kari jumped suddenly to grab for her waist. "It vibrates," she explained of the beeper she pulled from under her shirt. "Startles the hell out of me." She looked at the message window. "Someone's at the gate."

* * * *

Safe inside his car, Canterbury asked coolly, "Catch you at a bad time?"

Kari answered. "With you anytime's a bad time."

"Just trying to round up the dogs," Edward said easily despite the dash they had made to get back to the house and the time it had taken him to catch his breath. "Seems they wandered too far to hear."

"If you'd answered the call button, you'd have known where they were." Canterbury tried not to show how irritated he was over the wait and didn't succeed very well. The dogs, who had followed him from the gate to the house, still circled his car.

"Still having trouble with that thing?" Caroleigh asked Edward sweetly.

"Evidently," he answered just as glibly.

Canterbury wasn't buying their act. "If you didn't know who it was, why did you open the gate?" he asked hatefully.

"I did," Kari answered. She signaled the dogs to leave. "What do you want?"

"Right to the point."

"It isn't like we haven't already been over this multiple times."

"Not this time. I came to talk to him." Canterbury pointed at Steven.

"Why?" Steven asked on guard instantly.

"We could talk a little easier if I could get out." He pointed to where Sam lurked at the corner of the house.

Kari didn't need to look to say, "He doesn't trust you."

She didn't explain it was the gun he carried or how she could get the traumatized dog to accept an individual carrying one the way she had with Steven. She walked over to the corner and held Sam by the collar.

"A personality thing?" Edward asked.

"Very funny," Canterbury grumbled. "This is official business. I'm making a courtesy call for the Denver police."

"What do they want?" Steven asked.

"Why did you leave?

"No one told me not to."

"You best come on in." Edward interrupted. "Before either of them changes their mind."

Canterbury mumbled something under his breath and moved quickly from the car to the foyer. The others followed.

"I don't believe he has a sense of humor," Edward quipped dryly.

"I don't," Canterbury retorted, "when someone threatens me with a hundred pound dog."

"No one threatened you," Steven told him. "What do you want to see me for?"

Canterbury very pointedly looked at Caroleigh, Edward, and then Kari as she came in. "You don't mind discussing private matters in public?"

"Oh, dear, another character smear," Edward said in sing-song.

"Not at all," Canterbury responded with mock cheerfulness. "I'm not about to chance getting shoved out the door the way she did Maxwell when he told her something she didn't want to hear. Although I have to admit, I admire your tenacity." He spoke directly to Steven. "You didn't let a couple of deaths and attempted murders quell your pursuit of a lucrative business deal. Or are you going to pretend you don't know she has the authority to do anything she wants with the place?"

"I'm aware of it," Steven answered coolly.

"We could draw straws," Edward whispered, "to see who gets to shove."

"You did say," Kari pointed out tersely to Canterbury, "a character smear isn't what you're here for."

"Fine." He took a folded sheet of paper from his pocket and told Steven, "The Denver police are really funny about things like attempted murder. They tend to take it pretty serious."

Steven's response was a tart, "They never told me that was what they thought it was."

"Maybe because you didn't tell them about the last couple of times someone tried to kill you."

"Do you see some kind of connection?"

"Money," Canterbury said. He shook the paper open. "Lots of money. Do you recognize any of these names of Mercedes owners?"

Steven took the paper with Caroleigh moving to one side and Edward to the other, shamelessly looking over his shoulder.

Edward whistled. "Lots of money. There's Babs and Aaron and Old General Philips," he read and pointed.

"I didn't ask if you knew them," Canterbury told him and asked Steven, "Do you know any of them?"

"Honey," Caroleigh cooed, "Everyone knows these people."

Canterbury tried to drill Steven with his eyes. "Personally?"

"I did a job for the Benson-Hyatt Company and briefly met the Wethertons," Steven told him with little interest.

"Matthew and Elizabeth." Edward leaned around Steven to explain to Caroleigh. "They incorporated. They turned the old family home into a-ah, what do you call that, old boy?"

"Theme hotel and resort," Steven answered.

"Ah, yes, doing quite well, I hear."

"The one in Leadville?" Kari asked.

"No, love, the big one in Denver."

"They don't live there anymore?"

"They kept one wing, I believe."

"The west wing," Steven told her.

Canterbury couldn't stand it anymore. "I don't believe you people. You treat everything like it was a joke and lie through your teeth to anyone trying to help you."

"In just what way are you trying to help?" Kari asked.

"Someone tried to kill you."

"Or?" she challenged.

"There is no 'or.' If you hadn't stayed out of his reach, he'd have killed all four of you. Look, I know Eden came down pretty hard on you, but something didn't smell right. Still doesn't, especially now, weeks later and a Mercedes—a Mercedes for Christ's sake—tries to run him down. He comes running up here. You've barricaded yourselves in with electric gates and guard dogs. I don't see any weapons, but he…" He pointed at Steven. "…got a concealed permit right after it happened and he…," He pointed to Edward, "…has had one for years. I'm willing to bet one or both of you are carrying. You're scared. I don't care what you're lying about, I want to help."

"That was quite a speech," Edward drawled.

"You ass," he retorted as he turned for the door.

"Sam's out there," Kari said quietly.

He stopped with his hand on the knob, back to them. His head hung in defeat. "Is there a magic word to get out?"

Kari looked at Steven. He repeated Canterbury's question.

"Please would work," she answered.

He turned to face her. "Please," he said clearly.

"Why did you start by attacking Steven?"

"Two separate issues."

"When I pushed Max out the door I told him I wouldn't allow him to make me distrust the people I care about. I won't you either."

He looked like he wanted to argue. He didn't. "I'll remember that," he said instead.

"We're sure Caroleigh, Edward, and Steven got caught up in something aimed at me. The only person Caroleigh and I can think of that could be capable of such a thing is our ex-stepmother. Find her and you may find some answers."

"The people you hired couldn't find her?"

Kari showed no surprise over his knowledge of the private detectives. "No. She dropped out of sight after Jonathan, her husband, and Caroleigh's father, died. That was in Europe six years ago."

His eyes flickered back and forth between Caroleigh and Kari. "Motive?"

"Revenge is the only thing we can think of. She wanted the Meadow. When she married my father she thought she would get it. My grandfather blocked her. It was his home and his money. He wouldn't let her have any of it, especially after my father died. They had a vicious fight the day of the funeral, and she made a lot of threats."

"Then she moved on to my father," Caroleigh told him bitterly. "He gave her anything she wanted, but he didn't have that much of a fortune left. They were down to selling everything a piece at a time to maintain their standard of living. I've also heard stories of them being mixed up in some pretty shady dealings to keep them going."

"How do you maintain your way of life?" Canterbury asked, obviously bracing for a belligerent response.

"He already knows," Edward told her out of the side of his mouth.

Kari didn't seem to hear Edward, saying, "The last time Jonathan came to Grandpa to sell off a portion of his shares of the Glory, Grandpa would only agree if Jonathan used part of the money and the remaining shares to set up a trust for her. Jonathan took the money and left it up to Grandpa to set up the trust. He did, adding some of his shares and more cash. Her mother left her a small trust also. Anything else you want to know?"

"There's more I would like to know," Caroleigh said faintly. "How much did Grandpa add?"

"Thirty percent of the mine and five hundred thousand in cash."

"And all this time, I thought daddy dear had done one decent thing in his life. Fooled again." Her eyes filled with tears, rapidly spilling down her cheeks, and her hand groped for Kari's. "I was awful to Grandpa, Kay-Kay, and he did so much for me."

"You weren't awful."

"I was," she wailed. "I told him I didn't care what he did with his money or his house."

"Did you?"

"No, but I was hateful."

"You were just being yourself. He knew you're a bitch."

"She has a point there, my love." Edward patted her clumsily on the back. "You've always been a bitch."

"I have," she agreed and wailed even louder.

"There, there." Edward turned her to his chest and encircled her with his arms. "We love you anyway."

"I know." With one last wail, she subsided into noisy weeping.

"The stress," Edward told Canterbury.

He nodded a couple of times before he was able to finally pull his eyes away from Caroleigh. "If you will walk me out," he told Kari, "I'll get on this."

As soon as the door closed, Caroleigh pushed away from Edward. She sniffed once and wiped a little moisture from her eyes.

"I missed the signal," Steven said in wonder.

"So did I," Edward admitted, "but I know when my Caro is performing."

"She'd already told me that," she said in way of explanation, which explained nothing to the two men.

"So why did you make such an issue of it?" Steven asked.

"Because what Grandpa did was none of his business. She started it to distract him."

"From what?" Edward asked.

"Asking more questions, silly."

"Please," Edward said to Steven, "tell me you did not understand that."

"I think I did," he said with a weak smile. "I know one thing, if they get together and don't want us to know something, we're lost."

* * * *

Caroleigh let out an exaggerated sigh as she hung up the phone. "I can't believe we're actually pulling this together."

"I can't believe I let you talk me into trying." Kari grumbled from the table littered with mail. "Three more replies. The Gillermans will be here, Agnes Pippin, and Evelyn."

"Really?" Caroleigh said in surprise. "I never expected Evelyn to come back. Still she is quite the little social climber. As for the others, just late enough to let us know they had to really consider whether they should accept an invitation for such a tacky occasion."

"I think I'll call and tell them they waited too long, and their attendance is no longer desired."

"That would be an out and out lie." She glanced around as Emily entered the kitchen and nodded in greeting. "We never desired their attendance, just their presents."

Emily ducked her head and smiled shyly on her way to the refrigerator.

"Agnes," Caroleigh continued, "is such an old tight-wad we'll probably get the towels she got from her grandkids for Christmas."

"It's the thought that counts," Kari returned with a straight face.

"Of course it is," Caroleigh agreed just as they both burst out laughing.

Kari recovered first. "This is the last. The caterers said they can't add anymore after nine in the morning."

"How many haven't answered?"

"All but ten invitations, sixteen people."

"Helen Vanderman called, really to brag about some royalty she's picked up, but she did say the Kendersons and Chapels are abroad and Phoebe Casserman, remember her?" Kari shook her head. "Used to be Warren-Smyth, buck toothed—"

Kari stopped her rambling."Is she coming?"

"No. She said she never attends a reception for a wedding that in all probability never took place."

"Were you going somewhere with this when you started?" Kari asked.

"Just add five extras. That should cover any late entries. I swear you're getting snippier every day."

"And you're getting giddier."

"I think she's just nervous," Emily said timidly.

"She loves parties," Kari told her. "Don't let her fool you into thinking otherwise."

"I like the presents," Caroleigh teased before she took off on another tangent. "Are you fixing lunch? Is it that late already?" She pushed up and started out. "Emily have I told you how grateful we are that you agreed to come back?"

Her voice trailed off, hurrying out the door, and Kari leaned forward, rubbing her temples with her fingertips. "We do appreciate you coming to help, especially on such short notice."

"There's so little to do in the apartment when she isn't there, and as long as I didn't have to go back to that other place, I was happy to come. It is so pretty here. Her apartment is-oh, no!"

"What?"

"I wasn't supposed to tell you she has one. Now she will be mad at me."

"I won't tell her you slipped." She didn’t add she already knew about the apartment Caroleigh kept secretly despite the times she had claimed she had no funds for a hotel as an excuse to stay at the Meadows.

"Oh, thank you. It is so very hard to remember all the things she tells me not to tell people. I don't know how she keeps all those lies straight and some of them I just don't understand at all. It was so kind of you to forgive her for…for…for…" She stammered to a horrified stop.

Kari waved it away. "We had some things to settle. We did."

"That's so nice. Sisters should be friends, and I'm sure she never meant all those things she threatened the times she was-well-you know, drinking. People always say mean things when they're drinking that they would never actually do. It just seemed so strange when someone did do them. Was he really your brother?"

"No," Kari answered quietly, her fingertips still pressing at her temples.

"He just thought he was?"

"He was a complete psycho," she retorted. She got up to her feet. "And he was not an O’Keefe. He was too stupid."

* * * *

"Is it my imagination or does Kari seem preoccupied, distant, and withdrawn again?” Edward asked, keeping his voice low to avoid being overheard by Emily in the kitchen.

"I don't know what's happened," Caroleigh said miserably. "She was fine before lunch. Now she's as bad as she was before Steven got here."

They lapsed into a silence when Emily walked in. "Emily," Edward asked lazily as she sat a tray of coffee on the low table, "did you happen to notice if something upset Kari today?"

"I'm afraid I did. I just talk too much sometimes, and I don't think. I'm afraid I made her mad."

"What did you say?" Caroleigh asked.

"I asked if that horrible man was her brother. I had heard that, and it seemed so awful, a brother trying to kill his own sister. I should have thought of how she would feel bad about something like that."

"Emily," Edward asked patiently, "what did she say?"

"She said he was crazy and too stupid to be her brother, but it was in an angry voice, and she slammed the door. She was awfully quiet at dinner. Should I apologize?"

"No," Caroleigh told her quickly. "Leave her alone."

"I'm so sorry. Should I leave? I can call Vern."

"It isn't that serious. Just finish up in the kitchen and go to bed."

Before she could leave, Steven asked, "Was there a phone call or did someone come by that we didn't see?"

"No, sir, none that I know of." She fidgeted, and her chin quivered. "I really did do something wrong. I'm so sorry."

"No, it's fine," Edward assured her. "And we're fine. You go on now." Once she had gone, he whispered, "Maybe it was a mistake bringing her here."

"We needed the help, and I can't believe that is what's wrong," Caroleigh said.

"She has gotten to be quite a chatter box, a bit trying on the nerves."

"Maybe it's just a case of nerves," she said hopefully, "and nothing else is wrong."

"Should we call this whole thing off?" Edward asked.

"Maybe we should," Caroleigh said anxiously. "Do we even know what we're doing?"

"No," Steven answered. "We don't know what we're doing."

"What should we do instead?" Edward asked.

"I don't know." Caroleigh sank against Edward. "I'm just too tired to think."

Edward kissed her lightly on the head. "Go on to bed, my love. I'll just finish my coffee and join you."

They exchanged kisses. She and Steven told each other good night, and the room fell into silence after she left. A cup and saucer rattled as Edward took them from the tray and held them in Steven's direction. He kept them when Steven shook his head, but stared at the cup instead of drinking.

"This has got to be bloody hell on you," Edward commented to break the silence. "Not one kind word in two weeks unless you want to count what she said to Canterbury. You were the one he attacked so it would be safe to assume she was including you in those she cared about." Steven made no comment. Edward continued uncomfortably. "Pretty slender thread, though I held to one as slim for much longer."

Steven still made no comment. He gazed at Edward with a closed face. It prompted Edward to sit the cup down and lean forward with his elbows on his knees.

"Caro's pretty good at adding two and two, tunnels, greenhouse, you there, no sign of Kari.

"She saved my life that night."

"But she kept it a secret. They hadn't really spoken to each other for nearly five years, but Caro still knows her better than anyone. She says if saving your life was all it had been, Kari wouldn't have hid it. She also says Kari has never been casual about 'it', not in talking about it or doing it. That particular thing she only does from her heart. In less kind moments, Caro compared her to a frigid nun." Still met with silence, he added, "I'm not trying to pry."

"I know. There are just some things I don't talk about."

"I understand, private feelings and all that, but Caro is concerned that you might be so put off by the way Kari is behaving that you believe that garbage about it only being a fling for her. Kari doesn't believe in flings, Steven. Caro wanted you to know that, but she wasn't sure how you would take to her attempting to talk to you."

"I appreciate the thought."

Edward didn't press any further. To close the awkward conversation he said, "The O'Keefe blood breeds them stubborn and proud, but they're worth the wait. Now, if you will excuse me."

He made a quick exit and didn't slow until he reached their bedroom door. Caroleigh, who waited anxiously for him, opened it and pulled him in.

"Well?"

"Please do not ever insist I do that again, my love. It was quite uncomfortable."

"What did he say?"

"Apart from telling me very politely to mind my own business, nothing."

"He said something, Eddie. He had to have."

"He said, quote, 'She saved my life that night', unquote, and quote, 'There are just some things I don't talk about,' unquote."

"I knew it."

"I'm certainly glad you do," he said and unbuttoned his shirt.

"He loves her."

"Caro, he…"

"All you have to do is see the way he looks at her when he thinks no one is looking. He loves her, and she loves him."

"And you know this by the looks she gives him?" he queried lightly.

"I know," she said evasively.

"Has she said something to you?"

"That would be confidential."

He shook his head in wonder. "Let me get the ground rules straight. Anything you can surmise on your own or see, is okay to discuss and pass on, but anything she tells you is private?"

"I can't break a confidence, Eddie," she said apologetically.

"I'm not asking you to, my love. I just need to understand when I am or am not trespassing."

"She loves him," she insisted.

"Well, my love, I have done what you asked of me in an effort to repair whatever breach there is between them, but no more. Men have rules too you know. When one tells you he doesn't talk about it, you don't talk about it."

Caroleigh chewed the end of her finger, deep in thought.

"Caro, you look as if you're plotting."

"No," she said with a sigh. "I was just thinking it took you being nearly killed to make me admit how much I loved you. Let's hope it doesn't take that much for them."

Chapter Ten

Canterbury had to track Kari down at the Meadow. He started at the ranch, but didn't get any further without Caroleigh right behind him. Edward and Steven would have been as well, had they not been gone on a trip into town. Caroleigh was still right with them when Kari led Canterbury to the library and shut the door.

"Just as well tell you both at the same time." He took a notebook from his pocket. "I've got some information on the step-mother."

"You found her?" Caroleigh asked in a mixture of dread and excitement.

"I found where she's buried. From what I've heard of her being buried as an unknown in a pauper's grave seems like poetic justice."

"You're sure it's her?" Kari asked.

"The police over there are. None of your people found her because the gendarmes didn't know her by that name. One in particular recognized the pictures though from a time they were looking very hard for both husband and wife, under different names. They were hard on her heels when she missed a curve and went over a cliff. I'm not very good with French." He tore a sheet loose. "This is where she's buried."

"Why were they using different names?" Kari asked, making no move to take the paper.

"They had run a pretty cruel scam on a family over there and were on the run with the money they got."

"What kind of scam?"

"The family had lost a child in a kidnapping years before. They had paid the ransom, but never received the child back. These two showed up with a video of a young woman of the right age, along with some documentation, claiming it was the daughter. Before the police could prove the papers were forged, the desperate family had forked over a small fortune, supposedly for bribes and legal fees to get the girl back. What the officer who recognized those pictures really remembers is what it did to the family. The father killed himself, and the mother had a complete breakdown. She locked herself in the daughter's room until the servants finally called the police for help. When they broke down the door, she had hacked off all her hair with broken glass, cutting herself up with it. He says it's a sight he will carry with him to his grave."

Caroleigh shivered. "And have nightmares over. God, they were evil."

"The world won't miss them." He waved the slip of paper. Neither of them took it.

"We won't be sending flowers," Kari said coldly.

"I didn't think so, but I thought you might feel easier knowing where she is."

Caroleigh was struck with a new thought. "Kari, if it wasn't her, who was it?"

"No one," Canterbury told her. "We've investigated every angle we could think of. We can't find anything to prove anyone else was involved. We're closing the case."

"But-but..." Caroleigh stammered in confusion, "you said...what about the-the keys and the projector, and...and..."

"We did find the deadbolt keys in the debris. As for the projector he must have tossed it into one of those canyons either going to or coming from the ranch. The other keys had been lost for years. He didn't need them to get back in anyway with the deadbolt key to the apartment."

"You're saying you don't suspect any of us of anything anymore?" Kari asked.

"Just Steven Chase. I still think he's a self-serving opportunist. Be mad if you want, but I had a talk with his associate. The resort idea is not a dead issue. He's ingratiating himself, taking advantage of what's happened to con you into developing with him as a partner. He won't even have to come up with the money to buy the place that way. He's so sure of himself he even put his house up for sale."

"I don't believe that," Caroleigh said.

"Say that last again," Kari said quietly.

He repeated it and added, "He's never discussed you or expressed any special feelings for you with his friend and partner."

"You're right, I'm mad again."

"Mercedes aren't that common," Canterbury went on with, "but the police can't find any trace of the one that was supposed to have tried to run him down."

"You're done."

"He had a team of the best lawyers in town go over that..."

Kari didn't say anything more. She walked out.

He turned to Caroleigh. "He's going to hurt her."

"Because of assholes like you she won't let anyone close enough to hurt her," she retorted, but there was worry in her eyes as she went after Kari.

* * * *

Kari didn't join them for lunch. At dinner she was withdrawn. She made no effort to listen to their conversation or join in. She didn't talk at all until after Emily had served desert and left the kitchen. Then she gave up all her pretenses. She stood, scooped Rascal up in her arms and backed a few feet from the table. "I'm staying at the Meadow tonight. After the party I want you to pack up and leave by the next morning." She looked directly at Steven. "You can leave anytime."

"What? Why?" Caroleigh cried.

"I don't care anymore who did what or might do or why. I just want you all to go away and leave me alone. I mean it," Kari added when Caroleigh started to protest. "You can hold your grudges and plot to get your revenge and he can help you." The last was directed at Edward. The next went to Steven. "You can scheme for all the business deals you want, but not here, not with me."

Kari almost hit Emily with the kitchen door when she swung it open. Caroleigh followed her. Edward followed Caroleigh. All three rushed by a stunned Emily.

"Kari, Kari, wait," Caroleigh pleaded.

Steven stayed at the table and cringed when Caroleigh screamed, "She set the dog on me."

Edward's voice was lower. "She only put him in front of the door."

"She set the dog on me," she sobbed hysterically.

Emily eased into the kitchen. "She really is strange," she said in a stunned whisper.

Steven got to his feet. "I won't be here for breakfast."

"Aren't you going to stay for the party? There's going to be a lot of rich women."

For just a moment, Steven felt like he was going to explode.

Cowering, Emily said in a whimper, "I didn't mean anything."

"I think you did," he said in controlled anger. "I don't think you're nearly as simple as you pretend."

Her eyes filled with tears as she stared at him. "I didn't do anything for you to be mean to me. You're just mad because she kicked you out."

"And you," he reminded her.

* * * *

"Oh, my, you clean up nice," Caroleigh said in a weak attempt at humor.

Steven's mood was foul, and he made no effort to hide it. He had packed and nearly been to the door before he gave in to Edward's pleas to stay, at least through the party.

"You've seen me in a suit before," he grumbled.

"You need to put on your happy face to go with it," Edward teased.

"I'm not very good at acting."

"Oh, he's right," Caroleigh moaned. "I can't do this. We don't even have a reason anymore. It was for nothing. All of it."

"These people are coming here to help us celebrate our wedding. Please don't tell me you think that's nothing."

"Oh, Eddie." She leaned against him as Emily came in with Caroleigh's lace shawl. "How can she believe all those things?"

"Hush, my love," he warned.

"You look very pretty," Emily told her shyly.

Caroleigh straightened. "Thank you," she said briskly. She took the shawl and gave it a flamboyant swirl to settle it on her shoulders. "Let's go dazzle them."

"That's my girl," Edward said proudly.

"Ah," Emily began timidly. "I just wanted to ask, if it's okay, if no one would mind, would it be okay if I went for a little walk? Miss O'Keefe did say she was going to put those dreadful dogs up."

"She took all three of the dogs over to Max's this morning," Caroleigh told her. "You'll be perfectly safe until morning, but don't go into the woods. It's too easy to get lost."

* * * *

Edward, Caroleigh, and Kari formed the reception line, in that order. Steven absolutely refused to be a part of it. He moved off a short distance to watch and listen with his features set. Two of the three wore brilliant smiles for their guest. The men shook hands and the women embraced. All offered their congratulations to the newlyweds and eyed a somber Kari speculatively. Over and over Kari was introduced as their hostess. Over and over she was told they had met before. One heavily jeweled matron was tactless, cruel, or truthful, depending on your point of view when she added “before your illness.” Edward deftly ended the conversation telling the lady they would reminisce when there weren't people waiting. Evelyn came next, haughty and stiff. Of all the elegantly dressed men and woman there was only one Caroleigh was genuinely happy to see, the second to the last in line. The elderly lady seemed equally sincere in her warm wishes.

"Helene, I'm so happy you could come.” She turned to the woman beside her. “And is this your—” Caroleigh broke off with her hand to her mouth as she quickly turned to Edward with the color gone out of her face.

"Caroleigh, you look positively ill. Are you expecting already?"

"Helene," Edward pleaded, but his arm went around Caroleigh in concern.

"I'm…I'm okay," Caroleigh murmured and straightened. She smiled weakly. "It's…it's just…just…fatigue and excitment."

“Stress,” Edward agreed in concern. “The last few weeks have been hectic.”

While Caroliegh gave him an agreeing smile and grateful hug, Helene laughed in delight. "Don't worry, honey," she whispered loudly, "we all understand how so many first babies are premature."

Caroleigh leaned close and whispered something that made the little lady laugh again and nod sagely.

Helene patted her lovingly on the shoulder. “It will pass more quickly than you know,” she told her then changed subjects. "And this is our Kari, all grown up. What a lovely young lady you've become."

"Thank you," Kari murmured woodenly.

Helene tipped her head. She looked at her quizzically first, then Caroleigh. "We've always said the two of you looked enough a like to be sisters, but now that you're older, the resemblance is amazing. If not for your coloring, you could almost be twins."

Caroleigh had recovered quickly. She slipped her arm around Kari's waist and gave her stiff body a jerk to bring her to her side. "Almost as if we had the same father?"

"How could that be?” Helene asked in heightened interest.

Caroleigh flipped her eyebrows suggestively. "And who is this?"

With a short chuckle, Helene turned to the petite, elegantly dressed, silver-haired woman with her. She held her hand out motioning her closer. "I consider it my honor to introduce the Mar—"

"Gabriella, please," the lady pleaded in a heavy, French accent. "There is no need of antiqued titles."

"How gracious of you," Edward commented drolly. He took the hand she extended, in a position to be kissed. With a mischievous smile, he turned it slightly and gave it a slight shake. "How are you enjoying the crude ways of the Americans?"

Her laughter was the sound of tinkling glass. "I find many of the men to be outrageous rouges. I am very pleased to meet you, sir."

"Edward, by all means."

Kari walked away.

"Is she not much better?" Helene asked solicitously.

Caroleigh answered. "She doesn't mean to be rude, Helene. She doesn't hear well since that awful fever. It's very difficult for her to mingle with it isolating her so badly." She slipped her arm around her friend's waist. "She does read lips though. If you remember to…"

Edward gallantly offered Gabriella his arm to follow. It was Steven's turn to stiffen as they approached him.

"This is our friend, Steven Chase," Caroleigh said as introduction.

Helene eyes lit with curiosity."Mr. Chase or may I call you Steven?"

"Steven is fine, ma'am."

"Only if it's Helene, not ma'am." She looked him over from head to toe. "The stories have not been exaggerated. You are a handsome devil. If I were younger, I would give a go at getting through that cold reserve all the young girls complain of. Have you recovered from that nasty business?"

The last was asked with her eyes on his cane, but he was saved any kind of answer.

Caroleigh interceded. "Please, Helene, don't start talking about it. It upsets me too much."

"I shouldn't wonder." She touched her on the arm with compassion. "I won't say another word, but I doubt everyone in this room will be so considerate. You won't be able to shut them up quite so politely."

Edward drew Caroleigh up against him. "That's why I'm here. I excel at being rude."

* * * *

"For a high society, let's get all the dirt we can, it wasn't bad." Edward slid down into the deep cushions of the couch and propped his feet on the coffee table.

Caroleigh dropped her last shoe to the floor and cuddled up against him. "I'll have to start writing thank you notes tomorrow."

"Ah, yes, thank you, Joan, for the insipid gift."

"Not all of Joan's gifts are insipid."

"Yes, they are."

Steven sat in one of the chairs. His tie was loosened, but he was nearly rigid, legs crossed, and palms flat on each chair arm. "Just what does someone get someone who has everything?" he asked.

"Really, Steven, your temper has nothing to do with gifts," Caroleigh retorted. "You should have decked him, rather than taking your ill humor out on us."

"Would decking one of your guests have been proper?"

"Canterbury was not invited. We told you that. What did he say to you?"

"It doesn't matter." He pushed up out of the chair. "Just tell her she succeeded. I'm leaving."

"Oh," Emily said softly from behind him, "I don't think so."

She stood just inside the entrance from the hall. She was dressed in a bright pink running suit and had a large canvas bag in one hand. The other hand was behind her back.

"Emily?" Caroleigh questioned in puzzlement. "Are you going somewhere?"

"Not at the moment. Neither are any of you." Her hand came out. The automatic pistol was big, black, and ugly with the clip curled beneath her small hand.

"Good Lord, girl," Edward straightened with a jerk and would have gone straight to his feet if not for Caroleigh's hand clenched in his shirt front.

"I knew you weren't that simple," Steven said calmly.

"Yes, something you shouldn't have said and an observation you will pay for along with a few others things. We are not going to take the chance you saw something that would come back on us although you were so totally predictable. Dodge a little car and you came running back up here, right where we wanted you." She chuckled joyfully. "And you were so easy to divide and conquer."

"Emily and Dell?" Caroleigh asked incredulously.

"You're the one I saw just before Dell hit me," Steven said.

"I don't know who you saw. I was miles away establishing an alibi with that gullible, country trash and that snotty bitch." She sneered nastily. "No, we left it for that idiot to do on his own. Even after we prepared everything for him he botched it. He damn near killed me with his spur of the moment attempt to get rid of the pickup when the fire failed."

"I wondered about that," Edward mumbled.

"I'm sure you've wondered about a lot of things. If it's any consolation you would not have been involved at all if Dell had just done what he was told in the right order."

"I say, old boy…" Edward tipped forward to look around Caroleigh at Steven. "…any chance the safety is on?"

"No," Caroleigh cried and threw herself to cling to Edward with both hands.

"I can shoot all three of you with one squeeze of the trigger," Emily warned coldly. She jerked the barrel of the gun at Steven to move to sit beside Caroleigh.

Steven didn't move at all, except for the nerve that jumped in his clenched jaw.

"Steven, please," Caroleigh pleaded.

"Wouldn't shooting us spoil your plans?" he asked of Emily.

"Only plan A. It will work perfectly for plan B. Take your pick?"

"What is plan A?" Edward asked.

"Eddie," Caroleigh moaned.

"Just want to know the choices, my love."

Emily still waited for Steven to move as ordered and wiggled the gun. "This or a drink that puts you to sleep."

Steven considered it long enough for Caroleigh to plead with him again. "And don't get in the way?" he asked her bitterly but moved to sit beside her.

"Like a good boy," Emily told him. "But no lollipop for good behavior, or mansion, or ranch, or anything else you thought you were going to get out of this."

He crossed his right ankle casually over his left knee. "You think you will?" he asked.

Caroleigh relaxed a little once Steven was down and told Emily, "There's no way to break the trust, Emily."

"Yes, there is. That stingy old bastard wasn't nearly as clever as he thought."

"How?" Edward asked.

"You'll find out soon enough." She squatted with the bag in front of her, the gun trained on them. "This is the last time I will ever play servant for your sorry asses. Now shut up."

When she finished, a sliver tray held three crystal champagne glasses, each full. The half empty bottle sat with them on the coffee table. A square of mirror, a razor blade, a glass straw, and a scattering of white powder sat beside that. Emily finished setting up the scene, lighting the last of the candles she had scattered around the room as a vehicle drove up to the front door.

"That would be her now," Emily said.

"In a green Mercedes?" Steven asked.

"That's gone into storage, a waste of a perfectly good car. You really shouldn't have screwed up everything. If you had just left the next day like you were supposed to…" She ended with a shrug.

"I'm not the one who screwed up those stairs or that bomb."

"No, Dell screwed both those up too. The stairs were supposed to have gone down in the explosion."

"When was the bomb really supposed to go off?" Edward asked.

"It was supposed to go off an hour after he set it."

"It probably would have killed us, but you did something to it to keep it from doing any real damage to the house," Steven observed.

"Of course we did. I'm going to live there."

"I still don't understand how you think you can do that," Caroleigh said.

"I'll let Kari explain that to you." She smiled as Kari appeared in the doorway. "Won't you?"

Kari's eyes swept the room quickly. "It looks like you're about ready."

"No," Edward moaned with his hold of Caroleigh tightening. "No, no."

* * * *

"I am so sorry," Edward said contritely from his end of the sofa.

They sat four abreast. Caroleigh gripped Edward's hand with one of hers and the other gripped Kari's on the other side. Steven sat beside Kari, leaning away from her towards the arm of the couch.

Caroleigh whispered, "She can't hear you." She swallowed heavily; her gaze locked on the woman who propelled Kari into the room with a jab in her back with a pistol barrel. "Tell her later."

"There is no later," Gabrielle, told her, all trace of an accent gone. There was no longer any need for it. Gladys had revealed herself.

"Did you torture her before you killed her?" Kari asked.

"Who, dear, your mother or the Marquise?" She laughed at the collection of confused expressions. "It doesn't matter, the answer is no."

"You didn't kill them, or you didn't torture them?"

"Torture is so messy and difficult to explain without the right circumstances. I prefer drugs, so tidy and many so undetectable."

"Merrill?" Kari asked.

"My mother?" Caroleigh exclaimed.

"Your mother, my mother, Adam, and William," Kari answered.

"Not William," Gladys corrected. "Not that I wouldn't have liked to have been the one to give him a shove down those stairs, but, no. All I had to do was convince Jonathan we would never be able to marry as long as William was alive. Oh, and I didn't kill Adam, though I must admit, I did a rather tidy job of preparing him for his accident. He was so easy to incite into a blind rage, especially in his condition."

"And my mother?"

"She was in my way," she acknowledged indifferently.

"You're insane," Caroleigh cried. "How can you talk about killing as if it were no more than…than—"

"Everything is ready." Emily cut in. "Let's get this over with."

Gladys flipped her hand in a silencing motion.

"She enjoys it," Kari said.

"Not true," Gladys told her. "I only kill when I need to." She paused and then, with a glance at Steven, added maliciously, "Usually."

Emily stepped closer. "I think you're talking too much."

"When I want to know what you think about anything, I'll ask," she said in dismissal.

Emily was hurt, but before she could respond, Kari said, "There's no fun being the world's most clever killer if you can't brag. Who can appreciate your genius after you've killed all your partners?"

"What's she talking about?" Emily asked.

Kari answered again. "You sabotaged that bomb. That's why it went off too early."

"Oh, Kari, how bright you are, but not quite right." She flipped her hand as if shooing a fly away. "Had he done it the way he was instructed to do, all but you would all have died at once, and none of this would have been necessary."

Her expression and voice changed drastically. "Dell was lazy and incompetent. I don't know why the fool went back down there." She gave an exaggerated sigh. "At least the bomb's going off early got rid of him."

"Well," Edward quipped, "they always say if you want it done right, you have to do it yourself."

"Precisely," she agreed smugly.

"Just which one of you did he think he was going to marry?"

"Sophia, of course. I couldn't very well marry my own son."

"And William's?" Caroleigh asked.

"Who cares?" Gladys said indifferently.

"But you convinced him Adam was his father, even if Adam would only have been fifteen?"

"He had several fantasies," she stated indifferently. "One being that he was the rightful heir to the Meadows, the other that he was intelligent. He was putty in little Sophia's hands."

Edward indicated Emily with a tip of his head. "This would be Sophia, and though we haven't been properly introduced, you just have to be Gladys."

"Mommy Dearest," Caroleigh said in scorn. "Will Daddy be coming out of the woodwork as well?"

"Oh, no, he's quite dead as advertised."

"Helped along, was he?" Edward asked.

She smiled wickedly. "Now you are the clever one."

"You did?" Caroleigh asked in horror. "Why?"

"Do I hear regret in your voice?" She laughed again. "You of all people know what a tiresome boor he could be."

"That's about the nicest thing I would say about him, but why kill him?"

"He was in the way," she stated simply.

"Of becoming the Marquis?" Kari asked. "The one you mentioned killing?"

Emily demanded, "Why are you asking so many questions?"

"Stalling," Edward said to make Caroleigh gasp. "I'm in no hurry to die."

Gladys told him, "But you are going to die. You never should have married her. It puts you in line to inherit. Before it was just the two of them, and you were just—what do you call it?—collateral damage. Now your death is a necessity."

"I'm the one you want to kill?" Caroleigh asked in astonishment.

"You have always been a necessity. You first." Her eyes shifted to Kari. "Then you. I made that stingy old bastard a promise, and I always keep my promises."

Kari took her attention again. "When you said you'd keep the other one that time, you didn't mean Jonathan, you meant the baby you were carrying."

"Adam's child, the only true and rightful heir," she said in triumph "I have the only rightful heir, and I will have it all."

"It's all in trusts." Caroleigh argued and shook her head in confusion. "You wouldn't be heir anyway."

"She is for what matters," Kari said tonelessly. "The mine is what she's after."

"It's nearly worthless," Caroleigh exclaimed.

"Ask her how worthless it is," Gladys ordered.

Steven spoke for the first time since Kari arrived. "Dreams to insanity."

"It's there," Gladys insisted. "He will turn over in his rotting grave—all of you will—and I will have it all. I will find that map, or did you and that grandfather of yours really think Adam wouldn't have told me about it?"

"What map?" Caroleigh asked in confusion.

"She's never shared the family secrets with you? Shame, shame, Kari, hoarding it all to yourself?"

Steven moved. Emily swung the gun in his direction, but he only braced his elbow on the couch arm and lowered his face to press at his eyes, a maneuver to hide his expression and to keep from looking at the map on the wall behind Emily's head. He suddenly understood why Garvin's hand drawn map was out of proportion and the real significance of all of those tunnels.

Caroleigh held her breath until Emily swung the gun away from Steven, then asked of Kari, "What secret?"

"The lost vein," Gladys answered. "The old bastard told Adam about it, but he wouldn't tell him where. He called it their security. He said he would leave him a map."

"Knowing you were sitting on top of a gold mine would tend to make one feel secure," Edward commented dryly.

Caroleigh snorted. "Adam either lied to her, or they were wrong. That's what Dell was looking for." She looked at Emily. "You too no doubt while you were there. It was all for nothing. Grandpa had exploratory mining done in the fifties. Nothing is there," she said, but she looked sideways at Kari.

"That's why you had to die first and why Dell locked me in away from the rest of you," Kari stated emotionlessly. "She knows the mine is right of survivorship. You die, it goes to me. Then I die and everything goes to my sister, Adam's newly declared heir, a rightful heir that can challenge the trust and Grandpa's will. Your orders to Dell were to keep me insolated until you got there."

"Yes, that stupid ambulance nearly ran me off that despicable road. I knew then he had screwed everything up."

"You didn't tell him why, not the whole truth of it. You didn't want to wait for everything to go through probate to know you had that map in your hands."

"I know the old bastard told you where it is. After she..." Gladys tipped her head toward Caroleigh, "...was dead, your psycho stalker was going to torture you if you were stubborn, and kill you and then himself after you rejected him one time too many," she clarified smugly.

"Maybe you shouldn't have told him so many lies. His little improvisations nearly ruined your plans."

Gladys rolled her eyes. "He thought he was being clever."

"Must have been a real bother keeping up with all his blunders," Edward commented.

"Yes." she admitted, "He nearly destroyed everything we had set into place to wait for your next visit, but I am patient, and all is working out to my complete satisfaction. So your choice is to drink without giving us any difficulty, go to sleep—"

"And burn to death," Edward finished for her, his gaze on at the nearest candle.

"Yes," Gladys gloated. "And poor Kari will be so distraught, she kills herself."

"Or?" Kari asked.

"Overcome with the duplicity of their lies, you go insane, murder them all, then kill yourself. They can go peacefully or painfully."

Steven moved again, barely. He dropped his hand to his lap. "Hasn't this gone far enough?" he asked of Kari, his voice tight and controlled.

"Yes," Kari answered. She started to stand but froze when Emily's hand swung her way.

"What are you doing?" Emily asked in alarm.

"I'll show you where the mine is," she told Gladys. "You don't have to kill anyone. It's far enough from the original claim you can just make a new filing."

"This is a trick," Emily said with a nervous laugh. "Look at them. They're too calm."

"Shut up," Gladys told her.

"There's a tunnel under the house, this house. It's why he kept it when he tore all the others down."

"Show me."

"Mother." Emily moved forward and caught Gladys's arm as Kari stood.

Gladys threw her hand up, the barrel of the gun in her hand striking Emily in the face. Emily backed away, her free hand to her face and a trickle of blood on her cheek. Her gun hung limply in her other hand, and Gladys, so caught up in her greed, didn't notice. Nor did she notice Emily's attention was on Kari and Gladys as they left the room, not on those who remained on the couch.

Edward shifted for a better position and pried at Caroleigh's fingers to try to free his hand. Caroleigh shifted to grip both of his hands with both of hers, her gaze fixed on Emily.

Steven told Emily, "You're a fool if you think she won't kill you just as easily as she killed her son."

"He wasn't her son," she said numbly, but she had already heard too much from her mother.

"Florence Webber's son died within hours of its birth. Your mother paid her to take her son." He kept talking while the uniformed officer crept up behind Emily. "And she's lied to you about Morning Meadow. It was never what she was after. She doesn't care if you ever live there, and you won't. You heard her. All she cares about is the mine. She's your legal heir, and once you inherit it, she won't have anymore use for you."

She didn't want to believe him, but it was obvious she did. She listened in horror, her full attention on him as the cop slipped up behind her. She looked at him dumbly when he gripped her wrist with one hand and twisted the gun from her hand with the other. A few seconds later, Gladys screamed in insane rage from the basement.

* * * *

"I can't believe you did that to me," Edward exclaimed for the sixth time. He turned from where Kari stood near the door and stalked back to where Caroleigh sat on the couch. "I can't believe you let me go through that."

"Mr. Van Philips," Canterbury continued in his effort to placate him. "It was necessary. They had to believe your reactions."

Edward still raved at Caroleigh. "You made me believe our lives were in danger."

"They were," she said meekly.

"While I had to sit there like a castrated goose, doing nothing."

"Goose?" she asked with a giggle.

"You know what I mean!" he shouted at her.

"Yes, my love, but you caught on very quickly."

"The third time you nearly crushed my hand to keep me from moving. I went through a thousand hells before that. You could have told me. You told Steven so he wouldn't do anything heroic."

"We didn't tell him."

"I'm just not heroic," Steven grumbled. He still sat in the same position in the same place on the couch.

"Bull!" Edward exclaimed.

"Thank God he caught on as quickly as he did," Caroleigh said weakly.

Edward shook his finger in her face. "Don't you ever do anything like that to me again."

"No, my love." She took his hand in both of hers and pulled him down to her. He resisted only a moment before he sank down beside her and pulled her up against him. "I was so scared," she told him. "If the least little thing had gone wrong…"

"Hush, now, it's over." He sighed heavily. "I can't believe it happened so fast, so easily. He just plucked the gun out of her hand. She never even struggled. Rather anti-climactic actually."

"We took every precaution possible," Canterbury assured him. "The only time any of you were less than a few feet away from an officer was when the two drove over from the mansion. Everything was video taped and recorded, even Emily taking the champagne from the mansion and doctoring it up over here. We though she might let you leave." The last was said to Steven. "We aren't sure yet why they thought they had to include you."

"So glad I didn't mess things up by leaving last night," Steven said tartly.

"We were here then too, in the tunnels through the mine. There was the possibility none of you were to be included, just as Miss Goodman wasn't the first time," Canterbury said, simply to state a fact, not apologize. "We had no way of knowing until they made their move, but we were ready whenever it was."

"They tried to run him down," Caroleigh reminded.

Edward added, "That was a ploy, my love, remember?"

"I guess you know now how wrong you were," she told Canterbury with feeling. When Canterbury ignored it, she went on. "I almost gave it away at the party when I realized who was standing there. Seeing her like that, so brazen, just standing there like I would never recognize her. The face was a little different, but not those eyes."

As she shuddered, Edward hugged her close. "Bless that particular little twist to Helene's mind for giving you an excuse."

"Or perception," Kari murmured and turned to Canterbury. "Is Helene all right?"

"Nothing lethal, just an upset stomach. Gladys dropped her at the hospital and told everyone she was going on to Denver alone."

"Perception?" Edward asked and attempted to make Caroleigh sit up to look at him.

There had been a lot of men moving around collecting evidence. The small group had ignored them until one man came in to whisper in Canterbury's ear. Canterbury shook his head.

"Perception?" Edward asked again.

He jerked convulsively, as everyone else, when an enraged scream cut through the air.

"Let go of me!" Evelyn screamed and fought her way to the doorway with two men fighting to hold her back.

"We're busy here," Canterbury told her. "Come back some other time."

"I'm never coming back!" She gave one last jerk of her arm to free herself. "I'm going home where I belong, but not before I tell you what I think of you."

Edward shifted to shield Caroleigh since she was the one the tirade was aimed at. "Now is definitely not a good time, Evelyn, dear."

"Don't dear me, you phony ass," she retorted in a sidebar before she continued at Caroleigh. "I thought if I patterned myself after you, you would like and accept me, even when it made me sick. Well, this is me." She indicated the worn jeans and sweatshirt she wore. "You belittled someone you called sister, so I did. You talked about liking drugs, so I did."

"You should have picked a different mentor," Kari stood a few feet behind her. "No one likes her like that, not even her."

"Why would you want to anyway?" Caroleigh asked in confusion.

"I had this stupid idea we could be sisters. Since they told me you didn't have any family I thought you might even like the idea, but I've seen how you treat her."

"Jonathan's," Kari stated by way of explanation. "His American indiscretion."

"Bastard!" Evelyn shouted. "Why don't you just say it? Someone not good enough to associate with. Well, you can just go to hell. I lived all my life without a family. I can do so for the rest of it if it's a family like you. I hate everything you stand for."

She spun and ran, leaving a stunned silence behind her. A split second later, Caroleigh and Kari reacted in unison and ran in pursuit.

"Kari knew that?" Edward asked Canterbury in amazement with a vague point in the direction the women had gone.

"She suspected Miss Goodman after that business with her clothes. She thought she may have done it as an excuse to leave, create an alibi. We didn't find the family connection until Miss O'Keefe turned us in that direction. We also investigated Emily. On the surface there wasn't anything to make her look suspicious then either."

Edward grimaced. "In a way, it nearly was that old cliché. No one ever suspects the servants."

"Miss O'Keefe realized Emily was involved in some way when she attempted to throw suspicion on your wife with a story of threats she had supposedly made while drinking. She knew then you people were in over your head." He said the last in terse recrimination. Neither Steven nor Edward responded. "That was when she called and told me the truth. It was after Miss O'Keefe read through the background reports on both that we got on the right track. Miss Goodman had never been out of the country. Emily had been all over the world including France. I emailed a picture to the cops over there on the chance Emily had been seen with Gladys. Things fell into place pretty fast then. She was the girl in the video they used for their con. I went to the party to tell Kari, and she told me who was there." He smiled wryly. "She told me then that Gladys was after the mine because of some story about a lost vein of gold. I thought she was joking at first."

"Sometimes it's hard to tell," Edward murmured.

“Yeah, well, the cops over there would have liked for us to have gotten a little more detail on all that business, but once they knew about Emily, they already had a pretty good picture of what happened. The father had continued with his life after their daughter disappeared, but the wife had gone into seclusion. No one had seen her for seven years other than the servants and her husband, making it perfect for someone to take over her idenity. The scam was to give them access to the house, creating a plausible reason for the father to kill himself after all that time and for the mother to have a breakdown. It was probably Emily locked in the bedroom while Fitzhugh and Gladys put the real Marquise in the car in her place and led the police off. Then she got rid of him, checked him into the hospital under his real name with what was believed to be a heart attack. There was never any reason to connect a tourist’s death to what had happened. Then she went back and took the Marquise’s place. She hacked her hair off, nicked herself, and spread blood all over her face then made enough noise to terrify the servants into calling the police. All the servants and the police really saw was the blood. Small price to pay for a fortune. She stayed in a private sanitarium for a year, had some plastic surgery done, signed herself out, and started traveling to avoid anyone who might have known the difference. At her age, she could have lived the rest of her life in luxury after committing crimes no one ever knew happened. She threw it all away for a crazy dream and revenge on a dead man."

"Can I leave now?” Steven said suddenly.

"Leave?” Canterbury and Edward said together.

"It was a setup, Steven," Edward said quickly. "Kari never believed any of the things he told her."

"I'll need a statement," Canterbury told him.

"You know where I live."

"If your realtor hasn't already sold it."

"I'll leave a forwarding address."

The gauntlet was thrown. Canterbury picked it up. "If you really care anything about her, how is it you never mentioned her to your friend and business partner?"

"Because it was none of his business. Anything else you want to know that is none of yours?"

"No."

Edward stood when Steven stood. "Steven."

"Leave it alone," Steven told him quietly.

Edward watched him go and asked Canterbury, "Proud of yourself?”

"No."

"You don't have a chance, you know. She's in love with him."

Canterbury didn’t deny Edward's charge. "I know. I also know what I told her is not why he walked out on her just now. He finally realized she won't turn all this into some trashy tourist attraction."

"You've got a blind spot, old boy. Let's hope she doesn't.”

Chapter Eleven

As soon as Steven walked in the door, Robert engulfed him with an arm around his shoulder. He didn't even give Steven the opportunity to wave a greeting to Mary at the receptionist desk before he rushed him into the office and led him to the chair behind the desk. He also talked non-stop.

"I was afraid you were going to be late. I know you don't want to be here, but she insisted you were the only one she would talk to. She says she just wouldn't feel comfortable talking to anyone else."

"Why?" Steven asked as he was pushed down in the chair.

Robert skidded right over the question. "Just two minutes, two minutes, and you should be able to convince her of my superior qualities."

"Who?"

"Millions, Steven, millions, not just in this account but in the ones the publicity will bring in."

He grumbled, "If anyone cut your head open, nothing but dollar signs would fall out."

Robert laughed heartily. "I know money doesn't mean as much to you as it does to me. I can live with that. I can't live with the idea of ever going back to the slums I came from."

"Fat chance. Okay, I will dazzle her with your qualifications, but—"

Robert looked at his watch and headed for the door. "She'll be here any minute. Get yourself ready."

"Who is it?"

Robert stopped only long enough to give a double thumbs up signal and shut the door.

Steven punched the intercom button. "Mary, who am I seeing?"

"Mr. Brown didn't say, Mr. Chase. Shall I buzz-oh, here she is-oh, wow."

The intercom went dead. Puzzled as to what could have prompted such an unusual response from the unflappable Mary, Steven started out. Mary stepped in to hold the door open before he made it around the desk.

She rolled her eyes and pursed her lips in a silent whistle behind Kari before she pulled the door shut.

With a catch in his breath, Steven turned his back and returned to the chair.

Dressed in a royal blue sheath exhibiting her slender form to perfection, Kari was more beautiful than ever. Her thick long hair was pinned to the back of her head. Heavy curls trailing down her back with tentacles of loose hair placed artfully around her face. Her makeup was flawless, light, and natural. Even Rascal, cradled in her arms, was dressed for the occasion. A bright red vest peeked out from under her arm.

Her beauty only made him angrier because of his reaction to seeing her. His voice was sharp and his words clipped. "What do you want?"

"So much for impressing you with my ‘stop being a recluse look.’" She went to the chair in front of the desk. "May I sit down, or are you still too mad to be civil?"

"I think civil ended when you told me to get out."

She leaned forward to sit Rascal out of sight on the floor. As she sat back, she straightened to look him straight in the eyes, before she asked, "Which time?"

"Exactly."

She sucked the inside of her prettily painted lower lip between her teeth for the time it took to take a deep breath and let it out slowly. "After all that happened to you and all the time you invested in the Meadow, it's only fair you get the account."

A nerve jumped in his jaw before he told her coldly, "Chase and Brown will be only too happy to be of service."

"I was joking, Steven," she told him as he opened a drawer and took out a blank contract. When he looked up, his hostility clear, she added, "Trying to anyway."

"Will the contract be in your name or the trust?"

"The trust will be a partner. It's going to be a joint project. Once Evelyn stopped imitating Caro, she became quite a joy. Grandpa's even stopped locking the door on her." She waited for a response. When none came, she went on. "Caro's a little erratic now, even for her. She claims it’s all those pregnancy hormones. We tell her it's the strain of being nice."

"Four principals then?" he questioned curtly.

"Edward too, of course."

"Of course."

"We'd like to keep it just family. It will depend on how much capital you think we'll need."

"I won't be involved."

She blinked, hesitated, then asked, "Who would?"

"Robert Brown. He'll be in here in a few minutes. I'll introduce you."

"I never believed you were after anything, Steven."

"Whether you did or not didn't make any difference in the end."

"If I hurt your pride, I apologize."

"My pride is undamaged."

"Mine isn't," she said stiffly, then laughed ruefully. "There are so many O'Keefe bastards I—"

"You're pregnant?" he demanded.

Kari stared at him for a moment before she asked hotly. "Would that make any difference—in the end?"

"Yes and you know it would."

"If I were, I wouldn't need your help."

"No, you never need anyone's help. Or want it. You made that very clear."

"I was going to make some lame joke, not tell you I'm pregnant."

Rascal's head popped into Steven's view. The raised voices brought him up on his hind legs, his front feet on Kari's leg.

"Fine, then we don't have anything else to talk about." He punched the intercom button. "Mary, would you ask Robert to come in. "

Kari jerked Rascal up into her arms as she stood and walked quickly to the door. "I'll talk to him out there."

* * * *

Robert paced until Steven called. He nearly collided with her when Kari came out unexpectedly.

"Oh, ah, ma'am, ah, I'm Robert Brown." He suddenly grinned self-consciously and laughed. "I'm usually more articulate than that, but my, you're a beautiful woman. No wonder he sold out, loaded up his brand new four by four, and headed for the hills. Lovely, absolutely lovely. I didn't say anything to that cop though. I knew if Steven wouldn't talk to me about you, he certainly didn't want me telling that snoop I thought he was head over heels for you."

Movement drew his eyes when Rascal wiggled against Kari's tight hold. His gaze locked on the lettering on the jacket to realize it said hearing ear dog, and his eyes snapped back to her face. "I'm sorry. I didn't realize—"

"I understood most of what you said," Kari told him. "But if you could slow down a little it would help." Before he could think of what to say next she told him, "Steven can give you details and give you ideas. He can also tell you how to contact me when you're ready with a proposal."

"Yes, ma'am, but if I could just—"

"I really can't discuss it more now."

"I'll call soon," he called as she walked out the door.

Kari started at a fast stride. She slowed though, head tilted away from the loud noise of the traffic. In her anger she had mistakenly turned to walk with the traffic of a one way street. She couldn't see approaching vehicles without looking behind her to know when the sound would reach her, and some of those sounds were of such intensity to her they were equivalent to cymbals going off. She cringed over the loudest.

Rascal warned her of each with a bump against her leg as they walked, but he was nervous, both from the unaccustomed heavy demands in his new role and sensing her rapid increase in tension. As they reached the corner, an intersection with a two way street, the sounds came from all sides at Kari who had little ability to discern the direction of any of them.

She waited for the light only to nearly step in front of a car making a left hand turn off the one way despite Rascal pressing against her leg. She flinched and shied steps away from an impatient blare of the horn.

The way she flinched made her feel silly. "We can do this, baby. I can do this." She suddenly gave a short, bitter laugh, stooped down to scoop him up and buried her face in his fur. "We don't have to do this. It was all a waste of time. Let's get the hell out of this hell."

She looked to the sides and forward, but not behind. She knew she had passed nothing but office buildings. What she needed was a was a cafe, a coffee shop, anything with a public phone to call for a taxi, which she should have done before she stormed out of Steven's office.

Kari stood at the curb, eyes fixed on the lights, determined not to flinch again. She knew Rascal tried to warn her of everything, but with so many sounds, she ignored him. He twisted in her arms in an effort to look behind them while Kari stroked his head to calm him as much as herself. Rascal's efforts increased, but his struggles confused her. There were too many noises, too close together from too many directions. What to her was a low rumble came from the side. When it sounded too much like a threat she turned to locate the source and backed several steps when the skateboarder exploded into her peripheral vision. He kicked his board up to make a right angle turn and sped off again. Then the sound of what Rascal tried so valiantly to warn of hit her.

The dump truck driver probably saw her and thought nothing of it. He had a green light. He had no way of knowing what the sound of the heavy truck would do to her overwhelmed senses, and he probably didn't think anything at all of the sand blowing from the top of his load in a light spray.

Kari spun and backed a few feet before the truck reached the intersection. Her hand fly to her face, and she panicked, staggering blindly.

* * * *

The sidewalk was clear behind her, except for Steven. With his heart pounding, he increased his pace when he saw her nearly step out in front of the car. He knew she waited for the light and thought he would reach her before she crossed. When the truck passed, her recoil took her into the adjacent crosswalk into traffic already crowding a changing light with her hand to her eyes, and Steven started to run even before the waiting driver honked at her for being in his way. He ran in desperation when she spun yet again, completely disorientated. Blinded by sand in her eyes Kari backed up further, beyond the car that honked, out into the next lane. That was when Rascal wiggled free of her arms to leap to the ground and jump at her legs, an act that put him even further into the next lane.

With mulitpy horns blaring from different directions, Kari froze. Her hands pressed against her ears, she gasped when Steven caught her around the waist with one arm and swung her, her back against his chest. Locking both arms tight around her, he half-walked, half-carried her to the sidewalk.

“My dog!" She struggled against the arms in an effort to reach the ground, her arms flailing to find Rascal while Steven dragged her to the curb from in front of the waiting car, its driver looking on in astonishment. "Rascal? Where's my dog?"

"He's right here," Steven said in her ear, his voice strained with emotion.

Rascal ran circles around them, barking frantically. He jumped and hit her leg. Kari leaned down, hung over Steven’s arms, and swung her hands wildly trying to find him until Steven stopped, going with her when she dropped to her knees. With a leg on either side of her, he still held his arms around her waist. Rascal jumped at her chest. Kari, oblivious to everything but the dog her arms encircled, sat back on her feet and wept in huge, wrenching sobs.

A voice asked beside Steven, "Should someone call an ambulance or something?"

“No," Steven answered in a choke and had to clear his voice to finish. "She'll be all right."

"What happened?" another asked.

He looked around to see a small group had formed around them. He cleared his throat again. "Sand blew in her eyes, blinded her."

"That must have been terrifying," the first voice whispered, "to be deaf and then suddenly blind."

"How do you know she's deaf?" someone else whispered.

"It's on the dog's coat."

Steven looked over her shoulder at Rascal’s little red coat for the first time. Just as when she had walked into his office, her arm covered most of the lettering. Once he bothered to look, he could see enough to guess what it said. Part of her ‘stop being a recluse’ program included being accompanied by a well marked hearing ear dog.

"She'd have gone right into traffic if it hadn't been for that brave little thing," one woman said and moved a little closer.

Kari's sobs subsided, as she brushed trembling fingertips around her eyes. She blinked twice then closed her eyes again.

The same woman moved a few steps closer to hold out a tissue. Rascal growled.

Steven took the tissue. "He’s just telling her a stranger is close," he explained to the woman in a lowered voice. He didn’t think he was ready for Kari to know it was him.

"How if she can't hear?"

"She feels it, but she has partial hearing."

The woman told Rascal, "Its okay, sweetheart, I'm not going to hurt her.”

She smiled and backed away as he continued to growl until she was far enough for him to stop. He licked his mouth and nose nervously, then turned, giving Kari’s cheek a lick as well.

"I've got to get back to work," one of the on-lookers stated. "Glad she's okay."

He walked off and another joined him. Soon only the lady remained.

Kari put one hand on the ground for balance, and Steven moved with her. He got his own feet under him to lift her with his hands cupped under her elbows.

"Thank you," she murmured. She brushed again at her eyes, blinked between every few brushes to clean the grit away that floated in her tears. She was also stiff and rigid with embarrassment. "Would you please call a taxi for me? I can manage from here. You don't need to stay."

He put his fingers under her chin to raise her head. "It's me, Kari," he told her, his voice still thick with emotion.

She tipped her head towards him to hear over the traffic. At the same time her fingertips went back to her eyes. Steven knew she hadn't heard him.

"I could call for a cab," the lady offered. "I have a cell."

Steven shook his head. "My office is just down the street."

A little uncertain, she said, "Well, he doesn't growl at you, so I guess you aren't a stranger to her. You're Mr. Chase, aren't you?"

"Yes." He dropped his voice and whispered. "She's embarrassed."

"She doesn't have any reason to be. She's very brave." She hesitated and added, "And beautiful."

"Yes," he agreed. "Thank you."

Steven took a deep breath as the lady walked away and squared his shoulders. He pressed the tissue into Kari's hand and held it, much the way she had held his hand in the library. He wouldn't have thought she could stiffen more. She did when she realized it wasn't a stranger. With a twist of her hand, she pulled free and shrugged away his arm from where it laid around her back.

"If we stand here long enough, I won't need..." She snarled that word. "...you even to call a cab."

"How about want?"

"I don't need anything but a cab,"

He knew from her answer she hadn't heard what he said. She was, just as Edward had described the O'Keefe women, stubborn and proud. He didn't attempt to put his arm back around her. Instead he leaned closer and raised his voice to be heard over the traffic. "I'm going to take you back to the office to rinse your eyes out." He cupped his hand under her elbow and held his breath to see if she would allow him that much and let it out in a grateful sigh when she walked with him.

"You finally got to play hero," she said hatefully. "Must have done your ego worlds of good."

He leaned close again. "Stop being a bitch," he told her in a mimic of how she had talked to Caroleigh.

"Go to hell."

She didn't mean it as a joke, but then Caroleigh hadn't meant it as a joke the time he heard her say those words to Edward. It was a slender thread, and he held tight to it. He didn't have any choice, not after his heart had nearly wrenched out of his chest when he saw her step into the traffic.

The short walk back was silent. Kari displayed her refusal to accept anything more from him than she had to by shutting the bathroom door in his face once they reached his office. Only fair, he supposed, he'd shut his office door in the face of his confused partner and secretary.

He waited, perched on the edge of the desk. To a casual observer, with his arms and ankles crossed, he might have looked relaxed. Far from it, Steven knew he had a battle on his hands. After two months without any contact she had come to his world with her new look and "stop being a recluse program" willing, he realized too late, to sacrifice her own world for his. He had thrown it back in her face, refused to even hear what she had to say. Worse he had as much as told her he would not even consider talking to her unless she carried his child. She was angry and hurt just as he had been when he left the ranch. Now he had to find a way to bridge the large chasm filled with those angry and hurtful words.

She'd removed all the pins from her hair and shaken it free. The curls tumbled down her back and hung over her shoulders with damp tangles framing her face. The carefully applied makeup was gone along with the salon hair style, washed away with the girt and tears from her red, swollen eyes. Rascal, of course, was in her arms.

"Aren't you going to ask me what I want?" he asked when she stopped in the doorway, glaring at him. "That would be fair since it was the way I greeted you."

"I don't care."

"I would like to start that conversation over, Kari."

"We've had all the conversations we need."

She took one step before he launched off the desk to block her. She backed away, her features set and unyielding.

"You should ask me why I went after you," he told her.

"I told you, I am not pregnant."

He winced, but persevered. "I realized if you left like that I was letting you walk out of my life forever, that I would never see you again."

She tried to side-step by him. "You had that right. Congratulations," she retorted.

He matched her steps, staying in front of her. "I started thinking about what you had said, what it might have meant, what you might have said if I hadn't cut you off."

She stared blankly at him and didn't answer.

"Is that look because you're still putting together what I said or because you're deciding if you'll even talk to me?"

"The last."

"Damn it, Kari," he said in frustration. "When you told me to leave was it just to protect me or because you meant the things you said?"

"No," she cried and then corrected it in another cry. "Yes. You're talking too fast. I can't figure out what you're saying fast enough to answer, and my eyes hurt." When he took a step toward her she held her hand out to his chest. "I didn't want it to end with bitterness and anger. You did so much for us—me—and we—I-I was—you didn't deserve—there was a reason…reasons. I had to hold on so tight. I mean, I thought if you did—I don't expect…" She stopped to stare at him and took a deep breath, letting it out slowly. "I'm not making any sense."

"Do I need to take you to the doctor?"

"I'm not incoherent," she snapped. "I just sound like it."

Steven smiled slightly. "I meant for your eyes."

"Oh." Kari gave him a faint smile back. "I thought you might be suggesting I'm nuts."

"Because you see ghosts, believe in curses, and hide gold mines?"

She didn't deny any of it. "All that does sound pretty crazy," she said flippantly only to sober immediately and move slightly away from him. "When I realized it was Emily, I nearly panicked. I knew none of the things I had done, that we were doing, would mean anything. She could have drugged our food, set fire to the house while we slept—God knows what—so I called Canterbury. He was going to go right out to arrest her. He would have if he could have thought of any kind of a charge he could prove." She gave a slight, rueful smile. "He would have arrested us too when I told him what we were doing if he could have thought of a charge, especially when I told him he couldn't stop us, but he could take it over."

To give her the space and time she seemed to need, he sat on the edge of the desk again. "Bet that went over well," he commented for something to say.

She ducked her head to carefully brush grit from the corner of her eyes. She went to the chair in front of the desk, Rascal still in her arms. "I couldn't tell you, Steven," she said softly. "I'm sorry, but you don't role play." She looked back up, straight into his eyes. "Everything you think and feel is in your eyes and on your face. The closest you ever come to deceit is to close your features. If you had known, I was sure she would see it in your face when you looked at her, but I knew it was just as dangerous to have you stay without knowing. I was desperate to make you leave."

She ducked her head and brushed at her eyes to continue. "Caroleigh was sure she could control Edward, but I knew no one could control you, not after you tried to kick your way out of that basement." She gave him a sudden, quirky smile. "Turned out you were so pissed, that was all she saw. When did you figure it out?"

"I knew you were up to something when Caroleigh threw that hysterical fit. I don't know why Edward didn't. He was the one who told me she would never cry for real in front of anyone."

"He believed it because he knew how much it would have meant to her if it had been real. That was why I had to tell her even though Canterbury told me not to. I couldn't do that to her for even one day. I knew you and Edward would survive it and recover, but she's…she's more vulnerable than you realize. I couldn't do it to her. I don't know what she would have done if she had believed me, and she's role played all her life."

"It's okay to cry fake tears in public, but not real ones?" he asked in confusion.

"Real ones expose vulnerability. It's an advantage for someone to think one is there that isn't, but hell if you really expose yourself. Emily has a little twist in her. It wasn't necessary for what they were doing, but she wanted to hurt us by causing trouble between us, so we let her think she had."

He still didn't completely understand, but asked, "Did Emily tell you anything about me?"

"No, but she indirectly told you things. That was where Evelyn got the things she told you. It didn't come from Caroleigh. Canterbury was—"

He cut her off tartly. "He believes everything he said."

"I don't," she said without hesitation. "I knew how wrong he was when he told me you'd put your house up for sale, but I thought I'd made you hate me by then."

"No, I…when did he tell you that?

"The day before the party. I just wanted to tell you why I acted the way I did so you wouldn't be bitter or angry anymore."

"I know why you did it, Kari," he said quietly. "You didn't need me."

"I did," she exclaimed. "I drew strength from you being there, but if I had eased up, even a little, I would have lost it."

He went back to something she had said earlier. “Because you had to hold on so tight to keep control?”

“Maybe I made more sense than I thought,” she said with a nod.

“That’s why you backed away and shut me out the morning after the fire, to keep from crying?” She nodded again. “You let me hold you once before when you cried.”

She ducked her head to brush at her eyes again and mumbled, “You felt differently then. I’m sorry everything got so screwed up.”

“How do you feel about me now?’

She straightened with a deep breath. “My feelings for you haven’t changed.”

“Then you love me,” he stated. “You did say that.”

She blinked her eyes several times in surprise. “Guess you weren’t in as deep a coma as I thought.”

“Why can’t you just say it now?”

“That was before,” she stated simply.

“You shut me out, Kari. It was okay to have me around when things were good, but you didn’t want or need me when they weren’t. That was why I left. It has to be both, good and bad, happy or sad, tears or laughter. If you shut me out of one, you shut me out of everything. It has to be always, not just when it’s convenient.”

“Okay,” she said quietly.

“Okay?” he asked dubiously. “I don’t want anymore misunderstandings. I didn’t just put my house up for sale. I sold my share of this business to Robert. Development was not what I set out to do with my life. You reminded me of that when you said architecture was my passion. I have enough of a reputation now I can work freelance, and I can do that from anywhere. I went back up there to stay. I don’t care about any resort or ghosts or hidden gold mines.”

Kari giggled. “Grandpa always said the best place to hide something was out in plain view. The map I mean. He wasn’t looking for the vein in the fifties, he buried it.”

“You can tell me about that later,” he said impatiently.

“Okay.”

Puzzled by her behavior he asked, “Do you understand what I’m saying?”

“You haven’t actually said it, but I think you’re saying…”

"I love you," he blurted out. "I knew I wanted to marry you when I watched you fry eggs and bacon with one hand to keep the other hand free to comfort a dog you'd never seen before. Not quite ten minutes."

"It was when you took off my muddy boots for me."

He grinned at her. "Then you'll marry me?"

"When?"

"When?" he asked, perplexed again. "Does when make a difference in your answer?"

"The answer is yes, but I'm hoping you don't want a long engagement."

"You are pregnant?"

"No and if that's…"

"Don't do that," he told her quickly.

She tipped her head with a sly smile. "Do you want me to be?"

He considered it with a slow grin. "I wouldn't mind."

Kari smiled turned to shy. "I'm not, but we can work on it. Is the twenty-ninth too soon?"

"To work on it?" he asked, hoping he didn't have to wait that long to make love to her again.

"To get married."

Steven grinned at her in relief. "Okay."

"Aren't you going to ask me why I picked that date?"

"Later. For now, you'd better put him down."

Epilogue

Canterbury was one of the last to arrive at Morning Meadows Mansion primarily because he had debated with himself from the instant he opened the invitation as to whether he would even go. One moment he felt the invitation was a slap in the face from Chase, the next a genuine gesture of friendship or gratitude from Kari. He even thought at times it was a slap in the face from Kari. He was still at war with himself, lingering in the great hall with thoughts of leaving when he glanced casually at the fading photograph mounted on a golden easel, only to stare in fascination.

Judge Powell's wife stepped up next to a very surly Canterbury. "Kari's great grandmother," Eunice Powell told him. "Beautiful, isn't she? Kari looks so much like her." She didn't wait for a response. "Kari found it, hidden in the folds of the wedding dress when she unpacked it for Caroleigh to wear. They think it was the only likeness ever made of her. She wasn't considered pretty in her time, too tall, too slim, but Collin O'Keefe didn't care for the popular definition of pretty. They called her an old maid, a spinster school teacher, well past marrying age at twenty-five. She was considered too stubborn, too proud, too outspoken, and too independent to be suitable wife material.

"They called him a cold-hearted businessman who drank too much and was well past his prime at forty-five. But the night they met was magic. He took one look and walked straight up to her without waiting for a proper introduction to ask her to dance. She told him she'd not be having her feet tromped on by a drunken sod. He had his last drink that night, and they were married less than three months later, one hundred years ago today. So many made the mistake of thinking they didn't really love each other. So many interesting parallels with today. It's so right the bride and groom are wearing the same clothes and marrying on the same day. Kari's even had her hair done just like that." She looked at the photo reverently. "Our Kari, the last O'Keefe to ever live here, will leave with her new husband, as Collin should have done with Kari Anne, leaving the curse behind them."

Canterbury grunted. “I believe in that curse as much as I believe in Miss Goodman’s ghost stories.”

“Oh, I heard those. She’s quite wrong, of course. Gavin would have dealt with Adam in death just as he did in life, by avoiding him. Gavin locked the doors against threats just as he did then, but it was the first Kari Anne who stopped Adam from coming in.” She nodded toward the portrait. “That daughter of Johnathan’s gave Adam an opening into the house he hadn’t had before. It was Kari Anne who moved to protect her grandchildren from him and that Dell Webber just as easily as she took a horse whip to a teamster who was foolish enough to manhandle one of her sons when she was alive.”

He scoffed openly. “Next you’ll be telling me she not only chased Webber through the house, but set the bomb off too.”

“Of course not, he did that himself, but it didn’t do much damage, did it?”

Even knowing Gladys had shorted the powder in the sticks of dynamite she provided for Dell, Canterbury felt a chill run down his spine. He snorted defiantly, telling himself it had been dogs outside, not a ghost inside that kept Webber from escaping the house. His mind finally made up, he turned abruptly to leave and nearly collided with Martha.

Without batting an eye she told him, “It’s time to be seated. Follow the white ribbon.”

Reluctant to go around her, Canterbury completed his turn and moved away quickly. He muttered a “thank you” he didn’t mean and followed the white streamers leading the way to the back lawn.

“Why did you tell him all that?” Martha asked Eunice.

Eunice giggled impishly. “Men like that, my Zack included, live their lives all bound up in facts and proof. I like to just,” she waved her hands joyfully, “rattle their cages sometimes.” She looked back at the picture. “She was a great lady.”

“She died before you were ever born,” she said, but not unkindly.

“I wish I had known her the way my mother did. She loved to tell me the story of that first night. There he was, so arrogant and sure of himself, and he was drunk. When she refused him, he was so stunned it took him a moment to recover, and then he laughed and bowed to her. He told her she was quite right and when next he presented himself to her, he would be sober and ask her to marry him. He was and he did. It’s so romantic, just like Kari and her young man.” She grew sober. “He does love her, doesn’t he, Martha? We can celebrate without worry?”

“He does,” she stated without a doubt.

"They've survived bloody ghosts, murder, and crazy people. The curse won't affect them once they leave here. They'll be happy at Max's ranch." She looked again at the picture. "That's what she's wanted all these years, for the O'Keefes to leave this meadow." Her hand went out to Martha's arm. "Have you seen her? When you worked here all those years did you ever see her?"

"You're beginning to sound like a superstitious old woman," she said gently. "Go take your seat now. I'm just going to check the drawing room and library for stragglers."

"You would never say it if you had," she said knowingly and gave Martha's arm a slight squeeze before she left.

Left alone, Martha did not look for stragglers. "No," she said softly to the aged photo. "I never speak of those I see who others do not, just as I taught her not to." Her eyes lifted from the photo to the head of the stairs, the same spot on the landing Kari had stared at after Adam appeared. "It is done with, Kari Anne. Not an O'Keefe or any others will ever try to make a home here again. You can cross now and take all your children with you."

There were no strange drafts of cold wind or eerie noises. No lights flickered, no table rattled, no shadow moved. Yet Martha knew Kari Anne heard her.

THE END

About the Author

Multi-genre, multi-named, Larion aka Larriane Wills writes from the past into the future. With strong characters, no matter the setting, she drags you into intricate plots in genres you didn't think you liked with a fast moving style that keeps you reading. Visit her at her website to keep abreast of previously published and those coming. She welcomes visitors and loves to keep in touch.

http:/./www.larriane.com
larriane@larriane.com

Secret Cravings Publishing

www.secretcravingspublishing.com